Because You Are So Good

CYMMONE IMMS

Copyright © 2023 Cymmone Imms

ISBN: 979-8-8648-4576-9
Imprint: Independently published

DEDICATION

For Robin

ACKNOWLEDGMENTS

To those who have helped me on my way,
thank you.

PROLOGUE

1977

Freya got detention for not kissing the bishop's hand. Though, to be precise, and if she had been paying attention, she would have known it was his ring she was supposed to kiss – an innocent enough mistake but one that rang with consequences. During the school Preparation Mass for lent, the bishop gave a long and boring homily on the importance of giving up something they valued so they could be 'in communion with Our Lord' fasting in the desert for forty days and forty nights. Freya wondered why 'forty nights' were always tagged on. Even she knew that Jesus couldn't exactly pop home for his tea every night.

Freya lined up in the school foyer with the rest of her class to see the bishop off. A shiny black car waited outside while the headmaster presented him with a framed photograph of the whole school. She had seen it at lunchtime sitting on the display table and had searched the rows of tiny heads for her own. Disappointingly, when she found it, her left eye was covered by her long fringe and her chin seemed to have grown a beard because of curly John standing in front. A brass tag underneath read, *Our Lady of Perpetual Sorrow School 1977.*

She was busy thinking about what to give up for lent —sugar in tea, chocolate? (no, too hard) – when she realised the bishop's fat fingers were waggling under her nose. Her cousin had done the same thing when she got engaged and wanted to show off her new diamond ring. The bishop's though was gold with a purple stone, just like a boiled sweet, and seemed enormous. Some conversation she'd had with her mum about compliments and finding something nice to say, popped into her mind.

'Oooh, lovely ring, Bishop. What a whopper,' she said as she took his hand and peered closer.

The bishop eased it away and smiled. 'May the Lord bless you and keep you, my child.'

Everything might have been well had not Mr McGann noticed. When the Bishop's car swung away, and the class line-up dissolved, Freya felt the tug of trouble on her collar. Mr McGann lifted her by her blazer so that she had to stand on tiptoes to keep her balance. The rough woollen fabric cut into her armpits and brushed up against her ears. She felt like a puppet swinging on twisted strings.

Mr McGann cocked his head. 'What did I tell you?'

'Don't know, sir.'

'Don't know, sir,' he mimicked. 'Perhaps an after-school detention might refresh your memory?' He dropped her collar, and she stumbled backward but the fabric stayed stuck up around her ears as if she had suddenly lost her neck. Her cheeks glowed red.

After school, she reported to class five for the detention, completed three pages of lines – *I must listen to my teacher* – slapped the sheets on the teacher's desk and rushed out to collect her brother from his primary school. When she arrived, Beckett was sitting on the wall tossing pebbles onto the pavement and scowling. He opened his mouth to speak.

'Don't even think about it,' Freya said.

'But–'

'Just shut up, will you?' She ignored his hurt expression, pushing down the little voice that told her she was being unfair. After all, hadn't *she* been the one who had been treated unfairly? Still, the last thing she needed was Beckett whining on about things. She grabbed his arm and pulled him off the wall. 'All right. Promise not to tell Mum I was late, and I'll buy you a Sherbet Dip Dab?'

Beckett trailed behind her as they made their way to the sweetshop, then along Castle Street and on to the park. Freya tried not to dwell on the incident with the bishop, though she couldn't understand why she had to kiss the ring in the first place. Wasn't everyone supposed to be equal: the first last, the last first? And why couldn't she be an altar server just because she was a girl? Adults seemed to have the power to make things the way they wanted them to be even when it didn't make any sense.

Freya perched in her usual place on the backrest of the park bench. From here she had a better view of the park and town: the peeling red slide she had not been on for two summers which served as a rain shelter when needed, the sports field where she and Debbie sunbathed and made daisy chains, the woods on the other side of the road, and the large housing estate she called home. She knew every inch of the place, from the parade of shops with a Co-op, chippy and knitting store, to the identical rows of ginger brick houses you could tell apart only by the street names and local knowledge, she even knew the cracks in the pavements and the stamp-sized squares of grass you weren't allowed to play football on. She hadn't thought about where she lived much, it was home, her turf, her world.

Freya pulled out the pack of *Bay City Rollers* trading cards from her bag. The fuchsia-pink plastic wrapper was took out the bubble gum and popped it in her mouth. The tutti-frutti flavour didn't last long but the pay-off was in its stretchiness. She drew out a long strand of the chewed-up gunk, wound it around her finger, returned it, chewed some more and then with the tip of her tongue poking out, blew steadily to form a bubble the size of a tangerine until it popped. Success was all in the technique; blow steady, pop and droop rather than blow too hard, pop and it stick which would then need to be picked off her top lip in fragments.

She turned her attention to the photo cards inside: a group shot of the band members lined up in their trademark tartan-hemmed trousers swinging at calf length, another with them wearing kilts, holding up a sign saying Happy New Year! and three individual portraits, two of which she already owned but could swap with Debbie, and to her delight, a picture of Derek the blond one she had a crush on.

Freya checked her watch – 4.15pm and no sign of Debbie yet. She glared over to Beckett playing on the swing and resented his eight-year-old joy. He waved. She turned away. Debbie was rushing toward her from the daisy field with a red envelope in her hand.

'Thought you weren't coming,' Freya said. 'Where you been?'

'Sorry, Frey. Just seen you-know-who.'

'You're joking?'

'Nope. Said he had something for me.'

'Don't tell me, he stuck a wet finger in your ear and all his mates had a laugh?'

Debbie settled next to her on the bench. 'Better than that.'

'No way?'

'Yes way. For a start, Kev's mates weren't with him. And secondly, he went all shy like and gave me this.' She lifted the envelope. 'I'm too scared to open it.'

She knew Debbie was just playing nervous to rub it in. Freya's insides felt funny like when she had a maths test. She grabbed the envelope. 'I'll open it then.'

'Don't.' Debbie snatched it back and tore open the flap.

'Suit yourself. Bet it's a joke anyway.'

Debbie pulled out a white Valentine's card with the words *I ♥ You* embossed in red on the front. An arrow pierced through the heart. Inside was written *GUESS WHO?* in uneven capitals.

'Doesn't prove anything,' Freya said, examining

the letters for any evidence to disprove what she already knew. She'd sat next to Kevin in class for two years and could recognise his writing a mile away, could in fact pick out the biro that left its tell-tale blob on the cross-stroke of the H, and could, if need be, tell blindfolded if he had entered the room just by the washing powder smell that wafted around him. A fog of misery clouded in. Debbie had stolen Kev.

Debbie snapped the card shut. 'You're just jealous.'

'Suit yourself. If you want to go out with a spotty creep, it's up to you.' Freya grabbed her bag. 'Beckett, time to go.'

Beckett's answer was to make the swing go faster. 'Just a few more minutes. Give us a push, will you?'

'No. Come *on.*'

'He's only a kid, Frey,' Debbie said. 'Don't be so mean. I'll push him.'

'He doesn't want you he wants me. Leave him alone.'

Everything about Debbie seemed to disgust Freya: her shiny dark hair she'd flick from her eyes with the exaggerated jerk of her head, the way she wiggled her hips when she walked to make herself look sexy, her school skirt folded over at the waist to show her knees, her keyring collection which included a purple 'Debbie' made of bendy plastic – Freya had yet to find one for her own name. But most of all she hated the perfect seagull wing of her brows which Debbie plucked into shape in the girls' toilet at lunchtime.

'Suit yourself, Beck.' Freya walked away. 'I'm going now. You'll have to go home on your own. Mum'll give you what for when I tell her.'

'Just ignore her,' Debbie said and carried on pushing him. 'She's a spoilsport, isn't she? How high do you want to go?'

'Right over the top. Push harder.'

'No, Beck,' Freya said. 'It's too dangerous. Debbie, stop it!'

Within moments he soared level with the cross bar. 'More,' he shrieked.

But Debbie answered her with a sarcastic smile, stretched up with both arms and put all her weight behind the swing. Beckett flew. As he reached horizontal, the chains rattled and slackened. His bottom sailed away from the seat. He lost his grip and was dragged downward like a tumbling ragdoll and landed, skidding over the tarmac.

Freya held her breath. Beckett let out a long, pitiful howl. The left side of his face looked scuffed up like a pair of old shoes and his nose was swollen and bent, like her uncle Charlie's who broke his in a rugby match scoring the winning try for England – that's what he'd told her anyway. More blood than she had ever seen gushed from Beckett's nostrils.

Debbie grabbed the swing to stop it thrashing about. She was chewing her lip and her eyes were wide and watery and she didn't say anything at all which made Freya hate her even more.

'You're all right, Beck,' Freya said but somehow didn't believe. 'Shush now.' Her voice sounded older and didn't seem to belong to her. 'Let's get you home.' Though home was the last place she wanted to be. There would be blame and punishment. She'd be lucky if she escaped without a hiding.

Beckett turned pale and grey – monochrome like the kids on *Blue Peter* she watched on their black and white telly who got a badge for doing interesting stuff which she could never afford to do.

'She k–kept pushing and wouldn't stop,' Beckett said in a whimpering nasal voice like he had a bad cold. 'Am I in trouble?'

'Course not. It's not your fault.' She glared up at Debbie. 'It's hers.'

Debbie stepped back and dropped the swing, clunking it onto Freya's head.

'Right, that's it, Debbie. Just you wait.'

Freya lunged at her, briefly catching hold of her coat hood before she tugged away leaving only a handful of the fur trim in her fingers. Freya sprinted after her, gained ground, her sight fixed only on the source of everything wrong in her life – Debbie.

Freya chased Debbie across the road into the woods. Cars swerved, tyres squealed, horns bellowed, all serving to fuel her fury. She slowed down to a trot, her eyes taking a few seconds to adjust to the dim woodland light. She was aware of her new rosary beads they'd all been given in honour of the bishop's visit, jingle-jangling in their plastic tub. Panting, she came to a stop, took out the tub from her pocket and eased off the lid. Small pink beads coiled around a crucifix. They were cute, reassuring. But then she thought of how much she hated Debbie. The rosary was yet another reminder of how she failed to live up to the perfect holy life of sweet Saint Bernadette of Lourdes. The school was always going on about her, expecting all the girls to become nuns – well, they could get stuffed. She hurled the rosary tub at a tree and shouted, 'Debbie Monkcombe, you're dead.'

Freya squinted through the gloom taking in her surroundings: nettles, brambles, ferns still brown from winter, hazel rods breaking into bud, orange fungus on fallen tree stumps, smelt the earthiness of mushrooms and damp leaves.

She knew these woods well. The Wild Place, she called it. A path through the undergrowth led to Old Tramp's Cabin, a tumbledown disused signal box next to the railway tracks. Could Debbie be hiding there? She imagined her crouched in a corner behind the abandoned fridge, scared half to death, whimpering and her hair tugged all out of place. And this thought pleased her; to have power over little Miss Perfect and her perfect shiny hair and perfect brows that made her look permanently surprised – huh, she'd be surprised all right when she got hold of her. But deep-down Freya knew Debbie wasn't scared of anyone, had even punched Raymond Smith just for saying she looked chubby. Debbie, far from being afraid, would probably be hiding somewhere in the thicket waiting to jump out on *her*.

The trees stood tall and bare: great oaks and limes, and broken elms riddled with disease, crows circled overhead, trains rumbled in the distance, stinging nettles flopped over a path to the right of her and long bramble stems wound around fallen tree stumps. No, Debbie wouldn't have gone that way.

Years later, Freya wondered what might have been had she taken the overgrown path to her right. Would her wrath have been snagged and spent on the briars, her fury expended in the heat of nettle rash, her rage chilled in the cool evening light?

CHAPTER 1

Freya gathered up her handbag and coat, retrieved the small box of personal items from the backseat: books, pens, some obsolete chalk, confiscated debris from wayward students, letters of thanks, postcards from azure beaches she would never visit, and sat for a moment staring through the windscreen with the box upon her lap as if it were a sleeping cat she did not want to disturb. *How can memories weigh so heavy?*

'Don't take it personally,' Pat said, bringing her back. 'Scapegoating is never pretty.'

Freya winced. She had been grappling with that thought for a lifetime.

'We all knew the school needed to make cuts, Frey. Just a matter of where and when the axe would fall.'

'And you, will you be safe?'

'Ha! I saw it coming ages ago. Why do you think I took on curriculum liaison? The trick my dear, is to make yourself indispensable.'

'Right. Good. Indispensable.' Freya realised she had been sleep-walking these past few months.

'Mind you, it won't stop our mighty Head from giving himself a big fat pay rise.'

'Graham? No…he wouldn't…would he?'

'Really?' Pat raised an eyebrow and checked her hair in the rear-view mirror. 'That's precisely why you're such an easy target. And you're probably too expensive. Wages, agency fees, etcetera, etcetera. Anyway, let's hope the parasites have earned their fee and have a load of jobs lined up for you.' She turned and looked at her. 'Oh Freya, you haven't phoned them, have you? For heaven's sake why not?'

It was just this same question she had been asking herself. 'I will, I will…tomorrow.' But something niggled which had nothing to do with finding another contract. It was the stark and sudden realisation that she could no longer teach, or rather did not want to, a muddled bag of grief, fatigue, and uneasy restlessness.

Beckett once asked her why she loved to teach, as if he didn't know! Wasn't he the first to see her come alive with the sheer joy of sharing this mighty thing called knowledge? Hadn't he sat crossed legged in their nursery, lined up with all the dolls and superhero figurines while she acted teacher, precocious with hands on hips, coaxing him to recite his timetables? And wasn't she the first one to guide his chalky hand into a perfect 'a' on the blackboard? Playing 'schools', edifying and enriching, formed their unshakable bond.

She tried to pinpoint the moment when teaching slipped into a dull routine and the magic disappeared. When did she stop nurturing the wonder? But a beach does not simply wash into the sea on the turn of a tide, rather a slow erosive process of longshore drift occurs. The loss of Beckett was that final fatal storm which washed away the love.

'Thanks for the lift.' Freya gave a wane smile and climbed out.

Pat wound down the window. 'Promise?'

'Promise!' She knew it would end up being a white lie.

'And keep in touch.'

'Sure will, promise.' Another white lie. She trudged up the garden path toward her small, terraced house, didn't bother to look back and wave, let herself in, closed the door behind her with a gentle click, and breathed. The crushing sensation in her chest subsided.

Tea would help.

The kitchen, only ten feet square but bright and cheerful with its butler sink, shaker units and wooden worktops had been constructed in faith to an imagined bliss to be fulfilled by a husband and children. That it remained just that, an imaginary ideal yet to be grasped, she cared not to think about just now. It had once been within her reach but out of a dutiful conscience she let it slip away. This snug little kitchen would remain instead the belly of Jonah's whale, steadfast against the raucous sea and a motif to the demands of her conscience. It was here she retreated when the stresses and strains became too much, here she drank tea, baked, and made bunting to hang above the window.

Oh hell, the bunting! How she regretted letting her Year 10 class create a World War II wall display unsupervised. They were a hard class to win over in the first place and it seemed a way to create mutual trust. So much for that; the naivety of their swastika bunting festooning the walls and windows hung as if it were celebrating some jolly summer fete rather than glorifying the feared emblem of a tyrannical regime. Graham, of course, happened to be passing the classroom just as Freya returned from lunch and was removing the offending article. 'Hmm, interesting display,' he'd said without elaborating until he'd used it as further evidence for not renewing her temporary teaching contract, that, and the very small fact of a slight altercation in her classroom between two boys settling old scores. The damning moment came during a particularly dull history lesson – Chamberlain and appeasement.

That morning there had been a distraction in school. The statue of Our Lady of Perpetual Sorrow standing in the courtyard between the science and humanities blocks, received a make-over, a new pair of sunglasses courtesy of an artful student and a black marker pen. The class, over-excited and restless, marvelling at this show of audacity, wildly speculating on both culprit and due punishment, refused to settle. Boredom crept in; chaos broke out.

In truth, she hadn't been paying enough attention, had in fact been staring out of the window watching the caretaker attempt to remove the sunglasses with a wet rag and a bottle of kitchen cleaner. She thought of her brother, he would know what to do. And she caught herself – *dearest Beckett, gone!* A crevasse opened, her throat coughed out a tiny yelp and the caretaker outside went all blurry.

Whale belly or no, Freya stayed in the kitchen

until the grey light faded to pitch and supper time had long since passed. Tea gave way to wine. Thoughts rose like gaseous bile, vague half-formed things.

Freya poured another drink and took it upstairs to the spare room Beckett used on his visits. Why hadn't she just called it his room? She couldn't remember the last time anyone else stayed there. It might have given him ownership, anchored him, made him feel more.connected. She should make a start with the clearing. On the mantelpiece above the fireplace in a see-through plastic evidence bag the police returned to her was the debris from his coat pocket: a few coins, some garden twine, a betting slip from Ladbrokes – he had been at it again – a wooden rosary and a small buff-coloured seed packet. The letters *G&D B/M* were scrawled on it in Beckett's large handwriting. Her heart tugged. To sum him up in three words, if anyone had cared to ask, she might have said, trusting, magnanimous, generous.

She took a closer look: *Brassica Nigra ~ Black Mustard ~ Approximately 500 seeds.* She upended the packet and tapped out the remaining black seeds into her palm. So very tiny and yet significant, a parable of sorts. The faith of a mustard seed, perhaps he would want me to have faith, she thought, but in what? Faith in a cold distant God? Hope? Hope in Beckett's innocence of breaking the

6

commandment 'thou shalt not kill' – not even thyself? Faith that 'all shall be well, and all shall be well, and all manner of things shall be well'? But they were not and never could be. Beckett was gone and her life would never be the same again. She blew hard into her palm, scattering the seeds in a haphazard fashion. With her flash of anger satiated, she found to her bewilderment that the empty seed packet was still in her other hand, as if this too should have been scattered into the receptacle of the room. For no other reason than to ensure the complete purging of its contents, she looked inside. To her surprise there was a slip of paper on which Beckett had written *Jack and Gil went up the hill.* She sighed, *Gil* instead of Jill, the legacy of his dyslexia. Odd though, that he should write a nursery rhyme.

Freya laid back onto the bed and studied the halo the glass shade cast onto the ceiling. A chip on the rim threw the circle askew. She tried to imagine how it would look if it were unbroken, how she might smooth out the damage and make it whole again. It was with this thought that she dozed off and then awoke some hours later. With no resolution to the shade's imperfection, she rolled over foetal-like and groaned.

The wardrobe doors didn't quite fit flush due to the straps of Beckett's backpack she had unceremoniously dumped there after the police returned it along with the rest of his belongings. Sorting through it was yet another necessary task in the tying of loose ends.

She lay there for some minutes gathering the energy to get up, her will torn between curiosity for its contents and apathy. When at last she opened the wardrobe, the musty-canvas odour of scout jamborees flooded the room: campfires, tents billowing in the wind, sleep roused on dewy mornings by the smell of frying bacon. Good times. Inside the dirt smeared rucksack was Beckett's navy windcheater, the one with the orange hood she had bought for him at a country show, and an Ordnance Survey map of Dartmoor with curled and frayed corners. She tried spreading it out on the bed but it fell apart along the fold lines and she needed to fetch some sticky tape from the all-sorts drawer in the kitchen to piece it back together. Freya scanned the swirling orange contour lines and the pale no-colour wilderness areas that marked the moor. Beckett had ringed several places with a fat-leaded pencil: *Devil's Table, Wolf Down, Pail Pool, Margin Tor.*

Near to the bottom of the map where the moor met the gentler wooded hills of Devon, he had drawn a star beside a blue pint-jug icon and written *George & Dragon.* It stood along a lonely track with only a few buildings to mark out any hint of a settlement. She followed this track with her fingernail until it changed into a proper road, as if tracing the lines would bring her closer to the physical landscape where Beckett had once walked. The road soon hit a village to the north, a few centimetres on the map translating to roughly half a mile in real scale. The cluster of buildings were labelled as Brohn-In-The-Moor. Could this be what Beckett meant when he had written *G&D B/M* on the seed packet: The George and Dragon at Brohn-In-The-Moor?

Freya turned her attention back to the rucksack and unpacked the contents with an unexplained urgency. In the bottom, wrapped up in one of his checked shirts was a pocket-sized photo album. Flicking through it she reviewed the aeons of his life: Beckett as a baby on a sheepskin rug, him riding a tricycle, Akela handing him a scout badge, the family on a trip to London in front of Big Ben, his graduation, a photo of him with herself taken the previous summer at a fish restaurant on the coast. He had worn the windcheater that day and she an optimistic navy jacket with gilt sailor buttons. It was freezing and her warm smile did little to distract the attention away from her blue lips. The wind pummelled the shore and her hair danced in the wind. Even so, she remembered the sky a radiant blue, the sun sequinning the water trying hard to warm them, and diners pouring outside onto the promenade to eat at shiny tables with bowls of olives imagining they were on holiday in warmer climes.

One of the album pages bulged a little in its plastic pouch. Curious, she removed the photos. Sandwiched between them was a folded A4 piece of paper which read, *'Conscience betrays guilt' Latin Proverb,* and below that in Beckett's handwriting, *Freya, forgive me.*

She turned it over – no date, no explanation, nothing so why hadn't he put it somewhere more obvious if he wanted her to find it? And what use was it? It didn't even begin to explain the whys and wherefores of his death, but only added confusion and more weight to the police's version of events: probable suicide. The holding term remained at 'open', at least pending new evidence or until the cut-off point in December just two months from now when the coroner's inquest was due. The word 'suicide' was a final bureaucratic and damning judgement on a man who loved life, as if the word had no repercussions. But it did, invalidating all the principles by which he lived. It was ludicrous to even imagine that Beckett would have taken his own life. And if the unthinkable were true, what could possibly have pushed him to the abyss? She ran over the last few months in her head. Had they grown so far apart that she missed the signs? Why hadn't he shared his troubles? Was he so lost he could not even contemplate confiding with Father Paul, their mutual and long-standing priest friend?

Father Paul paid her a visit soon after Beckett's death. They drank tea in her little kitchen and ate scones fresh from the oven, though to her they were like dry cotton wool and impossible to swallow. Father Paul reminisced with all the conflicted gaiety of a person confident in his faith, as if Beckett had merely stepped through a veil into a parallel universe. Yet his voice cracked and faltered at one point, and he stopped to shed silent tears. She laid her hand upon his and squeezed, her own well of grief forgotten for now.

'Sorry, old girl, not much good to you, am I?' He dabbed at his eyes with a crisp white handkerchief.

'Paul. What's going to happen to him?'

He refolded the handkerchief in silence, returned it to the breast pocket of his jacket and stared into his teacup. 'They will do a post-mortem. Procedure I'm afraid. I take it you've seen him.'

'Yes, at the official identification.'

'Was he…peaceful?'

'Oh, Paul,' she shook her head. 'It didn't look like him at all. He was so…*absent*. Where do you think he's gone?'

Father Paul could not say in certainty what she wanted to hear, that Beckett now dwelt in Heaven, nor definitively what had happened to him if it had indeed been suicide. There were matters about the stewardship and sanctity of his life, of culpability, psychological and emotional factors, and his real intentions to consider, none of which anyone other than Beckett and God Himself could fathom. The phrase, 'God's mercy', dappled through his speech. He urged her to offer up her sufferings in prayer and supplication and think no more of these things for this route led only to more sorrow.

Freya had taken his advice at first, spent days in church, kneeling on the cold stone steps of the sanctuary until her knees were numb and her back ached with weariness, pleading, bargaining, as if her physical pain could atone for Beckett's transgression. Father Paul found her one evening as he came to lock up the church.

'My dear Freya,' he said, helping her up. 'Enough. Enough now.'

He led her to the front pew and sat with her. Votive candles flickered in the corner below a statue of Our Lady sending out an amber light into the gathering dusk, playing out the eternal struggle between light and dark. Under the upturned ark of the roof, a cavernous silence descended. An abandoned umbrella lay further along the bench and Freya couldn't help worrying that someone would be missing it by now.

'What's with all this?' he said in a voice to melt the soul, born from a lifetime of compassion.

'If I could just do this for him,' she said. 'Nothing else matters. I've got to know he's alright, that he's not…' Her eyes lowered to the tiled floor. As she delved into their past, a smile fleetingly crossed her lips. 'Seems silly now. We made a pact the way kids do, to look out for each other. Mother's illness meant we fended for ourselves most of the time. That was straight after the…' she stopped and pushed back the memories surfacing from a roiling sea: Beckett in the playground, the silent pause between a heartbeat, the sealing of a secret. 'It's my fault. I wasn't there for him. It should've been me that died, not him.'

'That's a silly thing to say, old girl. You are not responsible for his actions. Beckett alone must give an account of his life. What we do not know is the state of his mind at the time. However, I don't believe anyone really wants to take their own life. I think they just want the pain to go away. I'm comforted by the stories of suicide survivors, the bridge jumpers. They often change their minds on the way down.'

Freya looked away, unsure where her

responsibility began and ended. It was like unravelling a tangled ball of string that stretched back in time. 'But if I promised to be a better person, give my life to the poor, teach in a mission or something? Or if I became a nun, surely that would make up for things?'

'It's the mistake everyone makes.' Father Paul rapped his knuckles on the pew end. 'They think there are bargaining chips. There aren't!'

'So, it's hopeless!'

'Hardly. There aren't any because there is no debt, it's already been paid. Come on, you know all this. And for the record, so did Beckett. He need only accept it.'

But Freya could not accept it, was unable to reconcile her powerlessness with an omnipotent God who remained silent in her turmoil. So, she left her faith on a shelf in the closet of her soul while she pondered the little facts she did know about Beckett's death. Father Paul phoned from time to time, leaving messages on her answerphone that she never returned. Though Freya lamented blocking Father Paul out of her life, she saw no other way. He was a constant reminder of a God she could not trust and a faith she now lacked.

She turned her attention back to Beckett's cryptic note: *Conscience betrays guilt* and his tag line: *Freya, forgive me.* His ready admission of a guilty conscience set her mind racing. She couldn't conceive of Beckett ever needing *her* forgiveness, and as a suicide note, it didn't stand up. Something had to have happened prior to the s… she willed her mind to say 'accident' instead, something by definition beyond his control. Then there was the mustard seed packet. Why this of all seeds if it had not meant anything? And the backpack with the photo album and the map leading her to his location. But the strangest puzzle of all was the obscure nursery line: *Jack and Gil went up the hill.* Dismissing the rogue thought that these could all be mere coincidences, or just nonsense, the only action in her power to take was to follow Beckett to Brohn-In-The-Moor and discover what he had been trying to tell her.

Freya grabbed the rucksack, raced to her room, and stuffed into it an unconsidered assortment of clothes and toiletries. She returned to his room and cast a quick last look around and decided to take the photo album along with his navy and orange windcheater, despite it being so large that she would need to fold over the cuffs, then switched off the damaged light. In the kitchen she scribbled a note to her neighbour: *I have some time off work and a holiday offer has turned up out of the blue* – better to lie than to go into the convoluted details. *Don't know when I'll be back. Please could you keep an eye on the place? I'd be so grateful. Emergency cash in the cocoa tin by kettle. Thanks, Freya.* She popped it into an envelope along with her spare key and wrote *Bridget* on the front.

Dawn light nudged through the windows and the row of greeting cards sitting on the hall console table took on a luminescence. Freya walked past then stopped. She hovered a moment, turned back, scooped them into the rucksack and left without stopping to pick up the solitary card that flip-flopped onto the tiles. The cover, a cross entwined with a lily, lay half-open and inside were the copperplate words: *Thoughts and Prayers. Fr Paul x.*

CHAPTER 2

Freya caught a train to the little market town of Stannaton, as near as she could get to Dartmoor itself, the moor being too remote and wild to make a passenger line through it profitable. She had a few hours to kill before the bus was due which would take her onwards towards Brohn-In-The-Moor. She lingered in the camping and outdoors shop, stood in awe at the lightness and portability of hike tents, so different from the heavy canvas one she carted up and down Mount Snowdon on her Duke of Edinburgh expedition when she was seventeen. She bought a torch and batteries and then sipped hot chocolate in the tearoom until the allotted time.

The journey took much longer than expected and followed the natural contour lines of the landscape, alongside rivers strewn with boulders, through deep valleys and dark woods, skirting impassable moorland which could swallow up roads in heavy rainstorms. Passengers thinned. Freya listed towards the front of the bus to ask the driver where she should get off for The George and Dragon. He frowned, he wasn't going that far, that would be the Tuesday bus. What about a taxi? Unlikely around here. So, her impulsiveness had landed her in the middle of nowhere with night drawing in.

'Best phone and get someone to pick you up,' the driver said. 'Mind, you'd be lucky to get a signal round here. S'pose you could try up on the tor.'

'Thanks, but I'll manage. Not to worry,' she said without bothering to say she didn't have a mobile.

'Reckon you *should* be worried, my dear.' He looked out through the windscreen at the darkening sky. 'Moor's no place to be caught in the dark, not even if weather's half decent. Look, how's about you just stay onboard and I'll take you back to town? There's a small hotel along the High Street.'

She drew back her shoulders. 'I can't. I must get there tonight.'

A sigh came from the driver, and he pulled over to look at her map. 'See where that lane forks?' he said. 'I can't get the bus over the bridge but if you get off here,' he tapped the map, 'and if you're sharpish, you could nip

self-conscious and comforted at the same time, like saying prayers out loud in an empty room. The pony shuddered off the rain and with a toss of his mane, trotted away.

Freya stood inside the circle and checked the map. Three other such stone circles were close by, she could be at any one of them. And now, without the sun for navigation and no functioning compass, she accepted she was lost. Unease crept over her: to be lost and alone as darkness fell, a primitive fear re-surfaced. She sat on a fallen stone, kicked at the scree, held her head in her hands, then noticed a faint engraving on a fallen standing stone. She scraped the moss and lichen from the granite, felt the indentations of the past, a Celtic cross at odds with the pagan stone circle. Here at least the familiarity gave some comfort. As the demarcation softened between land and sky, day and night, summer and autumn, time and eternity, Freya experienced a fleeting moment of harmony. Despite the trauma of the last month, a sense of peace came upon her. All at once the mists lifted. In the distance, a cluster of lights twinkled momentarily from what she assumed to be a farm. She heaved the rucksack onto her back and headed towards it.

Fifty yards from the lights she saw her mistake, not a farm but a stone field shelter lit with floodlights operated by movement sensors. The byre door had been bolted with a heavy padlock. To the left was a high window covered by a simple wooden shutter made from old planks and secured only by a rusty nail through a metal hoop. Freya estimated it was perhaps six feet from the ground. Surely, she could scramble up. Anyway, it was a case of having to. She picked up a rock, dislodged the nail, and the shutter obediently swung free. She bundled her rucksack through the opening, jumped up and with fingertips on the windowsill and feet seeking traction on the rough stones, pulled herself through.

Inside, the dark seemed impenetrable. At least she had the foresight to buy the torch earlier. She switched it on and swept it around. The byre had a dirt floor and a tideline of dried dung lapped up the walls. An assortment of old farm utensils rusted in one corner and in the other was a fresh bale of hay which she loosened from its string to make up a bed for herself. She searched the rucksack for Beckett's microlite sleeping bag she thought to pack but evidently in her haste, had forgotten. She remembered it now sitting on the kitchen table as she wrote the letter to Bridget. Her new-found peace fell away along with the plummeting temperature. Dressing in what little additional clothing she had packed, she gathered up the hay around her and thought not of her shivering body or the fear coming over her in waves, but of Beckett lighting a fire for her when they were kids on a scout camp. Then, the ebony hills sat among the stars and their amber tinged faces wore the look of wonder.

Freya switched off the torch, unsure how long the batteries would last. Dark closed in around her and outside the sounds of the night carried across the moor: owls screeching, the claxon call of disturbed pheasants and the unearthly, terrifying rasps of what she hoped were nothing more benign than a cete of badgers. Sleep was fitful, dreamy, wrenched by spasms of cold which shuddered through her body. At one point, something set off the motion sensor and the outside light flashed on. Some unknown creature scraped at the door trying to claw its way in.

After many hours, when dawn surely was not far off, the sensor tripped once more. The byre filled with strands of light nudging in through the cracks in the window shutter. For a moment, she sensed rather than felt herself kneel in front of the light as if she had found hallowed ground. Sleep returned and when she awoke, she was lying on a sofa covered with a tartan rug, in a homely room with a low ceiling and blackened beams, and a fire roaring in the inglenook. A silver-haired man had his back to her and was cooking on a range.

'Ah, so you're awake,' he said turning around, his

smile full of warmth. 'How are you feeling?' He had the complexion of someone having lived outside most of his life, like a russet apple with a flush of red across his cheeks. He reminded her of Beckett though older. In twenty years, Beckett would look like this. She checked herself, could have looked like this. She gave a heavy sigh.

'Hey…hey now. What's wrong?' He went over to her and cocked his head, puzzlement on his face. 'Perhaps we should start again. I'm Jack.'

'Sorry,' she said. 'It's just you remind me of someone…sorry. I'm Freya.'

'Tch, nothing to be sorry about. You've had a shock, and near on hypothermia. You need a brew inside you. Milk and sugar?' He returned to the stove and put a blackened kettle on the hotplate. 'By the way,' he said over his shoulder, 'What in bally's name were you doing out there? Moor's no place to be alone in the dark, easy to lose your bearings. You're lucky I was out early checking on the hay stores so I could put the ewes out to pasture.'

Freya blushed. 'Yes, I realise that now. It was stupid of me… causing so much trouble for you. Sorry.'

'Well, no harm done, and you can stop apologising. You hungry?' He picked up the frying pan, tilting it so she could see the sausages, eggs, bacon, and black pudding glistening inside.

'Starving, but you can keep the black pudding,' she grimaced.

Jack helped her sit up, arranged a series of cushions behind her and tucked the rug over her legs. 'Best rest up and keep warm for today.' He placed the breakfast tray onto her lap and put a mug of tea on top of a boating magazine beside her on the coffee table, then knelt in front of her. 'May I?' he asked and dabbed at her forehead. 'You feel a bit hot. I should take you to the surgery in Stannaton.'

'I'm fine, really. Probably just a chill.'

'Hmm. We'll keep an eye on you. Eat up.'

Freya, though ravenous, struggled to swallow. 'Sorry, my eyes are bigger than my belly.'

'Thought we weren't apologising anymore! I'm in and out all day what with the animals and all the bally admin. But have a sleep. I'll try not to disturb you.'

'Thanks, but no. I'll be on my way now.' As she stood, the room swam around her and she fell back onto the sofa. 'Perhaps I'll feel better in an hour or so,' she said, though she knew this was unlikely.

Jack looked at her with a kindness she felt unable to refuse. He seemed genuine, safe. Her spirit of independence softened. 'Thank you, Jack,' she smiled. 'It's kind of you.'

'Expect you'd do the same for me,' he said, waving away the compliment. 'Stay…stay a while, at least until you're better? Where are you heading?'

'Brohn-In-The-Moor.'

'Then consider yourself arrived. Though why anyone should ever want to come to Brohn will remain forever a mystery to me. Nothing here but sheep and weather.' Jack moved to the door, stepped into his work boots, and bent to tie the laces. 'Allow me to be your guide when you've recovered that is. Tour shouldn't take more than ten minutes, fifteen if you stop to talk to the sheep. But that can wait, I've work to do.'

She giggled. 'Sorry, I'm stopping you. And Jack, yes, and yes to both questions. Thank you.'

He straightened up, took his coat from a hook, and popped on his hat. 'Be good, no partying till I get back!' he said and let himself out.

Freya smiled after him. She wasn't one for instant friendships, but he had an affability she couldn't resist. Warm and content, she sat a while gazing into the fire until it needed more logs and she more tea, and afterwards, she slept.

CHAPTER 3

The next day, with the brief tour of Brohn-In-The-Moor over, Freya and Jack stood side by side outside *The George and Dragon Inn*.

'Ready for this?' Jack asked.

'A lamb to the slaughter?'

'Not quite, more like the Spanish inquisition.'

Freya hoped he was joking. She looked up at the pub sign swinging over the entrance. A knight sat on a rearing white horse slaying a fire-breathing dragon. Its fangs and talons seemed too realistic for such a pastoral setting. The granite pub had a thatched roof and windows intercepting it like surprised eyes under lifted brows. It sat fronting a stable yard enclosed by barns and next to it ran a babbling brook. Jack opened the door for her and stood aside. She took a deep breath and crossed the threshold.

Inside, daylight struggled to illuminate the room and was supplemented by an array of wall lights and faux oil lamps set in various nooks and crannies. Blackened beams weighed down the ceiling making the space appear even darker. An inglenook fireplace, large enough to stand up in, housed a bread oven and an iron fire grate that could accommodate a small tree trunk – and no doubt had roasted whole pigs down the years – took up the whole sidewall.

Opposite the entrance was a bar behind which stood a dark-haired woman polishing a row of beer pumps. Jack made the introductions with minimal fuss. 'Freya, Susie our landlady, Susie, Freya.'

Susie stopped, her cloth marooned half-way up the enamel pump shaft. 'So, *this* is Freya?'

Jack coughed, an action not lost on Freya. News of her arrival had already spread around the village.

Susie resumed the polishing. 'I've heard a lot about you.'

'All good, eh Susie?' Jack said. 'Mine's a pint of Fitzwell's Folly. Freya, what'll you have?'

'Gossip travels fast around here,' Susie continued. 'Glad your night in the barn didn't do you too much harm. Strange things have been known to happen out there, all alone on the misty moors–'

'Susie, that'll do,' Jack interrupted. 'We don't want to be frightening her away, do we?'

'All I was saying is you wouldn't catch *me* out there after dark.'

'She's having you on, Freya, take no notice. And Susie, when you've quite finished putting the fear of God into our guest here,' he fished out his wallet and waved a ten-pound note, 'perhaps you can fetch her a pint of Wonky Wassail.' He turned to Freya. 'You okay with cider?'

They took their drinks to a table in the corner and spent a lazy hour getting to know each other. She told him about her 'break' in teaching but not about the humiliation of being 'let go' at Our Lady of Perpetual Sorrow School, made worse by the fact she had only reluctantly taken the job in the first place because there was nothing else on offer at the time. It had taken all her strength to overcome the memories of it as a schoolgirl. Her time there as a child had been unhappy and cut short because of what was termed a 'nervous breakdown' brought on, so the psychiatrists thought, by the sudden and tragic death of her friend Debbie. She explained her current career break to Jack as a sabbatical that had been on the cards for a while (though in truth it had been wishful thinking), then with her brother's passing she had decided to grasp the opportunity. Details were scant, washed over.

'You have a pretty name,' Jack said to fill a momentary lull. 'Freya means Lady or in Norse, the goddess of love and fertility.'

She had the distinct impression he was flirting. 'I'll go for Lady. I don't qualify for the other.'

'Oh, I've embarrassed you, sorry.' The easy-going mood between them dissolved and Jack seemed to be searching for something to say. 'Your parents had quite a thing for names: Freya and Beckett.'

'Beckett! But how…? I never told you his name.'

'Sure, you did.' Jack fingered the handle of his pint jug. 'How else would I know?'

Freya did a quick tally of all the conversations she'd had with him and frowned. 'I guess I've forgotten.' Though she was almost certain she had never used Beckett's actual name.

'Why did they choose Beckett?' he asked.

'From Thomas à Becket, Christian saint and martyr. Mum liked the sound of it, Beckett Greene. But he was always just Beck to me.'

'Even better, the name for a stream.' He took a swig of ale. 'Beck Greene – the mythical Green Man, symbol of man's union with nature, rebirth and transcendence.' There was a playful look in his eyes and

30

her misgivings melted away. She must have said his name at some point.

'Green Man. He would've loved that.' Freya smiled at Beckett's memory. 'He was happiest when he was outdoors in nature among the rivers and rocks and the plants and trees. How come you know all this mythical stuff?'

'Just a hobby. I do folklore, too, when the mood takes me.'

'And sailing?' she asked. Jack's breath caught momentarily in his throat. 'I saw the boating magazine on your coffee table,' she explained.

'There was I thinking you had the gift of foresight like ol' Cassandra. Ah, to be out at sea,' he sighed. 'But my adventure days are over. This old sea dog has washed ashore.' There seemed to be pain behind the comedy.

'I don't believe that for a minute…Hey, I once saw a care home called Dun-Roaming. Can you imagine?'

Jack laughed which gave her the confidence to ask, 'Seriously, have you really done with all your sea-faring adventures?' Then she felt ridiculous for using such an antiquated term.

'Strictly inshore now,' he shrugged. 'I've a small dinghy, *The Dragon,* out on the lake, that's all. Farm keeps me busy, only got thirty acres but that's quite enough for me thanks very much. And I read. It's my thing, folklores, myths and the storytelling.'

Jack as the raconteur; that she could imagine. His voice was deep with resonance, as spellbinding as any Shakespearean actor.

'It never ceases to amaze me,' he said, 'how people have always found stories to explain the great unexplainable.'

'You sound like a friend of mine.' Freya thought of Father Paul and pushed down the nub of guilt.

'Then your friend is a wise man. There's a saying;

'*We are all travellers on this ancient land,*

Forever old and forever new.

And when at time's final end,

We shall all dwell here anew'.'

'That's so beautiful. I wish Beckett had heard that. Too late.'

'It's never too late,' he murmured.

At supper that night Freya diverted Jack's increasing curiosity. They sat opposite each other at the kitchen table, the remnants of their fish and chips supper going cold on willow patterned plates. She regretted her earlier honesty, however guarded it had been. To be open was to be vulnerable. If being with Duncan her once-lover – if it had indeed amounted to such in its chasteness – had taught her anything it was this, if she were to reveal her true self, she would be rejected. No ifs or maybes, but a point of indisputable fact, empirically proven as well as any scientific study. She answered Jack's questions with barely adequate answers. 'Why teaching?' Easy. 'Wanted to since a child.' 'Why history?' 'Was good at it,' though this pat reply didn't satisfy him. 'What is it about history that grabs you?' Trickier question. 'Same as you really, it's about the stories we tell, or the lies.' Caution, she reminded herself, remain enigmatic. 'As a society I mean. How bias interprets facts,' she added quickly.

'And how does that work for you?' Jack asked, pushing his supper plate away and leaning forward to study her.

'What's that supposed to mean?'

'Freya, why have you come here? Not by chance, for sure. You said yourself, you were specifically on your way to Brohn-In-The-Moor when you got lost in the mist. There's nothing here and, forgive me for saying, but you hardly seem the outdoors type.'

She weighed up his trust for a moment before reaching into the back pocket of her jeans and tossing some folded pieces of paper onto the table in front of him. Jack stared and then picked them up. She gave him a minute to read and digest.

'Admittedly, it took me quite a while,' she said. 'Weeks in fact, to pluck up enough courage to go through Beckett's things. I found the seed packet on the mantel piece and that slip of paper inside, and then the note hidden in a photo album inside his rucksack. The police returned it ages ago and I'd just shoved into the wardrobe.' Her voice galloped along. 'You see, he was on his way to G and D, in B dash M. I looked it up on the Ordnance Survey map and it could only be here, The George and Dragon in Brohn-In-The-Moor. He'd ringed it and everything.' She drew a breath. 'The police think it was suicide.'

Jack winced. 'This one,' he flicked the corner of the A4 sheet, '*Conscience betrays guilt. Freya, forgive me*. Seems he had something on his mind. Doesn't that amount to a suicide note?'

'I don't believe the police's theory for a minute. He just wouldn't do that. Not my Beck.' She moved around to Jack's side of the table, 'Look!' she said, pointing to the words *Jack and Gil went up the hill* on the smaller slip of paper. 'I think he was trying to tell me something.'

'It's just a silly nursery rhyme. If you want my advice, I think you're on a fool's errand. Let the police do their job. Truth will out in the end.'

So that was what she got for her candour. She sniffed and considered her next move. If Jack wasn't to be an ally, fine, but perhaps he may be useful, nevertheless. 'Jack, the police said Beckett died on a Tor here in Dartmoor. Did he make it as far as Brohn-In-The-Moor?'

'The mists deliver all manner of folk to Brohn. It's a wild place. Some are running away, some running to, which is why I keep shtum. It's only when they've worked through their stuff that they move on. This is a staging post, that's all.'

'Did he come here?' she pressed.

'We all pass through here, Freya.'

She scooped up the dinner plates and shoved them on the kitchen side. 'What does that even mean? We all pass through here!'

'And yet it's true. You'll see.'

'Jack, can you help me out here?'

He walked over to the plates and scraped the leftovers into the bin.

'I didn't mean the dishes.' She plopped a plate into the washing up bowl and scrubbed hard.

When Jack had finished the scraping, he asked, 'Will you sit and have a glass of wine with me?'

She was tired and still recovering from her escapade on the moor. A cosy evening by the fire had not been part of the plan, but a gut feeling told her to stay. Very well, if Jack had a penchant for storytelling, she would just have to wait until he told the right story. She let him lead her to the sofa.

'You look like a red wine sort of girl to me,' he said. 'Malbec okay?' Before she could answer he had whipped out a wine bottle from the drink's cabinet in the corner of the room and presented it to her with all the flourish of a sommelier. 'Is that a little smile I see? And for the record, I am on your side. Heaven knows we have enough demons out there trying to get us.' He opened the wine, sniffed the cork, then poured two large glasses. 'To friendship,' he said clinking her glass.

'To friendship,' she replied, whatever that meant.

Later that evening when Jack went to refill for a third time, she covered her glass. 'You're getting me tipsy.'

'Just one more.'

'Not for me. Lots to do in the morning. Jack…You've been really sweet, letting me stay but– '

'But…Don't tell me, you've had a better offer?'

'Not exactly. I've arranged with Susie to stay in The Byre, the B&B behind the pub in the stable yard from tomorrow.'

Freya would have her own room but would need to share the lounge and kitchen with the other long-term guest, a guy she would meet later. Susie had given her a wink, though Freya was at a loss to its meaning. Her other gesture, however, was unmistakable. They had been talking about Jack when Susie mimed holding an invisible glass to her lips and waggling it: he liked the booze.

Jack poured himself another glass and smiled. 'Oh well, was nice while it lasted. I'll drop you off in the morning.'

CHAPTER 4

Susie unlocked the door to Freya's room in The Byre. 'It's a bit stuffy, been vacant for a while since the last chap…Never mind…I'll open the window. Best close it well before dusk if you don't want to catch your death. Brohn can get chilly this time of year.' She looked Freya up and down. 'You have a winter coat, I take it?'

'I didn't think I needed one. Is there a shop nearby?'

'You're not in the city now, love. We've a small post office cum store run on a Thursday and Saturday from The Old Forge. It's the only contact we have with the outside world now I'm afraid. The phone lines have been down since the last storm and the flood's taken out the internet, too. You might get a mobile signal up at the Jenkins' place.'

'The Jenkins' place?'

'Yes, that's right, Jack's place. Bit of a trek though.'

'It's okay, I've no one to ring.'

'Well then when you've settled come to the bar for a cuppa. Oh, and I've a wax coat I can lend you.' Susie placed the keys on the chest of drawers and left.

Freya stood hugging herself at the window, surveying the moor and the tor beyond. The wind felled the leached grass giving a forlorn barrenness to the landscape. Layers of granite boulders smoothed by centuries of erosion formed the tor itself and from this angle it appeared as a clenched fist thumping the ground in indignation. She sighed, wondering how Beckett could find such wilderness beguiling.

A cold breeze washed in through the window stealing the warmth from the room. She slammed the window shut, reached for a sweater, and stood looking at the sky – not nearly enough blue to make a sailor's collar. She regretted her decision not to stay at Jack's. This did not seem a place to dwell. If only Beckett were here.

In those long sleepless nights since Beckett's death, she had taken to poring over old photos from a sparse array of mismatched albums. How on earth did other people manage to remember their loved ones before photography? Even the few photos she had were barely enough for the rapidly fading memories of a shared life. If she looked hard enough in the mirror, she could just make out the similarities of him across her eyes, the familial slant of their noses, and their same flaxen hair. And if she peered long enough, by some heroic feat of her imagination, he would eventually seem to appear. Surely, it would then only take a small leap for her mind to imagine him as a living, sentient being again, moving around in this world he had abruptly left behind. A chill ran through her; there would be no Lazarus resurrection here.

The unpacking of her things could wait, now she needed tea. She grabbed her keys, though she couldn't think that they were necessary in such a remote place and headed back to the bar.

A fire had been lit in the grate to counter the dampness of the day, and Freya, like a faithful hound, drew near to it with gratitude. If she fancied that this place had escaped the rush of modernity, perhaps as a lost dream of Brigadoon, the whistles and screeches of the Italian coffee machine dispelled all such notions. Yet around her were nods to nostalgia: horseshoes nailed on blackened beams, a brass rail ringing the bar at ankle height to prop a lazy foot upon, chairs covered in cosy woolen tartan and carriage lamps sentinel on each side of the inglenook. Freya peeked inside a game's chest: Monopoly, Scrabble, Draughts, Bridge in a wooden box, and some playing cards with scenes of Dartmoor printed on the back of them. She was still holding them when Susie brought over a pot of tea and some oat biscuits balanced on the side of the saucer.

'You can take any of the games back to The Byre if you want. They could do with an airing,' Susie offered.

Freya put the cards back in the chest and shut the lid. 'Thanks, but there's no one to play with.'

'I expect Tom would. He's our local ratcatcher cum odd-job man. I think his preferred title is Sanitation and Pest Control Professional…whatever! He spends half his life here anyway. Oh, and don't let him talk you into buying any game meat even if he says he shot it fresh this morning. It's probably roadkill or worse.' She mouthed out the word, 'Rats'. 'Or there'll be Merc, he's partial to a game or two of cards. Mind you, keep your purse closed. He likes a good flutter, does he, would bet his grandma's last shilling if he thought he could get away with it.'

Freya remembered playing cards with Beckett as children, betting all their money on snap and happy families and seven-card brag, Beck with his fierce competitiveness, betting hard and fast on every hand regardless of the odds. And then mum making her give back all her winnings so he would have enough money for his school dinner. Occasionally, she would keep it so he'd go hungry just to teach him a lesson. 'Thanks for the tip, but cards aren't my thing,' Freya replied.

'Shame, it helps pass the time when the weather is against us. Still, it's nice to have a bit of female company for a change.' Susie sat down on the wooden settle next to her. 'Us girls together, eh?'

Freya gave a weak smile, female bonding wasn't for her. Though Susie might yet be useful, too. Where Jack had spoken enigmatically – he may as well have quoted riddles for all the help he had been – Susie seemed straight forward and a talker. She forced out a question, any question, to prolong the conversation. 'Have you always worked here?' It sounded indifferent, banal and half-hearted.

'Good lord, no,' Susie laughed. 'I was a PA to an executive and pretty good at it, too. Don't think the poor beggar could tie his shoelaces unless I'd written an itinerary and left an instruction leaflet for him. Hey ho, that was then.'

Freya's curiosity was piqued. She took in her surroundings with new interest: the mahogany bar, shiny like a new conker, rows of sparkling beer pumps, proud with their regimental badges, menu boards written in a perfect cursive font, tilted just so, and the condiments placed on the table with precision and paraded according to height. Susie, no doubt, had been a formidably organised secretary.

'What happened?' Freya asked.

Susie's face stuck midway in the act of smiling as if a camera had clicked the shutter too soon. Freya was aware she had moved from chit-chat to prying. 'Sorry, you don't need to answer that.'

'Well, you know how these things go…'

She didn't but an array of possibilities ran through her mind: an affair? Insubordination? Boredom? Hands in the till? – no, definitely not that.

'All good things come to an end as they say. Anyway, it got me to where I am now, owning and running my own pub. What about you? Do you think you'll go back to teaching?'

This time it was Freya's turn to be caught off guard. These people *knew* about her. The pot of tea, fresh and piping hot waiting to be poured served as an obligation tethering her to this unwanted turn in the conversation.

At that moment, the door opened delivering a swirl of leaves. An overcoated man in leather boots sauntered to the bar shedding pearls of rain in his wake.

'Hey, mind my clean floor,' Susie called. 'The rain's started then?'

'Aye, set in.' The man answered in a soft Scottish brogue. 'And the ford's up already. We'll be lucky if the riverbank holds, the rate it's coming down.'

Susie went to the bar, took a shot glass, pebbled in two ice cubes, and pushed the glass up to the inverted bottle of *Glenfiddich* single malt hanging on the wall. A glug of syrupy whisky dispensed down. 'Here you go, Merc, that'll warm you up.'

He downed it in one, wincing with satisfaction at the afterburn. 'That's grand. You'll get me another?'

His demeanor intrigued Freya so she joined them at the bar. Merc's gaze swept over her, summing her up in the three cruel seconds of first impressions, then flittered away to scan the room for some other item of more interest. For her part, she noted the upward tilt of his jaw, his hard eyes peering along the trajectory of his nose, his mouth seeming to snarl at one edge. He was about fiftyish, well-groomed, fragrant with expensive aftershave, and for all that, magnificent.

The introductions were made. Where Freya's looks failed to register, the mention of her name certainly did not.

'So, you're here then!'

44

'Apparently, I am. Were you expecting me?'

'You tell me?'

'Merc!' Susie intervened, 'Manners!' Then to her, 'Pay no attention, he's all het up with Jack. Hell will freeze over the day they see eye to eye.' She whisked Merc's glass away and refilled it. 'Here you go. On the house in return for a bit of civility, agreed?'

'Agreed.' But he took out his wallet, unpeeled a wodge of notes and threw one down on the counter. 'A drink for the lady. Some la-di-dah sherry or such like.'

Freya, mindful of how she had crumbled in front of Graham the Head at *Our Lady's* when he'd 'let her go' and determined not to repeat such a humiliation, picked up the note. With her elbow resting on the counter and her hand level with Merc's face, she rubbed the note between her thumb and forefinger. Looking him in the eye and exercising a defiance she had not mustered before, she said, 'Mine's a *Glenfiddich*, double!'

'Now you're talking,' Merc raised his eyebrows. 'You've just got a whole lot more interesting, lassie.'

Susie fetched the whisky and placed it on the counter in front of Freya. 'Here you go love, take it easy, eh?'

Struggling to drink the whisky at such an early hour, Freya took slow sips, rolled it around in her mouth, savoured the smoky taste. By contrast, Merc finished his in three large gulps, each followed by a grimace which stretched his mouth into a harsh elastic line. Fascinated, she studied him. Her mother might have warned her about such men: supercilious, preening, worldly-wise, cocky, would eat her up alive. Yet Freya was caught up by his charisma.

Uncharacteristically, she felt herself plying for his attention, as if in the giving of it, he would endow her with some great honour. But awareness of this did not amount to caution. Being in these new surroundings she reasoned, gave her licence, if not to re-invent herself, then at least to have some innocent fun. If thoughts that she might be out of her depth did arise, these she pushed out of her mind. She was mindful that Merc was nothing like her new friend Jack. Where Jack was a man she might have settled with given a different past, and therefore had to be held at bay, Merc was neither marriage material nor the sort who went for women like her – ordinary, mousey, insignificant, and well…crushed. Why not enjoy the moment, it wasn't going to lead anywhere?

Merc rested an elbow on the bar, and with his other hand, flipped out his business card from his top pocket. 'If you ever need some wheels, I could sort you out a stunning little convertible. Nice drive, mink coloured, cream leather trim. Just picture it, there you are, driving through the countryside,' he shifted position to animate some imaginary tableau with the sweep of his hand, 'the sun beating down, freedom at your fingertips.'

In this new spirit of fun, she ignored the fact that she couldn't drive. 'What make?'

'Mazda, sports.'

'Oh?'

'I could get you a Merc if you prefer?'

She frowned, 'A Merc?'

'Mercedes, lass.'

She began to feel the whisky's effects. 'Merc will find me a Merc?' she giggled. 'Anyway, what sort of name is Merc?'

'It's the sort of name for a second-hand car salesman, that's what. Some wise guy thought he was being funny. Now I'm stuck with it. Want to know my real name?'

He leant closer, his face brushing against her hair, his aftershave overwhelming her in a hijack of the senses. This was not some cheap scent from the local department store but classy, rich in tones of sandalwood and bergamot. Nor was the fat gold watch on his wrist some chain-store tat. Even she could tell it dripped with the flow of mammon.

47

'It's Gilbert. Or just Gil to you,' he whispered.

'Gil?' Startled, she drew back. She had thought Beckett meant to write Jill, that it had been a silly dyslexic spelling mistake, but he had meant Gil all along. 'You're kidding?' she managed to say.

'Not the usual reaction, I'll give you that.'

'Sorry. I didn't mean to…' She massaged her forehead with her fingertips. 'Gil. Yes, it's different, not very Scottish.' She was rambling but needed time to think. 'More like American.'

'At the risk of splitting hairs, it's Germanic.' He was amused, his face lit up, became softer, more animated and his snarl changed to a laugh.

Freya's stomach flipped, she felt woozy, swayed a little.

'You should sit down.' He steadied her with a hand on her arm and guided her to a bar stool. His touch sent a strange pulse through her. 'I'm fine. I just need some air… it's the whisky… not used to it, not at this hour anyway.' Not at all, she internally added.

Freya escaped from the bar with Beckett's nursery rhyme still ringing in her ears, *Jack and Gil went up the hill.* As she reached the corridor Susie spotted her from the kitchen. 'Is something up? Has Merc been annoying you?'

'No, nothing like that, he's been sweet.'

'Merc, sweet?'

'Yes, I thought so.'

'Well, be careful, love. That's all I'm saying.'

It was the second time Susie had warned her about Merc and Freya became curious.

'Noted. I think I'll go for a walk. I need some air.'

'Just a sec.' Susie twisted round and produced a cellophane wrapped sandwich from a basket on the kitchen side. 'Here,' she tossed it to her, 'to keep you going. And you'll need that coat I was on about. It's the wax one hanging over there.' She waved in the general direction of the back door. 'Take my advice and give the moor a miss today. Weather's against us. Best you take the path down the valley to the river. It's a lovely walk.'

CHAPTER 5

Susie's weather warning proved right, and the rain settled into a steady rhythm. Freya set out along Wagg Drove until she came to a T-junction by The Old Forge and hesitated. Should she take Susie's advice and go down the valley via the muddy track toward the river, which would mean a steep climb back up? Or should she take the stony path to the left and over the moors which looked much easier with its gravel track? But she risked getting lost in the low-lying cloud. The sky had turned a threatening purple and if the rain got worse, there would be no shelter. She pulled up the hood on the wax jacket, turned right and followed the way-marker sign down the muddy slope toward the river.

The rain gathered momentum and fell as steady silver dashes soaking her through. After a mile or so, the path widened to a woody glade canopied with trees which provided a natural umbrella. A carpet of beech nuts crunched under foot. She sat on a moss-covered tree stump to eat her sandwich and to think about Beckett, to try to re-imagine him into existence, however silly it seemed, either as a vision or a ghost, she didn't care which. Post-bereavement hallucinations were a well-known phenomenon, surely, she could make it happen for herself. If she could only see him again, even once, to know that he was happy, that he had not been denied heaven. But Father Paul had hinted at the hard climb on the mountain of purgatory. His words washed over her at the time, seeming melodramatic and apocalyptical. No, she mustn't think that way, of course he would be in heaven.

If Beckett had gone to the trouble of writing the nursery rhyme, and put it in the mustard seed packet at that, it had to mean something, didn't it? He must have been trying to tell her something, something about her new friend Jack and this Gil character. And if that was the case, wasn't the rest of the rhyme also relevant; *Jack fell down and broke his crown, and Jill/Gil came tumbling after*? It sounded more like a warning.

A chill accompanied the rain, and she was glad of Susie's jacket. She dug her hands deep into the pockets. In the right was a green handkerchief with an exquisite, embroidered figure of St George and the Dragon on it – elaborate in excess for a mere merchandising freebie. The bold saint George figure waved the banner of England: a bloody red cross on the white pall of purity. Beneath him writhed a defeated dragon. She traced the gold and scarlet threads with her finger, circled over the dragon's scales. The wind picked up, grabbed leaves from the woodland floor and swirled them into the air. Then, just as quickly, it settled as if by command. Freya took in her surroundings with new awareness. An overgrown path was set off from the glade, nettles and brambles vied for space, crisp brown ferns withered, and the earthy tang of mushrooms and damp leaves evoked a melancholy decay. She trembled. This place seemed familiar though she knew she had never been to Dartmoor before. Spooked, she shoved the handkerchief back into the pocket and ran.

After several hundred yards she stopped with the realisation that she should have gone the other way, up the hill rather than down. Now she would have to go back through the glade to return to the inn. Whatever had spooked her would have to be faced again. But had anything happened at all other than a puff of wind and a half-baked memory?

She was probably overtired, still grieving, and suffering the aftereffects of hypothermia from her night in the barn. And she had drunk that double whisky all too quick to be sensible. At this moment she wanted nothing more than to be at home in her little terrace house with all its safe familiarity. Why had she even thought that coming here would solve anything, let alone help her uncover the truth about Beckett's death, when the police with all their experience and resources had so far failed?

With trepidation, Freya began the slow climb back up the path, hoping to have enough energy saved to sprint right through the clearing. As she approached her limbs seemed weighted down as if by invisible shackles. There was a ripple of leaves and the crackle of twigs behind her. Then another sound, rattling in time to her own steps, like beads shaken in a plastic tub. Running from here seemed impossible, her boots slid and skated over the mud. She swung round, could see no one behind though heard someone panting close by. 'Oh no,' she groaned, and knew without a shadow of doubt what the next sound would be; the rap of plastic hitting wood and a twelve-year old girl's voice pitched to fury shouting, 'Debbie Monkcombe, you're dead!'

Still shaken, Freya would have preferred to return to her room in The Byre via the gate into the stable yard rather than going through the bar of The George and Dragon and risk bumping into Susie or Merc, but to her dismay it was locked. She stood a while outside, gathering her thoughts and composing a facial expression that would assume the cheerful lie of her feelings. She didn't want to appear vulnerable, not to these people she hardly knew, even though they somehow knew about *her*. For that, they held a distinct advantage. Her mother always said she wore her heart on her sleeve. Even more reason to keep up the pretence. As a child Freya took the literal meaning, imagining her beating red heart strapped to one arm, not unlike the painting of the Sacred Heart of Jesus hanging on Grandma's wall. Jesus smiled sweetly, and brilliant rays shone forth from his exposed and thorn-crowned heart nestled into his shining breast.

Merc was perched on a high stool at the bar, an open notebook and a half-drunk cafetière of coffee in front of him. Freya had not registered that he was in the middle of a call until he suddenly wished the empty bar a pleasant day and that he would speak to it later. But Susie had been adamant that there was no mobile signal here, that they were cut off from the world. If she had lied about that, what else might she be covering up?

'Success?' Susie asked Merc as she appeared from the cellar.

'Aye, perhaps. Time to call in a few favours, I

think.'

'Is that wise? The need to know and all that.'

'A wee precaution in case he blabs.'

'Ah, Freya,' Susie raised a warning hand to Merc. 'There you are. How was your walk? You look soaked through.' Before Freya could answer, she was ushered towards the fireplace where Susie peeled off her coat and pushed her down into a chair. 'Sit there, my lovely. Merc bring over the coffee and another cup, will you? We'll soon have you warm.' She threw on a large log and stoked up the fire with a poker.

Despite the warming heat, Freya shivered uncontrollably, whether from her encounter with her twelve-year-old self, the penetrating rain, or the overheard conversation, she could not say.

A cup of coffee materialised in her hand which she struggled to keep from spilling.

'You're trembling, lass.' Merc took the cup away and enveloped her hands between his, as if in prayer.

Freya took a sharp intake of breath. His hands were warm and smooth, free from the callouses of labour, his nails immaculate. She blushed and looked away. 'I'm fine…I'm okay,' she squeaked. 'Just shivery.'

'She doesn't look great,' Susie said. 'Probably set off that hypothermia again. Bed for you. Merc, give us a hand getting her back to her room.'

CHAPTER 6

Freya locked the door behind her as a figurative gesture against the wild Dartmoor landscape beyond and the intrusive attention by Susie and Merc from within. Light shrank from the room and in the twilight, she stripped off her wet clothes and ran a bath. The bubbles volumized into a shimmering foam. She slipped into the water and tried to relax but the incident at the clearing ran through her mind in a long continuous loop. She willed logical thought; there had to be a rational explanation. The footsteps, the jingle-jangle of the rosary beads in the plastic tub, the re-incarnation of herself as a twelve-year-old shouting, 'Debbie, you're dead', they couldn't be real, could they? She reached the same conclusion as earlier: whisky, weariness, grief, they did strange things to the mind. If she were going to prove everyone wrong about

Beckett's suicide, she needed to keep sane, and that could only mean leaving this place. Why stay when Brohn-In-The-Moor's silence proved impenetrable, and the unfamiliar surroundings conjured unhelpful memories? At least back home she and Father Paul might be able to formulate a plan together. And fortunately, he had many helpful contacts. She decided she should leave first thing in the morning.

After her bath, she sat in bed listening to the thrum of heavy rain on the roof, glad she had returned in good time before the worst came down. She switched on the TV – no signal, just a blue screen and a red *Freeview* banner floating across it. Listless, she picked up a Dartmoor Tourist Information brochure lying around on the chest of drawers and skimmed through the pages: things to do, places to eat, accommodation – a brief mention of The George and Dragon – legends and folklore – much more interesting. Jack probably knew all these tales by heart. Too bad she wouldn't be around to hear them.

Freya's imagination idled, dwelt on pixies and faeries, and magical stone circles. One story attracted her attention; Cutty Dyer, an evil sprite who preyed on lost souls on the moor, dragging them into the river, slitting their throats and drinking their warm blood. Not an encouraging omen. The temptation was to dismiss the story out of hand, but Jack had talked about the underlying truths of myths and allegories and how they pointed to a deeper wisdom designed to keep these countryfolk safe. It explained all the soothsaying about not being on the moor at night. And hadn't she got lost herself and had to be rescued by Jack?

She dozed off, at least she thought she had, and dreamt of Beckett sitting on the end of her bed flicking through that same magazine. 'You shouldn't have gone into the woods,' he said. 'You should have stayed with me.' Then he was gone.

She was awoken around midnight by an urgent rap at the door. She turned on the lamp, but the switch had no effect. The bulb must have blown. Being a moonless night in the heart of the wilderness and without the orange neon of streetlamps, the total darkness disorientated her. She climbed out of bed and yelped as her feet plunged into two inches of cold water. The knocking grew louder and persistent.

'Freya? Freya, you awake?' Jack's voice called out.

'I'm coming.' She moved forward and trod on her hike boot. 'Blast! Jack, I can't see anything. What's happening?'

'There's a hell of a storm out there. Power's off.

Here, I'm shining my torch at the door.'

A rectangle of light breached the frame. She paddled towards it, unlocked the door, and there stood Jack ghoul-like in the upturned torch beam. The brim of his sou'wester was turned up and his yellow oilskins were greased with rain. She could recognise the years at sea in him, mastering the tempest and taking command of the crew.

'The stream's already breached its banks,' he said, 'and it won't be long before the torrent comes down off the moor.'

'What can I do to help?' she asked.

'Get dressed for a start.' He strode across the room and shone his torch at the pile of clothes on the chair. 'Here,' he said, tossing her the jeans.

'Not those, they're wet.'

'Just get them on and come and help with the sandbags.' He was harsh, impatient, and his commanding voice no longer so gallant.

Outside she found Jack's bashed up old Land Rover running and the wipers scudding the windscreen at full pelt. Its headlights shone through the rain and illuminated a human chain in front of the pub passing heavy sandbags along the line. The last of the figures stacked them to form a perimeter wall around the stable yard to hold off the flood from the inn. Voices shouted to one another over a howling wind. For a moment, Freya dithered and was unsure where she could be of most help until Jack pulled her to the back of the vehicle and thrust a load of hessian sacks into her arms.

'Hold them open while I fill them,' he said.

Jack took up his shovel and sliced into the dumpy bag of sand he'd somehow managed to load into the back of the vehicle. Freya lifted the sack but when he shovelled in the first spade-full, its weight took her by surprise and the sack slipped from her hands. He swore.

'Sorry, sorry,' she said, aware of her ineptitude.

'Just keep it on the floor then, will you.'

He ladled in more sand, but the spade was larger than the sack and more of it ended up on the ground than inside. He cursed again. Freya let out an unexpected sob which was carried away in the storm. Tiredness, the day's events and eeriness of this place, Jack's curtness, the loss of Beckett – especially this – had all come together in a deluge. A grief too big for her heart spilled over and with it, the realisation of her utter aloneness. Jack continued shoveling and it was only when the first sack was full, tied and passed along the line, that she could pause to wipe away her tears.

Jack gave her a moment, neither acknowledging

nor condemning her distress, before nodding for her to hold out the next sack so they could carry on. For this she was grateful. The sand ran low. He tipped out the remainder onto the cobblestones and hopped into the vehicle to go back and fetch some more. But as he reversed out of the stable yard and swung around, Merc saw it would leave them without adequate light. The Land Rover was the only four by four in the village capable of going through the flood water. 'Hey, Jack!' he shouted, running after the vehicle. He just about caught up enough to bang the back of it with the flat of his hand before it sped away.

Now what? They wouldn't be able to carry on in the dark and the flood waters were rising by the minute.

'We need light. Have you got your mobiles?' Susie asked Freya and Merc.

'Why?' he answered. 'Are we going to string them all together like fairy lights?'

'I'll bear that in mind,' she said, dismissing his misplaced attempt at humour. 'There're some storm lamps in the cellar. It's pitch-black down there and I'd rather not break my neck in the process.'

Merc turned on his mobile and swiped for the torch app. 'Better?' He waved the beam around and it rippled over the water like moonlight on a lake. The flood crept further across the stable yard and was now only a few metres from the inn building. Susie groaned. Freya squeezed her arm. 'It'll be alright, you'll see.'

'Wish I could be so certain. We've the runoff from the moor to contend with yet.'

'But Jack will be back soon with more sandbags. He'll know what to do.' Freya hoped her confidence was not unfounded.

'Perfect,' Merc chipped in with unabashed contempt.

'Perhaps we could make a rill over to the brook on the other side of the road?' Freya suggested.

'The brook's almost full already, love. And it'll take all night filling enough sandbags. It's hopeless.'

'Then let's get started.' Merc said. His mobile gave off a weak blue light, not much brighter than the fly zapper in the kitchen but was enough to get by.

'I think it best if you two wait here in the bar. I know my cellar. There's a lot of pipework to trip over down there. I'll get the first storm lamp lit and bring up the rest.'

Left alone in the dark Freya sensed Merc unbearably near. His large and self-absorbed personality, which she found overwhelming yet captivating on so many levels, had porous boundaries as if he had somehow managed to escape the confines of his body and occupy more space than his allotted due. He seemed hungry even for more nudging into the limits of her own private space. And yet she struggled to resist. When his searching hand found hers, she jerked automatically away. 'Sorry,' she said, apologising in lieu of him, though the pain of longing lingered.

'Don't be scared, lass.'

'I'm not. I'm sure the stream will–'

'I wasn't talking about the stream.'

'Oh.'

'Why don't you have a think about it and let me know.' His offer was as casual as one of his second-hand car deals.

'Okay,' Freya found herself saying, as if she were one of her sixth form students fawning over the head boy. She should put him straight, but then again…Thoughts of being alone forever crowded in. With resolve she rejected the idea that there could be anything between them. She would be leaving soon and needed to focus on finding out the truth about Beckett's death. Besides, she was far too old to be playing around with silly little flirtations. She edged away, a chair scraped, tumbled, crashed onto the flagstones. Merc cleared his throat in a clumsy attempt to cover up a laugh. Freya suspected he thought her ridiculous, that perhaps the offer had been given out of pity, or just for his amusement.

A golden glow emanated from behind the bar as Susie climbed up the steps from the cellar. With the storm lamp held out in front and her long wax coat skimming the steps, she looked singularly like Old Father Time. The blackened ceiling beams with their glinting horse brasses, the inglenook fireplace, and the room bathed in half light, completed the timeless illusion.

Susie placed another five dusty lanterns onto the table and brushed away the cobwebs. Merc lit them with a cheap disposable lighter he had taken from his trouser pocket. The orange plastic seemed incongruent with his image, an item to be discarded at a whim, like some boiled sweet too long in the mouth and tired of. Would Merc likewise dispose of her?

They each took two of the lit lanterns and, bracing themselves, Susie opened the door. The wind tugged back at the heavy oak, yanking it from her hand and crashing it into the side wall. A deep gouge appeared in the plaster.

'Oh, for goodness' sake. That's all I need, more decorating,' Susie cried.

Outside in the storm, the lamps flickered and bent in the wind. They were placed at strategic intervals on the ground lighting up the chain line of helpers. Freya recognised some as locals who propped up the bar every evening. She knew only one by name: Tom the ratcatcher Susie had introduced her to. He was a local man 'born and bred', and proud to be a 'Moorlander', with his family going back generations, and with it, fascinating. He was wise in a country common sense sort of way and a living thread anchoring these Moorlanders to their agrarian past by his knowledge of the old ways. Yet not shy with new technologies either, anything which made life easier or more bearable: satellite TV, quadbikes, central heating. She loved Tom's weatherlore updates, *Rain before seven, fine by eleven*; *Dew on the grass, no rain will come to pass*; *When the wind is out to the east, tis neither good for man nor beast.* He was coarse with his colourful language, unsophisticated but no fool when it came to Susie's up-market pretentions for the pub. Freya had heard them arguing, 'It's a beef what?' he asked. 'Wellington, Tom. *Well-ing-ton*,' she enunciated. 'Why the hell do'ya want to be calling it that for? It's a bleeding pie. Anyone can see it's a pie. You got beef, you got pastry. It's a bleeding pie, I tells ya.'

Whilst they had been away fetching the lamps from the cellar, Tom had organised the others into a work force. He had managed to find a single old oil lamp, most likely in one of the tumbling down stables, and with that one light they had set about re-arranging the sandbags into a channel across the stable yard, over the road and to the brook on the other side. In effect, the rill Freya suggested earlier. He continued shouting out orders, 'Over there,' 'Not like that, ''Ere, I'll show you,' 'Put some back into it, you big girl's blouse.'

Progress was slow until Jack returned in his Land Rover with another load of sand. This time he'd hitched a trailer to the back, and this too was filled with sand piled up like a mini mountain. The headlights gave a more focused, stronger beam than the storm lamps and soon the sandbag chain functioned without effort and the pace quickened. Rain fell like long glass shards and broke out into concentric circles in the puddles.

Around four-thirty in the morning the rain eased off and the runoff from the moors slackened. The sandbag channel had reached right across the road funnelling most of the flood water into the brook on the other side and saving the inn from its threatened trajectory.

'Listen up,' Jack shouted over the wind as they finished. 'Job done for now, lads. Well done. Go home everyone, get some sleep. We'll reassemble at ten-thirty for the clean-up, earlier if we're needed again. Susie, send word if the situation deteriorates. Let's hope the moor's given up all she's got.' The helpers dissolved away and left Freya and the other four to gather up the lanterns and retreat inside.

'Got a nightcap to stave off the chills, my lover?' Tom asked Susie. 'Brandy will do.'

'For once, Tom,' Susie said, taking off her long coat, 'I think you're right. We all deserve one.' She fetched some drinks over on a tray and lifted a glass. 'A toast. To us and the tight-knit community of Brohn-In-The-Moor. May we all stick together.'

'Brohn-In-The-Moor!' they all repeated raising their glasses.

Merc swirled his around, the contents lapping up the sides of the glass like a perilous sea swell. He elevated it for another toast. 'And may we always remember that.' To Jack, he delivered a wry humourless wink.

Jack returned his gaze. His head dipped imperceptibly in a nod of confirmation before he raised his glass to his lips. Whatever the meaning of their communication, Freya sensed hostility. These two had history.

'I'm off home to bed,' Tom said, picking up one of the lamps. His wellington boots flapped and squelched as he made his way across the room. He helped himself to another brandy on the way out and would have headed onto the carpeted area had Susie not shouted, 'Tom, boots!'

'Philistine,' Merc muttered. 'Now then, Susie. The Byre's flooded and my room's ankle deep in it, any rooms here in the inn?'

Susie went over to the key rack and returned with a single set of dangling keys. 'I expect Freya's will be flooded too. The pair of you will have to fight for it.'

Merc took the keys. 'The lassie can share with me.'

Freya let out a nervous laugh. If he had not made a pass earlier, she would think he was joking. She resented the presumption, and at fifty-odd, though single, she was hardly a lassie. Jack bristled by her side, and she touched his arm in recognition of his concern. 'Hey now, I don't think so.'

'Ach no. Obviously, the room has twin beds, eh, Susie?'

'You're such a joker. Yes, as luck would have it, but–'

'I've a room at my place,' Jack said.

'Good, then it's sorted,' Merc said. 'I'll stay at yours. A chance for a bit of male bonding. Me and you, eh Jack? What do you say?' He squeezed Jack's shoulder with a white-knuckled hand.

Freya wondered if the room-sharing idea had been suggested for the sole purpose of cornering poor Jack. She considered rescuing him by offering to go herself, then

Susie spoke. 'Uh-uh, now-now boys,' she said. 'Safest bet is for Freya to go.'

Merc gave a grin and released his grip. Jack snorted in disgust and Freya was confused by his lack of gratitude. Anyone would think he was spoiling for a fight.

CHAPTER 7

On the way to Jenkin's Farm, Freya, quiet and reflective, stared at the road ahead through wide eyes. Jack chattered away his agitation, re-examining the evening's events and all the minutiae until he had got it out of his system and there was a momentary lull.

'Dawn's arrived,' he stated, more as a note of hope than fact. He pointed over to the east. A cleft of grey appeared on the horizon separating the darkness, land from sky. 'I'm famished, are you? It's too late for supper, too early for breakfast. There are some snacks in the glove compartment if you're hungry.'

'No thanks. I just need sleep. And tea.' But even as Freya answered she remembered she had not eaten anything since yesterday afternoon, the half-eaten sandwich Susie had given her abandoned on the tree stump. Her stomach gave an audible rumble.

'You sure about that?' Jack asked. 'Pass me one of those muesli bars, will you?'

She opened the glove compartment and looked for the bars among a packet of chewing gum, a tube of mints and a ten-pack of cigarettes. These she held up by one corner. 'What do you call these?'

'Emergency stash, that's what. A de-stressor. Haven't had one for weeks.'

Freya raised a questioning eyebrow.

'Honest, Miss, though I could do with one now. Anyway, what old seadog doesn't have the occasional puff now and again?' He peered through the windscreen. 'Best time of day, dawn-break. Out on the oceans the night watch seemed never ending. Could drive a man crazy. Cabin fever would set in. Watching all night without a point of reference, darkness like a solid wall all around you, putting blind trust in the instruments, hoping the power didn't cut out or the circuits blow.' His eyes swam with memories drawing her in.

'But didn't you have the stars to navigate by and that brass instrument thingy?'

'You mean a sextant,' Jack laughed. 'Bit before my time, and you'd need a whole cabin full of charts. That's why dawn was always so welcome, gave you a firm fix to the east. At a push, you could work out how far you'd travelled overnight given a constant speed.'

'Did you love it out there at sea?'

'Mostly, sometimes not. When the tempest came, the swell could easily reach thirty, forty feet high. But on clear nights, wow, the stars flung across the heavens, the moon enormous on the horizon.' He drew a great arc with his arm, daubed a blob of a moon with his hand. 'Made you feel puny yet part of it all at the same time.'

Though his manner had been brusque, and brittle with impatience earlier when he had barked orders with the sand, she now wondered at his depths. If Beckett had ever visited Brohn-In-The-Moor, she was sure he would have seen that in Jack too and would have gravitated toward him as a kindred spirit. Beckett had so loved the natural world. As for Merc, if Beckett had even passed the time of day with him let alone in pastoral contemplation, she would be surprised.

Freya handed Jack a muesli bar and took one for herself. As she put the empty wrapper back in the compartment, an emerald flash of fabric caught her eye. It was a silk handkerchief, like the one she had found in Susie's jacket pocket. She hesitated; she should just put it back. She didn't need another reminder of yesterday's flashback at the clearing. The Moorlanders spoke so much about myth and danger, but this magic nonsense had to stop. Yet she was drawn to it. Jack was miles away in some reverie of past adventures, so she took it out, opened it on her lap and smoothed away the creases. In one corner, coloured thread embroidered out the emblem of Saint George and the Dragon.

'Don't,' Jack said suddenly.

'Don't what?'

'Best put it back, eh? Probably full of germs and stuff.'

His warning emboldened her. 'So, if I do this…?' she laughed. Her finger hovered over the emblem, dabbed at the dragon. Though the night had been long, and the land no longer offered back any warmth, there was no dramatic drop in temperature, no sudden gust of wind. 'See!' she whispered to herself.

Jack shivered, turned up the heater and drove on in silence. The air grew fuggy, their breath condensing on the windows. He reached into the door side pocket for a tablet of chamois leather to clear the windscreen. Whilst his attention was diverted, a deer darted out across the Land Rover's path.

'Jack, watch out!' Freya shouted.

He yanked at the steering wheel, swerved hard right, missed the startled animal, but a swollen ford lay up ahead. The vehicle skidded and hit the ford at the wrong angle. Waves of water sprayed up either side propelling them across it like a hydrofoil at sea. The hiss and roar of water gave way to the rumble of tyres on tarmac as the Land Rover gained traction on the other side. On the incline, the engine spluttered, cut out and they juddered to a halt. Jack applied the handbrake, adjusted the gear lever to neutral and tried to start it. Just a cough. The headlights dimmed and flickered, the windscreen wipers scraped to a halt in mid-swipe and the car died. He tried again. Nothing this time except the metallic click of the key turning impotently in the lock. Howling wind filled the vacuum the engine noise left behind.

'What now?' she asked. She expected him to be in command and about to take up his coat and torch and fix the engine. Instead, she found him motionless, gripping the steering wheel, and his head bowed.

'It's alright, you missed it,' she said. 'Jack, did you hear me? You missed it. And we seem to be all in one piece, thank goodness.'

With an uncharacteristic slowness Jack raised his head. Freya started. He was ashen, dumb and loose jawed. 'What's wrong? Are you ill? Have you got any tablets to take?' She stretched for the glove compartment but was intercepted by his gentle touch, a lightness more remarkable from such strong laboured hands.

'No pills for what I have. I wish there were. It never ends.' He sighed out hopelessness, his face riven with sadness. He bore the haunted mournful look of sorrow as if tragedy had been his constant companion.

'What never ends? What is it? You're not making much sense.'

'Shakespeare had it right.

'Give sorrow words;

The grief that does not speak,

Whispers the o'erfraught heart and bids it break."

Jack's sudden change of mood bewildered her, yet she perceived a reverence in it, that whatever had happened in the past, the wounds ran deep and needed their due. This she understood.

'Oh, Jack.' She laid a hand over his.

He breathed deeply, shook his head to clear it. 'I knew you'd understand…Now, I suppose I need to get on and fix this.'

The blue-grey light of dawn still held shadows. Jack hunted behind the seat for his heavy-duty torch, gave it to her and went to the front of the vehicle and disappeared underneath the bonnet. Freya shone the torch over the engine in an ineffectual way and he needed to direct her. Whereas he had been forthright and commanding earlier at the inn, now his voice was hesitant and struggled from his throat. 'Could you shine it here at this point?'

She adjusted the beam while he poked at some wires. 'I see,' he said with certainty, then took a handkerchief from his pocket and pressed it onto a connection. 'Just wet, I think. Could you turn over the engine when I say so?'

For the first time in her life, Freya sat in the driver's seat. She took a few moments to find the ignition, then wound down the window. 'Ready when you are.'

'Okay. Now!'

She mouthed a prayer of hope and turned the key. The engine caught, coughed, and stopped.

'Just a sec,' Jack called. He bent back under the bonnet and reappeared. 'Try again.'

This time it purred into life. She expected him to slam down the bonnet and climb back in, but instead he disappeared under it again. After a few moments, she got out to investigate. Jack was staring without purpose at the jumble of wires and moving metal parts.

'It's all my fault,' he mumbled.

'It was just a silly deer, no one's fault. No harm done.'

'I should've warned him…'

'Warned *him*?' She raked back her hair as if clearing her face would offer clarity.

'I knew what could happen. I was just too darn…' His mouth twisted with disgust.

Now he chooses to speak, she thought. Surely, he must be talking about Beckett. Yet she hadn't even established that Jack knew him, had only the vague suspicion, let alone that he had something to do with his death. A pain stabbed at her heart. The details in the police report were perfunctory, matter of fact, unfurnished, cold. She had memorised them: *Beckett Greene died 4th August at the foot of a tor in the Dartmoor National Park. Emergency services pronounced him dead at the scene. He suffered head trauma consistent with a fall. Oedema and hyperaemia are indicative of the onset of hypothermia. Toxicology reports reveal alcohol levels above the legal drink drive limit. Police investigations exposed financial irregularities, erratic behaviour in the days leading up to his death and further evidence suggested he intended to take his own life, namely correspondence containing pre-emptive apologies and guilt. Additionally, all outstanding hotel invoices had been cleared earlier that day and an array of credit card bills had been discarded in the hotel refuse bins. All indicative of suicidal intentions.*

Freya struggled to breathe, the memories seeming to encase her in an airless stone tomb. She needed to ask Jack directly if he had known Beckett and this time she wouldn't be fobbed off with his enigmatic reply – *We all pass through here* – that wasn't good enough.

'You're talking about Beckett, aren't you,' she stated.

'Beckett? No, his name was Rigby.'

'He called himself Rigby?'

'Best first mate I'd ever had.' Jack placed his elbows on the vehicle's bodywork and leant forward. 'We went back years…and I let him down.'

Crossed purposes over. Beckett seldom sailed, although for a brief summer they had both joined a junior sailing club, but neither were great swimmers. Being a liability, they were politely asked to leave. If Beckett had known Jack before he came to Brohn-In-The-Moor and were old friends, she would have known about it, for sure. And poor Rigby, whoever he happened to be, was not her Beckett. She waited for Jack to continue, but he clamped his mouth shut, as far as he was concerned, the conversation was over.

The pull cords from the hood of his oilskin dangled precariously over the turning parts of the engine. 'Be careful!' Freya warned. 'It'll strangle you if it catches.'

'What of it? Perhaps no less than I deserve.'

'*Jack*!' She snatched the cords back and tucked them inside the collar of his jacket. 'Enough. Come on. It's been a long night. Let's get you home.'

When Freya woke a few hours later, the foul weather had given way to a subdued silence, as if nature had exhausted itself with the effort of so much wind and rain. The atmosphere reminded her of the calm sad space after crying. Why weep if not to feel better? Endorphins flood the body, a coping mechanism. Survival. And after Beckett's death, when detachment gave way to tears, it seemed the only sensible action to take in a senseless, surreal situation.

Freya went downstairs to the kitchen to retrieve her clothes drying above the range which she had swapped earlier for one of Jack's checked shirts. Wearing his clothing with the different washing powder smell and the ample huggable manliness of it, along with the strange unexplored conversation by the Land Rover, had changed their relationship without either of them intending it, binding them together in an unexpected intimacy. Would their next meeting be awkward with misgivings and regrets from either party?

A fire flickered in the grate and the smell of bacon and warm bread overlaid the muted weary texture of the morning. The kettle on the stove worked up to a whistling boil. She poured a splash of it into the teapot to warm it through and called upstairs, 'Jack, do you want a cup of tea? There was no reply. Then she saw Jack was outside striding across the yard with a bucket and a feeding bottle. A row of calves shifted in their stalls. Poor Jack. A gush of sympathy and admiration poured forth. He must have barely shut his eyes before the alarm went off and he had gotten up to tend to the animals.

Freya reached for the tea caddy, tossed in three bags, one each and one for the pot, then topped it up with boiling water. As she returned the tin to its place, she noticed a stash of dog-eared photographs tucked behind the sugar canister. She flicked through them smiling: Jack and Tom holding up a fish they'd caught out on the lake, a full side-on shot of a dinghy with the name *The Dragon* painted on the side – presumably belonging to Jack, a group photo of him smiling next to a pretty young redhead, and Merc with his arm around a woman bearing a passing resemblance to Jack. His sister perhaps? Were Merc and Jack related by marriage? It would explain a lot. Families were complicated affairs.

But she stiffened at the last photo: Jack in mid-speech, his mouth curled with amusement animating some joke with his big expressive hands. And beside him, throwing back his head with laughter, stood Beckett. He looked relaxed, at ease and not the picture of some

81

troubled and tormented soul considering ending it all. She flipped the photo over. Someone had scribbled in pencil, *Beck & Jack, The George & Dragon, 2nd August.* Two days before Beckett's death.

Freya considered the possibilities. Might Beckett simply have stumbled across Brohn-In-The-Moor, stopped for a pub lunch, and been captivated by the raconteur Jack and one of his amusing stories before then going on his way? It had to be that. She didn't want to contemplate the other more painful option; that Jack had known Beckett all along. That Beck had been staying at the inn long enough to form friendships, but Jack didn't want to tell her. The writing on the photo said Beck, not Beckett. Only a close friend would call him that. He was always so sparing with its usage. Although Jack bore his guilt for whatever had happened to Rigby like a flagellant might wear a cilice, she just could not believe he would lie to her.

She was so absorbed with the photos that she hadn't noticed Jack approaching the farmhouse. The door handle rattled, and she didn't have time to put them back before he came in. He was carrying a handful of fresh eggs and set them down on the counter next to the range. 'For breakfast,' he said and checked the side of the teapot with his palm. 'Good. Nice and strong, I hope? What you got there?'

Freya resisted the urge to hide the photos behind her back. 'Just some photos I found.' She re-arranged them and offered him the one of *The Dragon*. 'Nice one of the boat!'

He took it and smiled. 'She's a beauty, isn't she? Gaff rigged, wooden hulled, perfect for round here. Do you sail?'

'Not much. I did a bit as a kid. Wasn't much of a swimmer though.' She recalled standing at the side of the school swimming pool dripping wet, lips blue, body juddering from the cold, jaws aching where her teeth chattered so much. It had been even worse in the water, coughing up gallons of pool water, the strangling orange armbands, legs thrashing about all over the place. Her mum used the word 'akimbo', like it was a disability or something. 'Bless poor Freya, her limbs are all akimbo,' she had said. Freya tried to end the torment with the momentous decision of a twelve-year-old – it wasn't for her, and she wouldn't do it again. Yet by the end of the school year, she had somehow managed to pass her length certificate.

'Ha, the idea,' Jack said, 'is to stay on the water, not in it. There are such things as buoyancy aids, you know.' He poured out the tea and handed her a mug. 'Come sailing with me, you'd enjoy it. What about tomorrow, weather permitting?'

'That's kind but I'm leaving today. I ought to get home.'

'Oh. What about, you know…Beckett and the nursery rhyme and the proverb?'

Freya registered his disappointment. 'But there's no reason to stay. I can't seem to find out anything. This place is strange, odd.' She flopped down on the sofa curling her legs under her and cradling her mug. 'It's crazy I know, but I've started seeing things. I dunno…ghosts, hallucinations maybe. Or more like memories replaying themselves.'

'It's the grief, you'll get through it, I promise.' He sat down next to her and tilted his head to the side.

'Who is Rigby?' she asked.

'What? It's a different thing entirely.'

'Is it?'

He scratched the cheerful little boat design on his cup with a dirty fingernail. 'More tea?'

She shook her head, the intimacy at the ford long forgotten.

'Look Freya, I lost my wife to cancer. I like to think I know a thing or two about grief. At first, I kept seeing her standing at the sink, crossing the yard with the feed bucket, watching me while I shaved. It's perfectly normal. It will pass.'

'But Jack…' The truth was, she didn't want it to pass. She wanted to hold on to Beckett.

'I understand, that's all.'

She gazed at the glowing embers in the grate and sipped her tea. 'Why did Beckett have to go and die like that? Why did he do this to *me*?'

'To *you*? I wouldn't have thought you were at the foremost in his mind when he–' Jack stopped.

'Go on, say it. Everyone else does.' Freya got up and put another log on the fire. 'Suicide. Taken his own life. Ended it all.' They all said the same thing; her love wasn't enough to save him. 'Why didn't he just talk to me? How could he be so…*selfish*?'

'Good. Anger needs its due.'

'Same as your unresolved guilt?'

'Ouch.' He leant back on the sofa and crossed his arms, a look of submission on his face.

Freya's chest tightened. He didn't deserve that. 'I'm sorry about your wife. And for bringing up the other business. It's funny, us teachers have a saying, what's said in the staffroom, stays in the staffroom. I should've remembered that. What happens on the road, stays on the road.' The words tumbled out. 'Here…' She took a breath at last and thrust the rest of the photographs at him.

Jack sifted through them and stopped when he got to the photo of him and Beckett.

'Ah. You saw?'

'Yes.'

'He was a good man. He wouldn't have meant to hurt you.' Jack tucked that single photo into his chest pocket. 'I... listen, I was trying to protect you. Let sleeping dogs lie and all that.'

'Wasn't that up to me to decide?'

'Now I know you, yes, I suppose it was.'

'What else do you know?'

He finished the dregs of his tea and stood. 'A refill?' When Freya didn't answer he went to the range and poured another for himself. 'Beckett turned up late spring, pretty much the same way you did. I found him at dawn, curled up asleep, even in the same field byre as you. Ha, I ought to open it up as a bothy. He said he'd lost his way in the mist.'

As she listened, a nugget of uncertainty about this place lingered which she could not quite shift. And there was the mysterious moor itself: the stone circles, the sense of hallowedness she felt in the field byre, all the soothsaying going on, the dragon emblem on the handkerchiefs, the flashback at the clearing, the dream of Beckett in her room flicking through the boating magazine, and Jack's sudden memories of Rigby. What if Beckett had experienced that too? But this was fantastic, just magical nonsense. Her friend Father Paul would be the first person to put her right.

'From what I could gather,' Jack said, 'he'd been wandering around the moors for two days. He needed a bath but was happy enough. He seemed keen to get going, said he had some business to attend to, but I got the feeling he was more running from something. Anyway, the village soon worked its magic and he decided to stay.'

There was that word again, *magic.*

'I gave him a job mending the drystone walls. Very good at it, he was too.'

Warmed by the memory of Beckett, Freya felt more inclined to overlook and forgive Jack's omissions at their face value, though she still felt a sense of having had a wall thrown up to deliberately thwart her. It was as if these Moorlanders were closing ranks against her.

'Yes, he certainly would be. He used to wax lyrical about the tactile, elemental nature of the rocks. How they spoke to him of primeval beginnings and the connectedness of all things. A bit lost on me, I'm afraid. But it was the plants he loved most. He was a good gardener and nature seemed to respond to his touch.'

'Ah, I wonder,' Jack said 'if he might just have left

one of his plant catalogues lying around. Just a tick.' He searched among a heap of magazines and knick-knacks under the coffee table. 'Here.' He handed her a glossy pamphlet bursting forth with flowers of every hue and colour combination: blousy blush-pink peonies, to the delicate ivory bells of lily of the valley, the purple checkerboard of snake's head fritillary, to the ethereal palest blue of love in a mist, the garish magenta petunias, to the rainbow happy faces of pansies. Beckett had dog-eared some of the pages and marked plants of interest with an asterisk. Underneath the custard-yellow blooms of *Rudbeckia* he'd written *black-eyed Susan, say it with flowers*.

'Wonder what he meant by this.' Her mind leapt to astonishing conclusions. If Jack had gotten to know Beckett all through the summer, so too did the others – Merc, Tom the ratcatcher, and more interestingly, Susie. Why hadn't they said something? Freya imagined Susie serving Beckett a pint, their chit-chat moving to camaraderie (these locals stuck together after all), to goodness knows what next? Flirtations? Freya pointed at the page. 'Look at this. Black-eyed Susan, or maybe that should be Susie. Do you think it's possible Beckett and Susie were seeing each other?'

Jack peered at the entry and scoffed. 'Shouldn't think so. For one thing, Rudbeckia only flowers in the autumn. See? He'd hardly be able to court her with a shabby bunch of foliage, and like I said, he hadn't planned to stay around long. Secondly, it wouldn't surprise me if Susie was actually in some sort of liaison with Merc. But you didn't hear it from me.'

The phone rang in the other room and reverberated outside on the yard bell as a distant echo. While Jack went to answer it, she grappled with the idea of Susie and Merc together. She should have noticed it earlier. But why would she? It wasn't as if she had any claim on him. No wonder Susie was so eager for her to stay with Jack rather than share the room with Merc last night. His advances in the pub now seemed even more outrageous. How dare he. She closed her eyes and groaned. He had toyed with her. And she had made herself look stupid in front of Susie. How could she have been so naive?

Weariness ran through her like a troubled sleep. Brohn-In-The-Moor's pretty veneer was tarnished. Jack's admission of having known Beckett changed nothing. Home beckoned with its little shaker kitchen and bright floral bunting.

For the want of something to do, Freya fried up the eggs and buttered some bread. Jack's muffled voice carried along the corridor, then stopped. Moments later he burst through the door. 'That's settled then. That was old

Brian up at the top farm. Storm's carried away the bridge out by Margin Tor and the south road's flooded. We're marooned. You're not going anywhere today.'

'But I have to get home.' Having just settled on escaping, she didn't want to surrender.

'That's as maybe, but not today. Might even be days before it drains away. Still, worse things happen at sea.'

'I could go on foot,' she said, putting aside the time-honoured wisdom she had recently discovered from Moorlander folklore.

'Have you any idea how dangerous the moors are?' His voice reached a pitch of unnecessary incredulity. He stood barring the back door with outstretched arms, as if he was some heroic custodian of a dangerous beast.

'Jack don't be silly,' she giggled.

But he wasn't joking. 'We don't need any more accidents around here.'

'Any *more* accidents? What *other* accidents?'

'I was merely referring to some of the old folk stories. People disappearing in the bogs etcetera, getting attacked by wolves and all that stuff.'

'Wolves?' She imagined a pack of them, hungry-eyed and snapping at her heels.

He frowned. 'Well no, not exactly wolves as

such...Gah! Can't say anything around here.'

Freya conceded defeat. She didn't understand the landscape and envied Jack his sense of knowing the ground on which he stood. She dished up breakfast and they made stunted conversations between mouthfuls. Even so, she wondered why Jack seemed so keen to keep her in Brohn, her self-effacement unwilling to consider his interest went beyond kindness. So, if she were to be temporarily incarcerated here, she might as well try that bit harder to prove Beckett's death an accident and not suicide. That would solve, whilst not everything, a good many of her problems. She could then mourn in peace without fearing for him. He would of course be safely ensconced in heaven. But Beckett's last note to her belayed the peace she sought: *Conscience betrays guilt*. What on earth had he done? Maybe Jack was right, let sleeping dogs lie. But she owed Beckett the truth. He had stuck by her when he was alive at God knows what cost, she would stick by him in death. Jack may yet have more information to disclose.

CHAPTER 8

Freya marvelled at the handmade produce lined up in Jack's pantry as she searched for some tomato ketchup: honey crystallising in jars, pickled onions pale and translucent, malt-brown chutneys, cherries bloated in brandy, homemade quince jelly, runner beans in brine, brown paper sacks of flour and oats stacked in the corner, Tupperware boxes of muesli and cornflakes, salami and hams hanging from the beam, nameless grey meats entombed in fat. Enough supplies to get by in cold snaps when the winter blizzards piled snowdrifts high against the drystone walls or when heavy rains cascaded from the moors flooding the roads and tracks, cutting them off for days on end.

She began to appreciate how, when nature challenged Brohn-In-The-Moor, its residents rallied, such was their respect and reliance on the wilderness around them. Cars, electricity, and patchy phone signals were add-ons, not essentials. Being virtually off-grid, water came from natural springs and wells, sewage treatment from septic tanks, back-up power from generators stored in outhouses, heat from wood burning stoves. Jack had honed the skills needed for survival here on the moors out of necessity not whimsy, just as he had nurtured the Swiss-army-knife mentality for a life at sea.

A team of helpers had already begun the big clean up when Freya and Jack arrived back at The George and Dragon just after ten-thirty. Tom called everyone over and chin high and officious, rising on his heels, he de-briefed them. 'The flood peaked at around three this morning. The old pub was spared. Ta everyone, great team effort.' He broke off briefly to clap them. 'And the rill and gully method I suggested which we hobbled together from sandbags worked a treat. Shame about the stables though, and some of the rooms in The Byre which suffered a bit of water damage. Give yourselves a well-earned pat on the back. Well done Brohn folk!' All this was information they obviously knew but was dispensed for clarity, gratitude, and Tom's aggrandizement. For this, she did not begrudge him.

They all followed Tom into The Byre to survey

the damage. Jack stepped aside to hold the door open for her. The lounge remained untouched by the flood, although the sofas had been lifted onto block stilts and the rugs stored away upstairs as a precaution. Her room in the Byre and Merc's next door to hers displayed a three-inch tide mark around the bottom of the walls where the flood water had lapped and receded. The flagstone floors were still shiny with damp but unscathed except for sandy deposits along the joints. The windows were yawning wide open to help with the drying process. Hopefully, the rooms would be habitable by evening.

Out in the yard Merc pushed around a pole with a squeegee on the end, gathering up and then shoving the wet silt toward a mounting heap in the corner. He looked up and waved. Freya smiled, raised her hand self-consciously and then worried he had meant the wave for someone behind her. She lowered her arm as if it belonged to some errant schoolchild and checked over her shoulder – just Tom and a handful of volunteers bent over a pile of sandbags in the removal process. Merc waved again and returned her smile then turned his attention back to the mopping. Even at this early hour, after so little sleep, with his hair sticking up at the whorls and eyes puffy and small, he carried about him a presence, a self-assurance that he would be noticed. And Freya had not stopped noticing him.

Susie came into the yard carrying a tray of bacon baps and mugs of tea. Work halted and the helpers gathered around. Freya picked up a discarded squeegee and was about to begin mopping when Jack approached and took it out of her hand.

'Leave it for now, Freya. Let's be sociable.'

'But we've only just got here.'

'So, ten more minutes won't make much difference. Come.'

Conversation revolved around last night's heroism – prowess in the sandbag filling department as if the equivalent of a mountain had been moved, fighting back the torrents cascading from the moors, wading through water waist high – all with the jovial slant of exaggeration but coated with the thankful understanding of a disaster averted. Freya enjoyed the camaraderie of community, the communal chalice to be shared among them, whether good or bad. Could she stay here and drink from such a cup? Once teaching had given her a community of sorts. But when had her colleagues stopped congregating in the staffroom at lunch times to swap stories and offer support, preferring instead the disappointment of lukewarm flask tea and the isolation of yesterday's cold pasta eaten alone in the classroom?

After the tea break, Susie asked Freya to help prepare for the lunch time session. The chef had been seconded to the clean-up party leaving her to manage both front of house and food. In the sterile steel kitchen, Susie took some chef whites from the hook behind the door and tossed them to Freya. 'Here, put this on, you may as well look the part. And tie your hair back.'

Freya set to work on a tray of wild chanterelles and field mushrooms, brushing off the dry leaf mould and crumbly soil from the caps, gills, and stems. As she sliced and fried, the decayed earthy scent of a woodland floor filled the kitchen. Memories surfaced. She was twelve again, in the woods with a ferocious temper, stalking Debbie for having the cheek to fancy Kevin and wave that stupid Valentine's card under her nose. She sighed out the tragedy of that day; the sadness of all that Debbie could have been but never would.

'What's on the menu?' she said in an attempt at distraction.

Susie opened a drawer, pulled out a file and flipped through the plastic wallets. 'Ah, here we go.' She unclipped the clasp and passed her an A4 sheet. The bold typed heading read, *Supply Failure Menu, October.*

'You've actually got one for every month?'

'Got to around here.' Susie clicked her tongue.

'You never know when the weather's going to get the better of you.' She nodded to the mushrooms, 'Jack picked those yesterday. Seems he has some sort of sixth sense.'

'Does he know everything?'

'You name it, Jack's got some old wisdom for it. You should see him when he gets going with his folklore stories, a real crowd puller. Does wonders for my takings.'

'I'd like to see that.' Freya poked at the frying pan with a spatula. The mushrooms oozed a rich dark liquid. 'Will these do?'

'More heat needed, then flambé with some brandy.' Susie took a bottle of cheap wholesale brandy down from the shelf. 'You and Jack, you get on well, don't you?' She was fishing.

Freya let the ambiguity hang in the air. 'Doesn't everyone? He's kind, affable, a real gent.'

'But?'

'But nothing.'

'Perhaps someone else has caught your eye?' Susie turned up the heat to the cooker.

Steam rose in a great sizzling cloud to which Freya's face bore the brunt. She dabbed irritably with the stiff cotton of her sleeve.

'Oh, come on, not Merc? He'd eat you alive,' Susie laughed.

Freya resented the implication that she was some innocent little spinster at the mercy of a loveable rogue. She poured a great glug of brandy into the mushrooms and tipped the pan to the gas for ignition. Angry flames ballooned into the air. 'Well, you'd know about that, wouldn't you?' Freya said in an ill-judged riposte. And if she thought Susie might be magnanimous in her response, she was disappointed.

Susie popped an arm around her shoulders. 'Guess your little convent school doesn't see much of the likes of Merc and his ilk. As one friend to another, I'm telling you, he's dangerous. Now, be a love and get some lettuces from the garden.'

It might have been an exaggeration to describe the veg patch as a walled kitchen garden, but the moment Freya pushed open the gate and walked into the small, enclosed area, she felt at home. Not that she had ever managed a garden herself, but because she instantly sensed Beckett all around her. This was his territory. The raised beds with their straight rows of produce, bean poles dripping with fattened pods and the checkerboard of red and green lettuces planted grid-like, all celebrated Beckett's attention to detail. The rich soil once tilled to perfection but now full of weeds and gone to seed, exhumed his spirit. Nature at its most productive, ripe, and glorious; a cornucopia of grace.

Freya was drawn to the greenhouse, hesitated, and then stepped inside. Tomato plants hung limp on canes, their fruit taut and split on withered vines, and cucumbers, some the size of marrows, snaked along the floor among yellowing leaves. Geraniums in clay pots sat on the greenhouse staging, garish in fuchsia pinks and ice-lolly reds and going to seed. No one had thought to deadhead them, so Freya set to work until the plants looked presentable again.

She thought of Beckett on his increasingly rare visits to her little terrace house, sitting out on the patio surrounded by pots of them, sipping earl grey tea and chewing over their news. Thinking how perfect those moments seemed, their mutual understanding and easy silences, the sun always seeming to shine, she now saw how deluded she had been when all the time he had been holding back. If only she had known his true state of mind and what troubled him.

She pushed open the adjoining door which led to the potting shed. Rows of tools lined the walls on galvanised clips, each one shiny and oiled. Here at least Beckett's work persisted without decay. A Lloyd-loom chair like the one in grandma's porch, sat in the corner with a flattened seat cushion. Above the potting bench hung a rough-hewn wooden shelf with a library of garden reference books. Freya ran a finger along the spines and read aloud the titles as if to lure back his spirit: *Jekka's Complete Herb Book, Monty Don's Jewel Garden,* and *The Concise Book of Flower Meanings.* This one she removed and hugged to her chest.

'Beckett come back. Please…come back,' she said out loud to the books. She backed towards the chair and froze half-way down in the act of sitting. Sticking out from under her a pair of scuffed boots had appeared at the foot of the chair. Her eyes followed them up – brown corduroyed knees, check-shirted chest, and at last, Beckett's grinning face.

'Sheesh, Beck, you made me jump.'

'Hi, Sis,' he said. 'Welcome to my world.'

'Where have you been? We had a flood and could've done with your–' She remembered and stopped. Her imagination, the grief, tiredness, all had conjured up the illusion of him as sure as the sun rose at dawn. 'Never mind. You're just a hallucination, or maybe a ghost.' She upended a tin bucket and sat on it facing him. 'It all got a bit much,' she continued anyway. 'I got upset…and Jack was being mean.'

Beckett stuck out his bottom lip while he

considered. 'That's unlike him. He didn't strike me as scary.'

'I didn't say that. I said *mean*. Why does everything have to be so…*nuanced* with you, like you're trying to second guess me all the time? You're infuriating.'

She watched him run his thumbnail along the channels in the corduroy of his trousers. He had clamped up as always, and she knew he wasn't going to argue. If ever there was conflict, Beckett did his best to avoid it.

'Did you meet Merc?' she asked. 'He's a bit flash but…what d'you think, should I give it a go?'

Beckett's hand momentarily paused on the corduroy, then he set to brushing up the fabric the wrong way with the palm of his hand so that the nap laid in the opposite direction lightening the colour.

'Had a feeling you'd say that. But you've never liked anyone since Duncan.'

Duncan had diminished in her memory, like the sepia photographs of her grandparents, or the childhood friendships sealed with spit and grime, time eroding him to an irrelevance. Yet his impact remained by stealth, nurtured into a skeptical worldview; love is conditional, and by this code she lived. She thought she would be safe with Duncan, with his understated and uncomplicated sensible manner. She found companionship in his predictability, though passion remained an undeserved and unobtainable goal for both of them. One summer evening, when dusk held onto the sultry heat, they walked along the seashore and as the tide receded, he sat her down on a mooring post by the quayside and knelt before her. Silhouetted against the orange sky, he offered up a sapphire and diamond ring from a velvet box.

The engagement limped on for three months. Freya played at loving him, fooled herself into believing she had a right to be happy until her conscience niggled, nagged, screamed and at last compelled her to act; atonement being the only truth. She had practiced what she might say – *it's me not you, not ready for this, you're too good for me* – all trite excuses. In the end she didn't even say, *'I don't love you,'* or *'You don't really love me.'*

'Margaret's offered me promotion,' she had said to Duncan in the end. 'To Head of the history department.'

'About time. She's been getting freebies from you all term. Might as well get the recognition. And the pay.'

'It'll mean more work.'

'Obviously.' He refolded his newspaper, so the sports page was on top.

'I said I'd do the Masters' programme.'

'As well?'

'Always wanted to, why not now?' She gave a feeble smile.

'How on earth are you going to find time? You're working full-time and have a wedding to plan. We're supposed to be getting married, remember?' He set down his newspaper and removed his glasses, a gesture she knew preceded him making some point or other which he would inevitably win.

'*Supposed* to be?' She found the loose thread to pull. 'You don't sound too sure about that. I mean…I can understand. You've been on your own for a long time.'

'As have you. Freya, what's this all about?' He set his head to a quizzical slant.

She shrugged her shoulders and playing for time flicked through some student essays. 'You want to be sure you know what you're getting yourself into.'

'Well, I am sure. It's not like there's any secrets between us…' His voice trailed off. 'Are there?' She detected a slight tremor in his voice.

'We all have a past,' she said.

'Huh. You don't.'

Why did he always assume her life had only begun once they met? 'I'm not talking about sex.' The pretence of their relationship began to unravel.

He leant forward in a conciliatory manner. 'So,

there is something. Let's not have any secrets. Just say what it is and be done with it. Can't be as bad as all that. It's not like you robbed a bank, or killed anyone, or something, is it?' he joked.

Freya bowed her head, any last chance of happiness in tatters. What had she expected him to say, *'I couldn't care less so long as we're together'*? A small part of her hoped his love might be stronger than her guilt. Yet could she have accepted such a love?

'I'm sorry, Duncan.'

His terse response, 'I see,' were the last words he had spoken to her. The next day she received a note – *You're not the person I imagined you to be. It's obvious your conscience troubles you and I'm left imagining the worst. It's a matter of trust. I agree, it is best we go our separate ways. With sadness, Duncan x.*

Freya shook away the memories and turned back to Beckett. 'Me and Duncan. It wouldn't have worked. I'm glad I found out, saved a lot of heartache. Pity *you* never married though.'

Every time they had got close to the topic Beckett would take counter manoeuvres and bring the conversation back to the circumstances in her own life. Freya was left guessing the real reason he never committed. He'd had girlfriends in his twenties, but none who'd put up with his long silences, his solitary nature, or the wilderness weekends spent star gazing alone.

Freya remembered the lettuces for Susie. 'Just one thing before I go, does black-eyed Susan mean anything to you?' Beckett gave a shrug which she may have taken for a no had it not been for the slight lift of his brow. She understood the inference; silence is an answer too.

'Thanks Beck.' She grabbed the trug from the workbench on the way out.

'Bye Sis.'

She looked back over her shoulder. 'I need you.'

'I know.'

She blew him a kiss.

'Now get the lettuces before Susie gives you a bad mark.'

CHAPTER 9

After lunch service was over and only a few stragglers remained for the last of the clearing up, Freya snuck back to her room to take a nap. She closed the windows and drew the curtains on the lucent sky and curled up on the bed. But sleep didn't come despite exhaustion. Her thoughts whirled and fretted without settling – Susie's comments, Beckett, Merc, then imagining Susie with either of them, the black-eyed Susan plants and their indeterminate meanings. After three quarters of an hour, she abandoned sleep and turned her attention to the seed catalogue. She flipped to the ordering page in the middle. Beckett had par-filled it in with a blue biro: sweet peas, cosmos, zinnia, love-in-a-mist, then crossed through them diagonally in an apparent change of heart. Above this he'd written *Too late*. Only one plant remained on the list,

Rudbeckia. An arrow speared from the last letter to his next note, *Buy plants at nursery*. And then something strange, written in capital letters and underlined *JUSTICE!* Freya flicked back to the picture of the Rudbeckia and studied it. Large yellow-orange daisy heads with a dark centre smiled up at an invisible sun – the black-eyed Susans.

She tried to remember why the flowers seemed familiar, even significant, and then it came to her. A first-frost morning in October when she and Beckett were walking to school, hands shoved in woollen blazers, breath billowing in the crisp air. He had trotted ahead, his satchel banging against his side. He disappeared around the corner onto Chesterton Street. Debbie called out to Freya from the other side of the road, and she crossed over to join her. They stopped at the sweet shop to buy *Milky Ways* and *Polos*. By the time they reached Chesterton Street, Beckett was a tiny dot of a waif halfway down the road, dwarfed by tower blocks, and vulnerably exposed to the rush hour traffic. The burgundy blob of his blazer suddenly stopped and was swallowed by a mass of grey and blue, the blazers of the boys from the local comprehensive. The group were gathered outside the convent house which adjoined St Michael and All Angels' Church where she, Beckett and Debbie went to Mass every Sunday.

'We'd best get a move on,' she said to Debbie. 'Beck looks in trouble.'

Debbie jogged alongside her for a few paces, but her violin case flapped about and got caught up between her legs. 'I can't, Frey, you go on. I'll see you at school.'

Freya just arrived as the fattest boy grabbed Beckett by his hair. 'Pay day, dipstick. Hand it over.' His arm jerked up lifting her brother onto his tiptoes. Beckett squealed.

'I ain't got none,' Beckett said.

'He ain't got none.' The boy turned to his posse, and they sneered back. He rotated his hand and Beckett squealed with pain as his hair tore from the roots. 'Forgetful, are we? Guess we'll have to give you a reminder.'

Freya stepped forward. 'It's true,' she said in her most pleading voice. 'We've got sandwiches today.' She took out her Tupperware box, fumbled with the lid and offered it up. 'See, I've got crisps and a *Penguin* bar you can have.'

'Urgh, nobody likes *Penguins*.' The boy let go of Beckett's hair, grabbed the chocolate biscuit, tossed it on the floor and crushed it with the grinding motion of his ape-sized foot. At the click of his fingers, a goon scampered to retrieve it for him. He opened the wrapper, held it above Freya's head and sprinkled it upon her like sugar strands over a cupcake. Next, he smacked the lunchbox out of her hand. Triangles of beige ham and white bread somersaulted into the air.

'What d'you think?' he asked his mates, and when they jeered, he ordered them to grab hold of Beckett. He opened the crisps, and with a gorilla grin, tipped the whole lot down the front of Beckett's shirt.

Sensing some sport, two of them picked up the sandwiches and shoved them down Beckett's back and rubbed a buttery slice of bread in his face for good measure. Freya's temper flared. She shoved at the ringleader's chest, momentarily toppling him from his all-too solid base. In the tussle that followed Beckett was bulldozed. He stumbled backwards and tripped over the low garden wall of the convent garden. His feet traced a slow perfect arc in the air before he landed in a heap among the foliage. The boys ran off whooping and laughing at their early morning sport.

Freya peered over the wall. Beckett lay on his back partially hidden in a bed of waist-high yellow-orange flowers. Within seconds the convent door flew open, and a nun appeared wielding a walking stick. 'Holy Mary and Joseph,' the nun exclaimed. 'Jesus has eyes and thank the Lord, so do I.'

Freya rolled her own. Everyone knew Sister Martha Mary was so very old and almost blind. Sister crossed herself. 'I know what's going on here and shame on you. Filthy little heathen. Get up out of my precious flowers. Oh, my poor black-eyed Susans.' She raised her stick above her head, and thinking she might use it, Beckett scrambled to his feet cowering away from her and creating even more damage to the flowerbed. The old lady stabbed forward and grabbed him by the ear with a gnarled hand. 'Father Llewellyn will be wanting to hear about this.'

'But it weren't his fault, Sister Martha Mary. It was those other boys. Honestly!' She couldn't understand why Sister was getting all het up about a few daisies anyways, they didn't look anything special.

The nun turned a beaky face towards her. 'Hush your lying mouth, Freya Greene.'

It was Freya's bad luck that Sister Martha Mary had been blessed not only with 'good eyesight' but also a sharp memory for names.

'It's true though, isn't it, Beck?'

Sister narrowed her eyes. 'You would add corrupting your little brother to your list of sins too young lady? Now, the pair of you, off to confession. Let's see if Father can knock the devil out of you.'

Father Llewellyn stood at his front door listening

as Sister Martha Mary relayed the tragic events. All the while, Freya stood beside her shaking her head and hoping he'd see the nun's version was all lies. After the third round of repetition, and suggestions of suitable punishment for the heathens, Father raised a hand to intervene.

'Your input as always is most valued, Sister. You can safely leave it with me now.'

He stepped off the doorstep into the street and closed the front door behind him. He signalled for them to follow him over to the church where he waved them in before entering himself. As he was closing the door, Sister Martha Mary shoved a surprisingly strong foot into the opening. 'You'll be wanting my help now, Father,' she said.

Father Llewellyn pushed the door closed a fraction more, so sister's face became a narrow slit. 'No, no, I'm sure I'll be fine. Thank you.'

'But there's two of the little rascals.'

Father looked over his shoulder and winked at Freya. He was definitely on *her* side. 'Oh yes, so there is,' he said, turning back to Sister. 'Nevertheless, I must soldier on alone, fulfilling this most sacred of duties for the salvation of souls. The sacrament of reconciliation, though it be both heart rending and sometimes painful,' Sister Martha Mary oozed a look of sympathy, 'will need a careful examination of conscience,' he said. 'And these children will want a period of peace and quiet to reflect and consider how they have offended Our Lord.'

Sister crossed herself again. 'Well, Father, I'm sure you know best.'

'Indeed. Obviously, your prayers will be most appreciated for these little ones of Jesus. Could I suggest you light a candle in the convent oratory? And perhaps, if you could possibly bear it, say a decade or two of the rosary?'

Just as the door was closing, Freya succumbed to the urge and poked her tongue out.

'Okay you two, sit here.' Father pointed to a bench in the Lady Chapel. 'Who's for orange squash and biscuits?' he asked.

Father Llewellyn popped to the sacristy and returned with the refreshments. He sat on the pew in front and pivoted round to face them. He reminded them they were in church, which Freya thought a strange thing to say since they obviously were. And besides, they went there every Sunday for Mass and knew how to behave. He leant forward and with his thumb, traced the shape of a cross on their foreheads and blessed them.

Father invited Freya to give her account of the incident. She described in detail, Beckett running ahead, she and Debbie stopping for sweets, and him disappearing out of sight. She pulled out her packet of *Polos* and offered him one. He declined. In her version, the four boys had turned into six goons and each one of them had taken a pot shot at Beckett before dumping him into the flower bed. 'Honest to God,' she added.

Father Llewellyn turned to Beckett. 'Is this true?'

Beckett nodded his head. 'And the boys were at least six feet tall, weren't they Frey?'

One side of Freya's mouth twitched in irritation. He'd gone too far and now Father would know.

'I see,' Father said.

'Sister Martha Mary didn't even see the boys though, Father,' she said. 'She only saw Beckett falling into the flowers, so she was lying.'

Father closed his eyes in disgust. A sense of doom descended on her. If only she hadn't called Sister Margaret Mary a liar.

'I'm going to phone your schools and tell them you'll be late,' he said, 'then I'll get ready to hear your confessions. You're to come along to the confessional box in a couple of minutes when the green light comes on. I'll be on the other side.' He pointed unnecessarily to a dark curtained box in the corner. 'While I'm gone, I want you to think carefully about truthfulness, whether you've been judging others or taking Our Lord's name in vain. Remember, it's God who's listening, not me.' He picked up their empty glasses and returned to the sacristy, his rubber soles squeaking on the floor.

Freya rolled her eyes. Everyone knew it couldn't physically be God, so Father had to be taking His place. And if it wasn't physically God, what if Father didn't always manage to close his own ears so he could be God's ears, in which case he'd be listening too, right? Though to be fair, Father had never mentioned any of her sins outside the confessional. Besides, it was a lot to ask of God who probably had better things to do than listen to her going on about how she argued with Beckett and how she wanted to kiss Kev at school. The issue had grown to unmanageable proportions, and she hadn't felt like going to confession anymore. She asked her mum about this. Mum grabbed a coffee and sat her down, so Freya knew it would be a long conversation. She talked about Father Llewellyn being *in persona Christi*, and mystery and faith and loads of other stuff and that one day she would understand. She doubted whether she ever would.

Freya's confession took a lot longer than normal because Father kept asking her more questions. 'Are you sure that's all?' 'Have you taken full responsibility for your part in this?' 'What about the way you talked to Sister

Martha Mary?' 'Do you think you treated her with respect and compassion? She is very old after all,' 'Could you have acted differently today?' While Freya thought about the last one, she looked around the box for inspiration. A wooden crucifix hung above the grill which separated them. Jesus looked so sad that she wanted to say the right answer, only she didn't know what that was supposed to be. She toyed with a plastic covered card sitting on a plinth in front of her with the act of contrition written upon it. She'd have to say that in a minute – *O my God, because You are so good, I am very sorry that I have sinned against You, and by the help of Your grace, I will not sin again. Amen.*

Father spent a while sympathising with her, explaining that perhaps it wasn't always easy to do the right thing when someone had hurt us or if things seemed unfair. When he was a boy – Freya yawned – a similar thing had happened to him and all he could think about was getting justice, so he knew how it felt. She tried to listen but kept getting distracted by the *Polos* in her blazer. Her hand drifted down to her pocket, stroked the tube, fiddled with the straggly end of the foil, and managed to wriggle one out which she then popped into her mouth. Father raised a hand in benediction. 'Amen,' she said too quickly.

'What kept you?' Beckett asked when she came

out.

'He wanted to know all the ins and outs. I set him straight, so you won't have to. You owe me now.'

Beckett's confession by comparison was short. Afterwards he sat sulking in the pews while Freya completed her three Hail Mary's and two Our Father's. She restarted the Our Father twice because she'd been trying to say it carefully, thinking about the words like she was supposed to. But saying it slowly put the rhythm out and she couldn't remember them.

When they were back out in the sunshine, Freya asked Beckett what he said in his confession.

'None of your business. It's private,' he said.

'Didn't you say it wasn't your fault, that it was the boys'?'

'No point.' He kicked a stone. 'Nobody listens anyway. S'not fair.'

'All we want is a bit of justice, don't we?' Freya said in sympathy. She used Father Llewellyn's own word so it couldn't be wrong, could it?

'What's that?' Beckett asked.

'It means being fair, people getting what they deserve.'

Beckett seemed to taste the idea, rolled the word around his mouth. 'Just-iss,' he said, repeating it all the way to school, as if saying it enough might make it happen.

Freya opened *The Concise Book of Flower Meanings,* searched through the index, and thumbed to the page for Rudbeckia. Underneath the picture of a meadow bathed in golden flowers, the entry read *Rudbeckia, hirta, common name, black-eyed Susan. North American species of perennial herb with showy cone-shaped orange-yellow flower heads. Flower meaning: Justice. Also noted to convey encouragement, motivation, and impartiality.*

It couldn't be a mere coincidence. Beckett had been angry for months about that flowerbed incident and had spurted out the word 'justice' at every opportunity, until at last their mother banned him from using it. He screamed it for one last time, 'All I want is some justice,' which earned him a clip round the ear.

Freya decided to draw on Jack's wisdom. She found him in the bar playing dominoes with Tom and sharing together not a pint of beer but a humble pot of tea. He shifted along the bench so she could sit down. His great paw of a hand cupped three dominoes, none of which could be placed. He tapped the table with an unusable two/three – a pass, which meant he had to pick up a spare. Tom rubbed his hands together with glee and set down one of his, a double blank, so Jack missed another turn.

'Sorry,' she said to Jack, 'I'm bringing you bad luck.'

'His loss is my gain,' Tom said, his deep lined face crinkling with mischief. He held up a domino between his curled fingers and thumb. ''Ere, my lover, rub my bone for luck, will you?'

She shuddered in mock disgust. 'You really are quite revolting at times, Tom.' And though it was true, she also envied his visceral earthiness, the uninhibited behaviour she could never imagine she or Duncan displaying. It had been as if their relationship played out solely in the intellect, never quite translating to a true emotional or physical response, with neither of them free enough to take the initiative.

'Now, now, Tom,' Jack warned, 'Ladies present.'

'She don't mind, do ya? Are you going to pick one up Jack, or what?'

'Nope. I fold. Pot's yours.'

'You're playing for money?' Freya asked, but as she said it, she clocked the heap of matchsticks on the table. 'Ah. My mistake.'

'Let's go!' Jack stood and ushered her out of the bench. As they were leaving Tom called over, 'Settle up with ya later, eh?'

'So, you are playing for money?' She hadn't meant to sound quite so appalled.

'Relax, it's just for pennies, or the next round. Tom's always skint.'

'Yes…and so was Beckett.'

'Like I said, just for pennies.' Jack held open the door for her, 'I'd best get on with the fencing repairs back at the farm.'

'Of course, sorry.' Consulting the oracle would have to wait. 'Maybe see you later?'

He took a few steps away then swung round. 'Heck, it can wait, what's up?'

Freya explained the significance of the Rudbeckia flower and the word justice. She omitted to mention her recent hallucination of Beckett in the potting shed, though Jack of all people would understand. At first, he seemed doubtful the two were connected. 'Hmm. Still thinking about those black-eyed Susans?'

Freya hugged her jacket around her and shrugged.

'You could be right about the justice bit though,' he said with more kindness. 'Who knows what childhood trauma shapes us? Come on, follow me. There's something I think you should see.' He led her around the perimeter of the stable yard, past The Byre's outer wall and along to the veg patch where she had harvested the lettuces.

'I was here earlier. There's nothing,' she said.

'You haven't looked hard enough.' He went over to an ivy-covered wall at the far end and tapped out a straight line on it at ankle height with his toecap. The thud of leather on stone changed to a hollow knocking sound on wood. 'Here we go. We'll need a key though. Check the shed.'

Freya searched the shelves in the shed: spiders, discarded clay pots, empty seed packets but no key. She tried a drawer under the potting bench – locked. And most likely it contained the key to the old door in the wall. 'Oh, come on,' she grumbled. A grimy but well-used gardening apron hung on a peg by the tool rack. She guessed it was Beckett's and popped it on, crossed over the tapes at the back and brought them to the front where she tied a bow. In the front pocket she found a bunch of rusty keys which looked like they hadn't been used for years. As she was leaving, she caught a glimpse of Beckett in the same Lloyd loom chair as before, giving her the thumbs up. Wishful thinking perhaps, but it was worth a try. 'Thanks Beck.'

She and Jack set to work pulling ivy from the door. Dust and pollen spewed into the air and danced as dust motes in the afternoon sun. The first key wouldn't even fit into the lock, the second went in but there was no room to turn. The last looked more promising, slotting in fine but sticking when it engaged with the mechanism.

'There's some *WD40* on the workbench,' Freya said. 'I'll get it.'

Beckett was no longer in the shed, but she felt his presence lingering. She grabbed the can and said to the ether, 'You know I'll look an idiot if there's nothing there.'

Jack attached the red straw nozzle onto the can and squirted inside the lock, then directly onto the key. He used the tail end of his shirt to rub off the rust. 'Fingers crossed.' He inserted the key, wriggled it back and forth a few times then the inner workings slid back with a satisfied click though the door did not open.

'How long do you think since the door's been used?' Freya asked.

'Probably not as long as you think.' He tugged away at the ivy. 'We've had a good summer, sunshine and showers. Ivy grows at a fair old pace of knots. It's possible Beckett was the last person to use it and he's been gone...'

'Since August.' She had her doubts; ivy didn't grow that fast. 'Maybe there's another door in from round the back.'

'Not that I know of.'

She was about to suggest they give up on the fool's errand when Jack gave an almighty shove at the door with his shoulder, and it swung open. The momentum, however, carried him on sideways for a few steps as if he were a dancer in a chorus line. Freya smirked.

Jack rubbed his shoulder. 'I'd do it again to see you smile.' Freya blushed.

A small private courtyard garden lay before them surrounded by stone walls higher than Jack's head. The sun struck one corner where this part had been devoted to a seating area with a lattice-work table and two metal chairs. Cream paint flaked off exposing a rusty skeletal core. They stood on recently laid flagstones with still-clean grout lines – Beckett's handiwork no doubt. Had he and Susie spent snatched moments here away from the tittle-tattle of the inn? Paving ebbed out toward a central flower bed filled with plants at various stages of decline. Weeds infiltrated everything. Freya sighed. It had been pure fantasy to expect a whimsical secret garden behind the door, blooming away in Beckett's absence as a monument to his memory.

'It's a bit of a mess,' Jack stated needlessly.

'Not Beck's finest work, that's true, though I suppose it could have been nice originally. It's too random and unkempt to be a message. You've humoured me enough, Jack. We're wasting our time. No point trying to read into something that isn't there.' She sat on one of the old chairs.

'At least you have your Rudbeckia over there.'

She managed a half smile, a small consolation. 'Oh well, I won't be needing this.' She put the flower book on the table and stared at the chaos of the garden. Jack picked it up and flicked through the pages, pausing to read any that caught his attention and glancing up from time to time to look at the plants. He frowned as if he were trying to work out a puzzle. In a large terracotta pot next to Freya stood a specimen bay tree shaped like a lollipop. An untidy mass of weeds grew in the potting compost underneath it and she began clearing these while she waited.

'Be careful of those,' Jack snapped. 'They're pretty deadly.'

'What these little things?' She raised a handful of leaves and tendrils. Some had purple star-shaped flowers with a yellow central cone, others had shiny black berries.

'It's Belladonna. Highly poisonous.'

'Urgh!' She dropped them quickly and rubbed her hand along her thigh to remove any last traces. 'Looks like Beckett's warning me off.'

'Maybe not.' Jack thumbed through the book and found the entry for Belladonna. 'It says *silence*. Interesting. Well of course there's bound to be silence after the poison has finished us off.'

She sniggered for the second time that afternoon.

Laughter had been in such short supply in her life. She struggled to remember Beckett ever collapsing with the sheer joy of amusement. 'Perhaps silence is its own answer,' she mused.

'Maybe. Look where it's growing though, under the bay tree.' He flipped through to the entry for bay in the book. '*Laurus nobilis, common name, bay tree or sweet bay. Aromatic evergreen shrub originating from Mediterranean regions. Plant meaning, I change but in death, no change till death, I change but in dying.*'

'I know the flavour of bay intensifies when it's dried out for cooking but other than that, it makes no sense.'

'I'm no preacher but it makes every sense if you read it with the eyes of faith.'

'Faith!' she said. 'I have faith that Beckett wouldn't have killed himself, faith that he wants justice, and faith that he'd lead me to the truth. Is that good enough for you?'

'You tell me?'

She looked away as if they were strangers. He failed to understand what he had asked of her. Could anyone?

After an uncomfortable pause he asked, 'Why have you *really* come?' His question had a validity she could not deny. Was it really to get justice for Beckett by finding out the truth? And didn't she want the comfort of knowing he basked in eternal life? Or was it because she could not bear the thought that he had committed suicide and she had not meant as much to him as he did to her? Another question, nebulous and dark, shrank from articulation and had everything to do with silence and guilt from those wild places of her memory.

While she grappled with the unthinkable, Jack at last said, 'I'm sorry, I've no right…Let's see what other clues he's left lying around.'

He moved to a central position in front of the flowerbed where he could get an overview of the entire garden. A low box hedge framed the perimeter, four small cypress trees stood foursquare at each corner, and running perpendicular through the plot, Beckett had laid gravel paths edged with chamomile. Swathes of yellows and blues at various heights occupied the central areas and honeysuckle climbed the wall at the far end.

'Got the book?' he asked. 'Let's make some sense of this.' He raised his hands and dabbed at an imaginary canvas in mid-air. 'Cypress. What does it say?'

Freya searched in the book. 'Basically, it's a symbol of death and mourning.'

'Cheerful old soul, your Beckett.'

'So, it seems. Jack, do you think he could have known his fate, what he was going to do?' Somehow it seemed much worse knowing he'd been thinking about it for some time. She shivered with misery.

'Doubt it… What else have we? This silvery plant it's rue. What does it say?'

She read through the entry and paraphrased it. '*An itchy and irritating plant*…blah, blah, *a natural insect repellent which allowed people to rob from plague victims, hence it is regarded with disdain.* I guess that's where the phrase, 'rue the day' comes from. Next one?'

Jack stepped into the flowerbed to take a closer look. 'I think this is golden rod.'

Freya took longer to find this one and needed to comb through the pictures until she found it under its proper name. 'It's solidago and stands for encouragement.'

'Well, we need that alright.' He bent down to a shrubby plant, picked a frond and brought it over to her. 'No blooms on this one.'

She twirled it around between her fingers. 'I've no idea and the pictures don't help either. If only Beckett were here, he'd have it identified in a jiffy.'

'If Beckett were here, we wouldn't be doing this. Okay, leaving aside this one, what's the chamomile say?'

After a moment Freya found the entry. 'No way.

It says *energy in adversity*. Code word patience, d'you think? Guess that means we'll have to look through all the pictures to find the meaning of the other one.' She poked a finger at the nameless plant set aside. 'So, what have we got? Pairs of leaves situated along the stem and a single leaf at the apex.'

They sat at the table, side by side over the book with their heads bowed and almost touching. A few minutes later, Jack tapped a photo with his fingernail. 'It's got to be this one, coronilla, but it flowers in early spring, and he wasn't even here then. I think we might be barking up the wrong tree. Why would he plant this if no one was going to see it bloom?'

'But in the seed catalogue he'd written *buy plants at nursery* so he must have done just that in anticipation for next year.' With this her logic fell away. 'But Beckett never stayed anywhere long enough to see the fruits of his labour. Though look at this, the gumpf says it means *success to you*. That's got to be it. We're nearly there. Are there anymore?'

'See those patches of lilac and blue,' he pointed over to the far side of the garden, 'they're Michaelmas daisies.'

'I know. And Beckett knew I loved them,' she smiled.

Jack consulted the book. 'You're not going to like this. They say *farewell.*'

'Is that all I'm worth, a measly bunch of flowers?'

'You said you loved them.'

'Some consolation. I'd rather have him a million times over.'

'I know you would…I know.' He patted the back of her hand, but his sympathy was short lived. Distracted, he returned to the book and after some minutes, during which Freya held back threatening tears, he snapped the book closed. 'That honeysuckle on the wall, it's woodbine and stands for fraternal love. So, if we run through these and re-arrange, we have cypress, belladonna, rue,' he counted them off on his fingers, 'black-eyed Susan, bay, goldenrod, chamomile, coronilla, Michaelmas daisies and honeysuckle. Don't you see?' he laughed.

'I'm not with you.'

'The clever old beggar! You were right. He's left you a message, and with a bit of poetic licence, I think it goes something like this – *In death there is mourning, but a poisonous silence brings irritation and disdain. Justice comes from dying to oneself. I offer you encouragement, patience, and energy in adversity. I hope this brings you success. Farewell, my dearest sister.*'

The sun dropped below the west wall and the shadows of evening embraced them. They sat in silence, digging the layers of Beckett's words, the pale discs of their faces taut with concentration. Once Jack had processed them, he rubbed an exasperated hand over his face. 'Darn it, Beck,' he said. 'What more do you want from me?' He got up, made his excuses and left. She watched his retreat with puzzlement. What had Jack meant? Things were left hanging and unsaid. There seemed to be more secrets.

Left alone in the courtyard her thoughts dipped into a pool of memories. Amongst the hidden places a forgotten face, that of Debbie's mother, distraught and knotted with grief. Unable to bear it, Freya ran out of the courtyard, away from the inn, and from Brohn-In-The-Moor where so many memories seemed to surface, over the fields, along the track and up high towards Margin Tor.

The gentle countryside of trees and pasture gave way to the wilder terrain of grass cleaving to scree, and boulders set awkward by some great conflict with nature. Fragile in the wind, her small frame leant onto the slope, climbed higher, her thigh muscles burning with effort, until she reached the summit. The wind roared all around her swallowing her cries. 'Why? Why now?' She fell to her knees, tipped her face to the heavens. 'I can't undo the past. Am I to be punished for ever? I hate you. Do you hear?' Yet through this tirade, a kernel of hope remained.

Perspective needed logic. Hate was simply another overused word, hyperbole for strong angry feelings. Father Paul once said that love and hate were flipsides of the same coin. It was when love disappoints that hate – if indeed it could be called that – steps in. Freya edged around the tor looking for a respite out of the wind. In the calm space between the rocks, she began to understand. Disappointment came from her unfulfilled expectations of God, of Beckett, but most of all from herself.

CHAPTER 10

A few days later when the aftereffects of the flood had subsided and Freya was returning from an early morning walk around the village, she found a posy of purple heather left at her door. She raised it to her nose and inhaled the honey and smoked lavender aroma. The gift tag read *Hope you slept well!* Two thoughts occurred, they were from Jack, and the heather held a secret meaning. Resisting the temptation to look it up in the flower book, she instead decided to accept the gift at face value.

Someone was whistling a familiar tune in the kitchen – *All Together in the Floral Dance*, a silly old-fashioned staple from her childhood. It seemed the day would be dominated by flowers. She walked into the kitchen and found Merc filling the kettle. He turned and smiled, and a frisson of unexpected and startling desire seared through her.

'A wee cup of tea for the lassie?' he asked. The collar of his polo shirt was turned up and his sunglasses were pushed back onto his head like a tourist in Rome. A yellow sweater draped over his shoulders with the arms looped in front as if he were out to play a round of golf in summer, not to go about his business on a chilly October's day.

'Lovely morning. Hope you slept well,' he said.

'Ah, so these are from you.' Freya waved the heather posy, and he gave a small bow. An irresistible warmth glowed inside her. 'You must have been up early for these?'

'Best part of the day. I thought I'd lost something up on the tor. Wasn't there so I guess not.'

'I could help you look.'

'Ach, leave it, it'll turn up. Besides, the exercise will do me good.' He patted his clenched stomach muscles. For a man in his fifties, he was indeed in good shape. 'You keep yourself nice,' he said to her as a point of fact not open for contradiction.

'I could do with losing–' She stopped and remembered her negative response when Jack had once complimented her on her hair. 'Suit yourself'', Jack had said in disappointment, as if she had questioned his judgement.

'The bridge is mended so I'm away to Exeter on business. Want to come along for the ride?'

Freya weighed up the advantages; the chance to get to know Merc better and a few hours shopping for a new jacket (that way she wouldn't have to borrow Susie's again), versus the negatives; having to sound interested all day if he turned out to be a narcissistic bore. But what clinched it in the end was the need to contact Father Paul and ask him a favour. The phone lines were still down in the village and showed little sign of being mended.

Half an hour later Freya found herself a passenger in the sports convertible of a Mercedes-Benz. Merc handed her a baseball cap embroidered with the brand's three-pointed star logo. 'To keep your hair in place,' he said, his own short, clipped hair untroubled by any such back draught.

She put it on and tucked her hair behind her ears. 'Any good?'

Merc frowned. 'It's a wee bit big. Here.' He took it off and fiddled with the adjuster at the back and popped it back on her head. 'Grand. Just a sec.' He stroked away a lock of hair from her eye while she filed away the memory of his warm fingers to savour later. 'Ready?'

'I guess so.'

He turned the ignition, revved the engine, slipped it into gear and sped away from the village. With the car roof folded down and the raw wind pummelling them, she had the illusion of travelling at great speed. When Merc took a blind corner whilst accelerating, she yelped. He threw his head back in amusement.

'Not scared, are you?'

'Course not.'

'You do want to have fun, don't you?'

'Sure, I do,' she answered, instantly regretting it as he slipped up a gear and pressed his foot to the floor. The embankments and hedgerows blurred in her peripheral vision. She scrunched up her eyes, grabbed the seatbelt with one hand and the middle armrest with the other.

'Do you trust me?'

'No!'

'Good,' he laughed and his left hand slid from the steering wheel to her knee and squeezed.

For a few seconds, she played between eyes open, and eyes closed, testing whether she had either adjusted to the speed they were travelling or if the pace had slackened. When at last she thought she had overcome fear, Merc rounded a bend into the path of an oncoming tractor. Freya shrieked. Her arms instinctively flailed into a cross-armed, face-protecting posture, that through some herculean feat of strength, they might provide a level of invisible protection from the near-certain head-on crash and death. But Merc's reactions were swift and controlled. The car stopped in an instant. He yanked the gear lever into reverse, glided into the passing place ten yards back and waved on the farmer to pass with a nonchalant beckoning gesture usually reserved for a child.

She leant back onto the headrest and concentrated on breathing. So, this was what they called fun. She considered her options: fake it or say something. No, driving along at high speed down single-track roads designed for a horse and cart was reckless, no matter which way she looked at it. '*Now* will you slow down?' she said, with more than a hint of irritation.

Had it been Jack, she would have expected an apology. But being Merc, he turned to her, smirked, and cocked her a wink. He was infuriating yet despite herself she smiled back. How could she be so easily swayed? She had a further half an hour to think about this as they left the moor behind and cruised along the dual carriageway where only shouted conversation was possible.

As they approached Exeter, Merc drove past the exit slip road leading into the city centre, and on to the adjoining motorway. Freya fixed her gaze to the receding exit, her head pivoting over her left shoulder. 'Weren't we supposed to come off there?'

'Didn't I say? We're not for the city. This'll be more fun.'

Fun, there was that word again. All she could muster was an inadequate, 'Oh.'

'My client has a little boutique hotel just north of here. I thought you might amuse yourself in the spa while I get on with some business.'

Amuse herself? Was she some accessory to be thrown a few distractions to be getting on with while the men got on with the real business?

Merc swung the car into the tree-lined drive of a Georgian manor house sited next to a private chapel. A shiny red car was parked to one side. Everything about the place spoke of confidence, luxury, and money, even down to the delicious rumble of tyres on freshly raked gravel. He pulled up in front of the house, skipped around to her side of the car and opened the door. Taking her hand, he led her up the steps, through the stone columned porch and into the hotel lobby. A table held an overlarge vase bursting with flowers: fragrant lilies, roses, lisianthus, amni and eucalyptus leaves – she resisted tagging a meaning to them. A staircase decorated with old black and white photos of classic sports cars swept up to the first floor. To the left, a room stuffed with chintz sofas and antiques served as a guest lounge, and to the right, a library converted into a gentleman's bar with leather chesterfields and a snooker table. She had only ever been once to such a place and that was in a posh frock with a wedding present tucked under her arm.

The hotelier came into the hallway with two bounding hounds at her side and greeted Merc with a two-cheeked kiss. He held her out in front of himself for inspection. 'Allegra, stunning as always.' And indeed, she was, with her dark wavy hair and a complexion that spoke of hot summers and lazy lunches under a pergola. Freya had been wrong to assume the business associate would be a man. Merc gave the introductions with a superfluous flourish, 'Freya, may I introduce you to the resplendent and much revered Allegra. Allegra, this is the delightful Freya. Isn't she adorable?' Unsure of etiquette, Freya offered her hand then wished she had managed a casual 'Hi' instead. Handshakes were for interviews or in Mass at the sign of peace, seldom between women socially. Had she imagined Allegra's mouth twitch with a suppressed smirk?

'Your Porsche looks in good shape,' Merc said. 'Should fetch a fair bit.'

'Cheeky, *mio caro*. You know that is not the one for sale. One moment, please.' Allegra called over the concierge and spoke in rapid Italian to him. The man nodded and asked Freya to follow. He led her through the marbled corridors to an annex housing a swimming pool, pausing only at the spa reception to hand her a white robe, towel, and a brand-new bathing suit. 'After you change, Carmela will take good care of you. Any treatment you prefer, it is on the house. Will there be anything else?'

'Is there a phone I can use?'

'Here, there is good mobile signal, but as you wish.' He indicated the one on the desk.

'Is there somewhere more private?' she asked. The intended call would be difficult.

'*Sì, certo.*' He led her back into the corridor and used his master key to open one of the bedrooms. 'Dial nine for outside line. I send champagne to spa.'

'But I didn't order–' she stopped; it must have been from Merc. Her misgivings multiplied. Should she read more into this? What then would be expected in return?

'Compliments of Allegra, madam,' he said and left.

Freya misjudged her. Polite hospitality would have been fulfilled with a simple pot of tea in the lounge, instead she was being indulged with generosity beyond her means to repay. She considered Allegra's intentions, whether they be out of respect for her friendship with

Merc, or the consolation prize for being another one of his disposable girlfriends he had brought along to the hotel. Girlfriend? Since when had she given herself that title? Girlfriend indeed!

She returned her concentration to the difficult phone call she was about to make to Father Paul but only he could help. Though he was a busy well-respected theologian and a postulator for the Vatican Curia investigating the causes of saints, and less glamorously, a locum filling in for sick priests just outside Salisbury, she knew she could rely on him. Besides, he openly cherished the locum role the most and said it kept him in touch with *real* people. He had not expanded but Freya wondered if he somehow thought his curia work made him a little detached and aloof.

As she dialled his number a fit of nerves overcame her. It had been months since she had last spoken to him and then she'd given him the cold shoulder. She hung up. Most likely he would be out anyway, and she hated talking to those dreaded answer machines. What would she say and where should she say for him to contact her anyway, the lines were down in the village and she didn't have a mobile? He would worry if she garbled something about being in a remote pub in Dartmoor trying to find out about the last days of Beckett's life. However, this time what she intended to ask had nothing to do with Beckett. She took a deep breath and dialled again.

Father Paul's phone rang and clicked to answerphone. She hesitated, knowing he often allowed the long answerphone message of confession times and Masses to play out as a filtering mechanism for the time hoarders. The casual chit-chat people gave up. Those urgently needing the Sacrament of the Sick and all but the determined hung on to leave a message. She'd had coffee with him once as a call came through and he had waited with patient concentration for the caller to be identified before picking up.

She let his answer message play out and as predicted, when she started to talk, he answered.

'Freya, is that you?'

'Yes, Paul, thank God, you're there.' Her voice collapsed in relief.

'What is it, old girl? Where are you, you sound miles away?'

'Yes. Yes, I am. I'm in Dartmoor. Well, not at this precise moment. I'm in a hotel near Exeter.'

'What? I can't hear you, the line's bad. You're in a hotel on Dartmoor?'

'Yes. No, I'm on an outing.'

'An outing?'

'Yes, but that's not important. I wanted to–'

'What on earth are you doing on Dartmoor? Tell me you're not on a fool's errand about Beckett's death, are you?'

Freya held the receiver away from her while she tried to gather herself, his voice chiding from a distance.

'Freya…? Are you alright…? Listen, I'm coming to collect you. Hang on and I can be there in a couple of hours. Freya?'

She took a deep breath. 'No need. I'm fine, really, I am.' Her voice sounded wobbly and frail. 'That's not why I phoned you. I wanted to ask a favour, for your help, if you weren't too busy.'

'Dearest Freya, you need only ask, you know that. What is it?'

She explained only what she thought necessary. 'I need to find someone. Please don't ask me why at the moment. I'll explain when the time comes. Trust me on this. The phone lines are down where I'm staying so I can't do it myself and there's no internet either.' She gave him the scant details and added, 'I just hope it isn't too late. Thank you, Paul.' She sighed, knowing that when he eventually found out the truth about her, she would no longer be able to count him as her friend.

'It might take a few days, but I'll do my best,'

Father Paul said, rounding off the conversation. 'Let's hope we can get it done and dusted before my trip to Rome at the end of the month.' And as an afterthought he added, 'Say you'll come with me, to Rome that is. Do come. I can have the nun's make up another room in the convent for you. It'll do you good, put a bit of distance between you and this whole sorry business.'

'Oh, Paul, I'm so grateful. I'll try and ring again on Thursday. And I'll think about Rome.' She knew it would never be an option. They said their goodbyes and Freya went to change into the swimming costume, feeling a little lighter than she had for some time.

CHAPTER 11

Freya made good use of the spa facilities, enjoying a swim, back massage and facial. She lay on the masseuse's table contemplating the luxurious feel of being pampered and wondered if the experience was enhanced or diminished the more frequently it occurred. Allegra was constantly surrounded by so much...*pleasure*. Did it make her happy?

Around 1pm, as Freya was relaxing by the poolside wrapped in her towelling robe and reaching for her second glass of champagne, the Italian concierge approached her bearing a single red rose tied with a ribbon. A card read *Join me for lunch. You must be ravenous. I know I am! M.* Freya allowed herself an indulgent smile. Another flower, his second gesture today, and a rose of all things. Whilst she might have wondered about the double entendre of 'ravenous', the meaning of the rose was unmistakable – he liked her. Bewilderingly, it felt validating as if at last she had shed her invisibility and become someone worthy of interest.

Merc, although a smooth operator, had the old-fashioned manners to stand as she approached the dining table which was set in an intimate spot at the far end of the orangery, away from the knowing gaze of older couples staid in their affections, and where the low autumn sun skimmed through the windows and warmed their budding relationship. He kissed her on the hand, beamed a smile, and said how wonderful she looked. Freya set aside her reservations and delighted in the fairy-tale, for what harm could there be in just one romantic day amongst the grey days of her grief?

He chose from the menu for her, a light lunch of sea bass and samphire, complimented by chilled Chablis. They talked, Freya about teaching, Merc about the customers he had once served – celebrities and aristocracy, crooks and lottery winners. He told her stories of yachts in the Mediterranean and fast cars at Goodwood. Freya felt the pull of aspiration, of wanting to shed her dreary life for excitement and that unknown entity Merc had offered her – fun.

He apologised for having another appointment after lunch, this time with one of the guests. 'About a

Bentley,' he said tapping the side of his nose.

Freya nodded. 'Ah, nice,' she said, though she had just a vague recollection of the name and no mental image of the car. Her vehicle knowledge consisted of Fords and Vauxhalls, or at a push, Audis and BMWs, anything commonplace in the staff car park.

They finished their coffees and took a stroll on the lawn. A large black car scrunched over the gravel and parked next to his Mercedes. 'There he is, right on cue,' Merc said, turning to her and lifting her chin, 'I'll try not to be long, lass.'

She observed him for a few moments, noted how he approached the driver with an outstretched hand a few paces before he reached him, then planted it with conviction as he found the target. At the same time, his left hand grasped the other man's upper arm in a display of bonhomie. He gave the impression of someone in control, confident and affable. But perhaps because of the words of warning from Susie, or the echo of her mother's opinions about men like Merc, she intuited a dark flinty side to him. She had no doubts that should he ever be crossed, he would make a formidable opponent.

Freya wandered over to the chapel and went inside. The space was smaller than imagined, and truncated, the nave ending prematurely two thirds of the way along and the transept and the chancel missing altogether, most likely because of the turmoil of war, and a stray bomb intent on destroying beauty. A brick wall served to plug the hole where the building's limbs had been severed. The stone floors and walls wicked away any trace of warmth but the fragrance of incense and a thousand extinguished candles gave the unmistakable ambience of peace. Pews the colour of cocoa faced a small altar, and to her surprise, a sanctuary candle glowed in the dim light beside a miniature brass tabernacle. Here dwelt the Blessed Sacrament.

With sincerity and respect rather than habit, she genuflected, made the sign of the cross and slipped into a pew. She tried praying, found herself distracted and unsettled, mesmerized by the patterns of mulberry, gold and pomegranate cast by the stained-glass windows struggling to illuminate the nave. Were it not for the sound of someone sighing, Freya wouldn't have noticed the dark figure knelt on a prie-dieu in the bell tower behind her. She glanced over her shoulder, mouthed a simple 'sorry', and with exaggerated care, eased out of the pew.

'No, do stay. I am all finished,' Allegra said, her too-loud voice sacrilegious in the silence. She rose and approached Freya with a basket of fresh roses on her arm. 'He is charming, isn't he?'

'Merc?' Why had he been her first thought when Allegra might just as well be talking about the concierge who had taken her to the spa or the figure of St Francis sitting in its niche?

'Yes of course, Merc. He is charming, no?' she said, the matter finally being settled.

'Yes, I guess he is.' Freya wondered where this was leading.

Allegra tipped back her head. 'Ha. I like you. Now then, I must prepare these flowers for a wedding but please stay. Let's talk.'

Freya feared a repetition of the Susie conversation where she was reminded of her inexperience and that Merc would 'eat her alive'. 'I won't hog your time. You must be very busy.'

'Sure, I am busy. The hotel takes all my time. The staff argue constantly. These passionate Europeans! And as for the guests, they are so demanding.' She clicked her tongue. 'And the paperwork, ah, the paperwork. It is my job, but it is not my life. This chapel is the only peace I find. Please, sit down.'

Freya dutifully slipped back into the pew. 'Yes, I can imagine,' she said hoping to sound convincing. Her experience of managing staff, let alone the challenges of the hospitality industry was limited. Come to think of it, her experience even as a guest at such a place was pretty limited too. Her life seemed to have slipped by in some buffered bubble of home and school, largely of her own making.

Allegra set to work on the floral display poking rose stems into a pedestal half full of foliage. 'No, I don't think you can.'

A sense of impending conflict descended on Freya, and she shrank in her seat.

'You see all this, the beautiful house, the gardens, the limitless…' Allegra searched for the right word, 'pleasure. And rightly I am privileged. If you think it is glamorous, then yes, it is.' Her nostrils flared as if privilege had a distinctive scent. 'It is not just glamorous, it is *intoxicating*.' She let the word hang in the air.

Freya felt the pull of all those riches promised: lifestyle, luxury, influence, honour, friends. Then with a sudden anger Allegra stabbed a white rose into the arrangement and turned to her with weary eyes. 'I think I can trust you. You are not like the others.' Freya had been right about Merc's girlfriends. 'I once had everything I needed to be happy. But I did not know it. I wanted more. Look where it has got me, a crook for an ex-husband, a string of love affairs, an untenable lifestyle…Everything seemed lost. Then out of the blue a gift, a second chance.

148

But before I knew it, it was taken from me. Why do we do these things?'

In the silence Allegra bowed her head into her hands, and Freya sat motionless trying to pluck words of wisdom from a vacuum of experience, every thought seemingly inept and inadequate. When the natural interval appeared exhausted, she said, 'A priest friend of mine thinks it's because we're searching. There is a great ache that wants to be filled and our souls are restless until they rest in Him. It doesn't bode well, does it? I don't suppose we will ever be happy.'

Allegra straightened up. 'You are a strange one. What is that saying? Doctor heal thyself. Think, *per favore*. And be sure you can afford what Merc has to offer.'

Freya paused in the hotel lobby to browse through some glossy magazines scattered on the table. A yachting one caught her eye. Most of the photos were of drinks parties and glamourous women against backdrops of turquoise seas and white sands. Was this the world Allegra and Merc craved? Likewise, was this the life she wanted if she dared to step outside of her dull little life? Towards the back the magazine became more informative and technical. There were interviews with young crew members in navy polo shirts and white shorts lamenting the difficulties of marina locks at midnight. A picture showed an exploded diagram of an engine and another was titled 'head', or loos from the look of it, and had its internal gubbins splayed out to illustrate how it all worked. Jack would love this. She rolled it up and looked for someone to take payment for it.

The bar stood empty, as did the lounge. Then she heard hushed spat voices from a room behind the reception desk. She tried a tentative hello and waited. No answer. Bolstered by her new familiarity with the owner – Allegra wouldn't mind after all – she went behind the counter and was about to call out again when she recognised Merc's voice. Curiosity compelled her to listen. She pressed herself flat against the wall in a comedic fashion where she could hear what was going on but not be seen.

Merc had his back to her, but she had a good view of the other person, the Italian concierge who had helped her earlier. His slackened tie hung beneath an open collar and his jacket was strewn on the back of a chair. He had parked his bottom on the desk on top of some scattered paperwork and his arms were crossed in a defensive gesture which contradicted his poker-face. 'It is no problem,' he said, 'I get it for next week. *Normale!*'

'Look, pal,' Merc replied, 'it may be *normale* where you come from, but that's not how I do business. My old

Da' would think I'd gone soft. You've had your week's grace. Now, you wouldn't want me to be letting him down, would you?' He took a step closer and the Italian straightened. Merc extended a curled finger and lifted the man's chin in malice. The Italian jerked his head away and amongst the bravado, Freya saw fear in his eyes.

She sighed. Her brief hope in Merc as an icon of what life might be, upended. But hadn't she half-expected that anyway? Wasn't it best to know now before she was too committed to her fantasy that such a subversion would be unbearable? No, best to know now, at least that way she stood a chance of detaching herself without too much damage and with her dignity still intact.

Merc gave a sudden cough. 'Since business is sweet and I'm feeling generous, you've got a week. No excuses, *capiche?*'

The man gave a curt nod. '*Si, capisco.*'

'Good,' Merc said, then called out, 'Freya, lass, are you ready to get going?'

Back at the car, Freya made an excuse to return to the hotel. 'I've left my brush in the changing rooms.'

'Leave it, I'll get you another, silver handled, whatever you like, you name it.'

'I won't be a minute,' she called over her shoulder as she trotted back to the entrance. She found the concierge sitting at his desk with his chin propped in his hand. 'Please, take it,' she said, holding out three twenty-pound notes. 'It's the only cash I have, but if it helps.' He looked up confused for a moment and weighed up her gift, then nodded and took the cash. '*Grazie, grazie.*'

Merc was uneasy on the journey home, uncommunicative and pre-occupied. She wondered if he were berating himself for letting the proverbial halo slip.

'I liked Allegra,' she said. 'I wasn't sure at first, but she's nice.'

'Aye. Allegra's canny. Someone I can do business with.' He switched on the radio; white-noised music and adverts, channel hopped, listened to a few bars of *Fantastic Day*, switched off.

'Are you two still seeing each other?' she asked.

'You're a perceptive lassie. But no, it was a while ago.'

Though she guessed right she expected more of a reaction. She considered her next words. 'And the concierge? What was that about?'

Merc's eyes left the road to look straight at her. 'It's business, don't worry about it.'

He may as well have gone the whole condescending hog and tagged on, *your pretty little head*, and be done with it. 'I see,' she said.

'Nothing personal. You get used to guys trying to screw you, that's all. I'm merely protecting my interests.'

'And the Bentley guy?' she asked, instantly regretting her trespass into his business affairs.

'Just routine. He needed to liquidate some of his assets, I helped him. Simple,' he said with casual indifference.

'But you gave him the going rate, didn't you?' she said provocatively, but now the subject was raised, she had to know for her own peace of mind.

Merc coughed out a laugh. 'Bless you, lass. That's not how it works. I gave him what he needs in return for a fee.'

'Then you're a pirate.' She hated the thought of him taking advantage of someone down on their luck.

'I'm no Captain Hook. When the Bentley guy's better fixed, he'll come back to me to replace the said assets. I reciprocate with an equally good deal for him. We know where we stand.' His hand shifted from the steering wheel and patted her on the knee. 'It's all above board.'

Though his reassurance calmed her, she couldn't help but feel her small life had not prepared her for encountering either the savvy or cunning. Until now, if she had ever thought about the business world at all, it had been through the lenses of a fixed-profit mercantile mentality of shopping; goods are priced x allowing for cost price plus fixed percentage profit, therefore customer pays y, no haggling. Perhaps Merc was not dishonest but just a shrewd businessman. The distinction was subtle and made all the difference. 'I'm sorry I called you a pirate,' Freya said.

'No worries. Well, Tinkerbell, should you ever fancy a bit of role play...'

Her feelings for him morphed into something akin to shame and she blushed. How could he keep disarming her like this?

As they said their goodbyes at her room door, Freya was a stammering teenager, flustered and outmaneuvered. She thanked him for the outing, for lunch, for a lovely day – and to her surprise it was true. When she turned to go inside, he caught hold of her hand and spun her around. He leant in towards her and then in a sudden change of heart raised her hand to his lips and planted a kiss. 'Hope you've had fun. I have. Until later.'

CHAPTER 12

The day away from Brohn-In-The-Moor unsettled Freya. She was excited, restless, hounded by intense self-doubt, brooding, and on the lookout for Merc, both dreading and desiring his presence. She had allowed herself to be distracted at the hotel by novelty, pleasure, wealth, the beautiful Allegra and by Merc, and so had forgotten the serious job of grieving for Beckett. Had it not been for the phone call with Father Paul, the day could have been written off as an unproductive waste of time, bringing her no closer to finding out the truth.

After lunch she went for a walk to get away from The George and Dragon. She headed for the lake Jack had told her so much about. Out here in the wild barren landscape, Freya struggled to understand Beckett's love affair with this natural world. She regarded Margin Tor with foreboding, the moors as merely an escape from the claustrophobic atmosphere of the village, and the walk down to the river as a necessary form of exercise. None were beauty for its own sake.

She took the path up toward the summit of Seven Moor. Here the track forked to the right for the tor, and downward to the left for the valley following the route of the running streams. In between, smaller sheep trails radiated star-like in every direction. She stood a while facing the wind, her hair dancing behind her. Clouds ebbed past in a mackerel sky. From this vantage point she could take in the vast landscape. Jack's lake shimmered silver to the east. To the west, farmsteads and hamlets nestled into junctions of interlocking spurs. She stepped forward, took the path downhill, disturbed grouse among the heather and sent alarmed pheasants into the air. A herd of Dartmoor ponies grazed peacefully among the rusting bracken. Harmonious and pastoral, all was as it should be. The landscape began to work its charm and she sensed an inkling into Beckett's world, beauty as peace.

Freya wandered away from the path to explore a stone circle. She wanted to finally dispel the myth of magic she had created. When lost on the moor in the impenetrable fog, the moor had grown in her mind to mystical proportions: a night of faeries and fantasy, of monsters clawing at the barn door and of rescue by…Jack as her knight in shining armour? She chuckled – hardly.

A circle of standing stones sat squat in the grass like twisted and angled tombstones. Freya moved among them hesitant for the same occurrences as that night lost on the moor. But this time there was no ethereal grey pony, no carving of a Celtic cross, no strange happenings at all. Perhaps this place, the tors, and Dartmoor itself was no more than a conduit for memories and the space to explore all that was silenced? Satisfied at last, she returned to the path and set her sights on the lake.

After about a mile the lake became less of a puddle in the distance and more of a prominent feature of the landscape. A dam sat at the nearest point of the lake dispelling the notion that nature had graced this scenery with the blessing of a body of water. The lake, or rather reservoir, covered perhaps a hundred hectares, maybe less, but enough water for an interesting sail. Out on the far side a dinghy with red sails and a white spinnaker leant into the wind. It travelled at a fair speed changing direction when the shore loomed, and in this way crisscrossed the water towards her.

The dinghy reached the jetty just as she approached. Its spinnaker was slack in the bow and the mainsail lowered. Jack waved and shouted over, 'Ahoy,' and Freya called back, 'Ahoy there,' for what else would she say.

He tossed a coiled rope to her. 'Here, catch this and loop it round the mooring post over there.' The rope unfurled in mid-air as if it had been endowed with the grace of a skylark in flight. Freya leant forward, grabbed at it but missed and it plopped into the water. 'Sorry!'

The Dragon drifted past the jetty. 'I'll come in again,' Jack said. He pulled in the rope, coiled it over his bent elbow and up to the crook of his hand and back again forming half a dozen loops, then laid it on the seat beside him. His sleeves were wet and darker now where the water had soaked in and seemed not to belong to his shirt anymore. He tugged at the jib sheet, caught the wind, set the tiller to its new course, and sailed away from the jetty in a perfect arc, re-approaching a few minutes later at drifting speed. Jack's expertise and ease suggested the rope catching and mooring request had just been a ploy to include her in his hobby.

He threw the rope again and this time she caught it and slipped it round the mooring post. She tied-off with no idea if it was a half-hitch, reef, or granny knot, but it held, and Jack seemed satisfied. She stood on the jetty looking down at him in the belly of boat, he with his hands on his hips, staring out across the lake and making no attempt to come ashore.

'You're itching to get back out there, aren't you?' Freya said.

'It's a great day for sailing, perfect wind. You getting in or what?' His wistful eyes crinkled at the corners.

She shook her head. 'I'm not dressed for it.'

'I won't give you a dunking if that's what you're thinking. There'll not be too many good days left before winter sets in. Be a shame to miss out. What do you say?'

Freya followed his gaze across the water. The wind ruffled the surface into repeating rows of w. She recalled her naïve drawings of the sea as a child and through a combination of nostalgia and a longing to be back in those innocent years, she changed her mind.

'Sure. Love to.' She gripped his outstretched hand and stepped aboard. Jack handed her a buoyancy aid from under the seat. 'Not sure I remember much,' she said.

'You don't need to. Let's start by you holding the jib sheet.' He handed her a rope joined to the front sail and cleated off to the side, its counterpart being on the opposite side. 'Just tug on it to keep the sheet straight and when I say, let it loose. As we go about, swap seats and pull on the one opposite. And mind the boom. Don't worry, it'll all come back, you'll see.'

Jack took her through a few basic techniques

which she picked up quickly and then felt confident enough to set out. Soon he let out the mainsail and caught the wind. The dinghy zig-zagged across the lake, the breeze steady and the hull cambering with the billowing sails. 'Told you it would come back. You're a natural,' he yelled.

'I love this,' Freya laughed. She studied him, noted the swell of pride, his chin lifted with confidence, the command of his strong arms bearing down on the boat, and she felt safe.

'We're ready for a bit more leaning. Sit up on the side and lean back using the jib sheet to pull against.' Jack tightened the sails to brace the wind. The boat listed further.

Freya became snagged in memories. She and Beckett as teenagers out on the Solent, a dozen small boats bobbing past as the junior sailing club race got underway in a cacophony of horn blasts. Light bounced off the waves and their little red sails flapped and dithered in the breeze. She had insisted on taking the helm that day and Beckett hadn't stopped complaining saying he thought now that he was twelve, he ought to have a go. The dinghy started slowly and through a combination of confused commands and ineptitude, they were soon so far behind they would never catch up.

'If only you'd just pulled on the sheet, Beck, when

I'd said.'

'You said starboard then steered port. How was I to know?'

'Come on, you could feel it turning, couldn't you?' But he had a point, she was always getting her left from right mixed up.

He went quiet and she could tell he was in a mood. He sat with his shoulders hunched and his back turned away from her like she was invisible or something. And he wouldn't join in with her favourite bit when she said in her silly posh voice, 'Ready about,' and he was supposed to say, 'Ready,' and she'd give the order, 'Lee Ho,' and push the tiller away and the boom would swing over and they'd change direction. And they'd laugh at the snootiness of it.

Then, with the sun shining and an increasing breeze, Freya felt they might be in with a chance of catching up after all. She held the tiller hard against the water and the dinghy heeled. Beckett yelped in alarm, and she couldn't help laughing.

'Don't Frey. You're doing it on purpose.'

'What's up, not scared, are you?' She pushed the tiller harder still, the rudder straining against the water, then she tightened the mainsail. The boat gained speed. Waves splashed up against the side drenching poor Beckett huddled in the gut of the boat. His skinny body jerked and trembled with cold, and he let out a whimper. 'Then get over to the other side, will you,' Freya shouted. 'You're supposed to be there anyway.'

'No, you're trying to drown me.'

Her temper flared. 'Oh, come on. Just do it, moron. We're gonna look like complete idiots when we get back to the club house. And it's all your fault.'

He had half-stood to move across when Freya let out the sail. She had meant to help him by slowing the boat down but the sudden change in speed flopped the boat back down horizontally on the water. Beckett fell forward and banged his head on the mast. He pressed the wound with an angry hand as he waited for the pain to go. He looked down at the sticky blood on his fingers and turned pale. His mouth twisted into an ugly fish-pout. She thought he was going to yell but instead he stared at her with wide marble eyes.

She stretched out her hand in sympathy. 'Beck, come here,' and softer this time, 'Come here, eh?'

He backed away, scrambling on his bottom to the furthermost point of the boat. 'Keep away from me,' he said, trembling. His eyes darted to the water and back up to her as if he were weighing up his chances – the devil or the deep blue sea. Freya's chest tightened. She had seen that look before, her last glimpse of Debbie, eyeing the cold iron railway tracks versus the cold steel look on her own face.

Freya couldn't understand what had come over him. It was an accident; anyone could see that. 'What?' she half-laughed, he had to be joking. 'I'm not going to let anything bad happen to you, you know that *don't you?*'

Beckett hugged his knees to his chest and burrowed his face in them. He started to hum a soft tune which Freya strained to hear.

'Beck, you're too old for this. Stop it.' He hummed louder and the familiar tune came back to her, *Hush little baby, don't say a word, Freya's going to buy you a mockingbird.*

The wind dropped; the light faded. Jack loosened the sails, pulled on the tiller, and headed for shore. To cast away the memory of Beckett's fear, Freya told Jack about her trip to the hotel with Merc, the pool and spa, the champagne, sea bass for lunch and meeting Allegra.

'Ah, I wondered where you'd gone. Sounds like you had a nice day. Kind of fancy. Good for you. I'm glad.' His tone was flat, as if his energy had dissipated along with the wind.

'Yes, it made a nice change. I won't say I didn't

enjoy it. I felt quite treated…pampered, a bit special. Not that I'm used to that though…Well…I probably won't do it again.'

'Oh, no, I wasn't suggesting–'

'I know you weren't. I'm just trying to say…I didn't feel that comfortable.'

Jack brought the boat up to the jetty, slipped the rope around the mooring post without needing her help, and climbed out. He offered his hand to her from the jetty. 'Nothing wrong with a bit of luxury once in a while. What did you make of Allegra?'

Freya took his hand and climbed out. 'You know her? She seemed intimidating at first, but I caught her having a quick pray in the chapel and we had a chat. Stressed out with the hotel and everything, I guess. And I felt sorry for her.' She didn't go into what 'everything' meant.

'And Merc? How was he?'

'What is it between the two of you? And don't say I'm imagining it? You two have history.'

'Better ask him.'

'I'm asking you.'

He busied himself removing the sails and spread them out on the jetty, intent on smoothing out the creases. He nodded for Freya to help with the folding. 'We're lucky they're dry enough to put straight away. Since you're asking, he's a rogue, some would say a loveable one.'

'But not you?'

'No. Since you asked, he's a womaniser and a gambler.'

'But you gamble too.' Jack's hypocrisy stunned her.

'Yes, but not to the same extent. Blimey, the losses he's gone through. But O boy, when he's lucky…unbelievable.' Jack whistled through his teeth.

'So, it's ok if you don't lose much, is that what you're saying?' Freya straightened up and planted her hands on her hips.

'No, that's not what I'm saying.' Jack stood to be level with her. 'All I mean is that you don't gamble when you've a wife and kids to feed.'

'He didn't tell me he was married!' Her voice rose. 'And had kids!'

'How convenient of him. Merc's my brother-in-law, rather my ex-brother-in-law. He was married to my sister. Anyway, they divorced long ago, and she's passed away, God rest her soul. The kids are in their twenties so it shouldn't affect your…thing with him. Did you really expect a man like Merc to be a bachelor?'

Freya looked away. 'Well, no, not now that I think

about it. I suppose I did see the photo of you and him together and thought maybe you were family. Though I couldn't see it really, Merc being married.'

'Exactly.'

'Well…perhaps he just married the wrong woman, or he's like my brother, waiting for the right woman to come along.'

'You've got to be joking? They were leagues apart. Beck was a top bloke, but no saint.'

What was that supposed to mean? She knew Beckett better than anyone.

'Look, for the record, Merc's a chancer who would screw you at the first opportunity. And Beck wasn't like that. Take for instance the time me and Merc were on holiday together. My wife and sister got on well, loved the whole happy family thing, unfortunately. Rain stopped play so me and Merc would amuse ourselves with a friendly game or two of cards. We had a few beers, a laugh, and kept a pot on the table. So far, so good. A couple of weeks after the holiday, an anything *but* friendly solicitor's letter arrived asking me to cough up the £200 I so cavalierly bet on four-of-a-kind. If I'd thought for a second, it was for keeps...'

'Perhaps he's got an addiction and can't help it.'

'Stick around Freya and the last thing you'll be

doing is defending him. Trouble is you're too nice, always ready to make excuses for people. I take it Beck never told you about *his* little problem?' One side of Jack's mouth attempted an ironic smile.

'Oh no, Jack. Not more revelation. You think he had a gambling problem too, don't you?' She paused and saw Jack's relief. 'Thought so. I suspected as much when I found the odd betting slips here and there. I'd been waiting for him to say something. That and the fact he never seemed to have much money. He'd get a bit agitated sometimes, constantly checking his phone. In hindsight, I wished I'd raised it with him.'

'Pity. I urged him to get some help, gave him a leaflet on it, said he should talk to you. Got the impression he thought he'd be letting you down though.'

'For goodness' sake, he could never do that. He meant everything to me.'

Jack loaded the sail bags into the Land Rover. 'Hop in, I'll give you a lift back.' After a few minutes on the road, Jack drummed his fingers on the steering wheel. 'Maybe that's the problem?'

'What is?'

'He meant everything. You can't let go.'

'Not true,' she said, though she knew it was. Jack wasn't out to hurt her. She clamped up for the rest of the journey and when they arrived back, she hesitated before inviting him in for coffee. 'Though if you need to get back for the calves or something?'

'Nope. My day off. Tom's on duty.'

They sat in the lounge of The Byre and decided on something stronger to warm them up – whisky, what the Scots call the water of life. She curled into the armchair cradling her glass, still swaying with the memory of waves. Amber light layered around the room: gold on russet, copper on orange, lamplight, firelight, whisky, tawny rugs scattered over furniture. A gilded dusk reached in through the window reflecting the golden bracken on the autumn hills beyond. Freya, warmed through yet tired, idled away the time with small chit-chat and enormous thoughts. She remembered the yachting magazine she picked up at the hotel for Jack and went to fetch it.

'What's this?' he asked.

'I thought you'd like it.'

'You thought about me when you were out enjoying yourself?'

Freya found genuine warmth in his smile. 'There's a bit at the back, here, let me show you.' She flicked through and found the exploding diagram of the 'head'. 'Where does all the waste go when you're out in the middle of the ocean?'

'Well, me old landlubber,' Jack laughed, 'there are holding tanks or treatment devices or both, depends. You're not really interested, are you? But I appreciate you trying to be.'

Freya topped up their whiskies – she'd gotten a taste for it – found some snacks, suggested a game of scrabble and set it out on a small table between them. When the opportune moment arrived, she asked, 'What happened to Rigby?'

Jack nodded, as if he had been expecting the question all along. He picked up his glass and stretched back in his armchair, his face illuminated by the lamp. 'I'd been a skipper chartering out my yacht for decades, mainly to rich Americans. I had a good crew, the best. We worked together for many years.' He swirled the whisky around and held it to the light, so it shone like honey. 'And I think that was our undoing. We got complacent. It's funny, I had a bad feeling as soon as that Columbian guy stepped on board. Should've refused the job there and then but business had been a bit slow. There was something lifeless about him. Have you ever met anyone who chills you to the point of utter despair?'

'Blank people?' Freya asked.

'Yes…no, more like hard-eyed, like the light had gone out of their eyes and their heart had somehow withered away. If I believed it to be possible, I'd say he had no soul.' Freya shuddered and took a sip of the whisky.

'He needed to get to Florida a.s.a.p. I checked the weather, a possible storm fifty miles to the north. We'd be very unlucky if it dipped toward us. If I hadn't been so wary of the guy though, I'd probably have waited for it to pass, just to be sure. But I'm a coward. I didn't want the confrontation and aggro.'

Freya raised her glass to him. 'Aren't we all? Anything for a quiet life. It doesn't make us bad people.'

'Merc thrives on confrontation.'

'Oh, Jack,' she sighed. 'I understand your grievances, but you do seem so set against him.' Merc couldn't be as bad as everyone made out. He'd treated Jack badly, yes, been a bit mean to the concierge, was presumptuous, but she was drawn to him so he must have *some* good points. The small fact of her being flattered by his attention didn't really come into it.

'You don't know him.' Jack said no more, and Freya needed to coax him back to the story. 'Well, six hours in and the storm changes course, heads right into us. We get kitted up, storm gear, heavy duty life jackets, send the passengers inside, get the ropes and carabiners out.' He was out at sea again, reliving each agonising detail. He stood, mimed putting on a life jacket, snapping the clasps, tightening the straps, and clipping harness to the rail. His face was tight with concentration. Freya worried for him.

'It wasn't a huge deal, we'd been in worse, we knew the drill. That's when you rely on your crew. We took on water, the self-bailers weren't working properly. I sent Rigby down to the engine room to sort it out. Oh God–' Jack stopped, scanned the room horrified as if judge and jury had entered for judgement. He searched for an escape from his memories and, finding none, collapsed back into the chair. 'I should've said. I should have *reminded* him. You never go into the engine compartment with a life jacket on…Then the unthinkable happened. A loose strap got caught in the moving parts, pulled him into the engine and…oh God.'

Freya waited while he composed himself. She recognised a man defeated by hindsight and traumatised by what he had seen. She closed her eyes and pushed back her own visions of blood and gore. 'It wasn't your fault, Jack. You said yourself he was an experienced crew member. He should've known as well as anyone. It wasn't your responsibility.'

'I wouldn't feel so guilty if I hadn't thought about the jacket beforehand. But I had. And I didn't say anything. I guess I thought it would be demeaning, reminding him of something so mundane and routine. I really thought he'd take it off when he got below deck.'

She looked for a way to take away his suffering. 'There must have been an inquest. Surely, they found it wasn't your fault?'

'Officially, I was exonerated. Somehow it doesn't take away the pain though. Huh, and to top it all, all that psycho-Columbian guy could say after the accident was, *how long till we get a replacement boat to Florida.* God only knows how I didn't punch his face in. I dunno, reckon he was a drugs baron or something and used to people being expendable.'

'Surely, that's just in movies? Maybe something wasn't quite right with him.'

'Or maybe he was just an evil git.'

'Jack!'

'I say it again, Freya, you're too nice. Not everyone lives in your fluffy bunny world.' He raised his glass in a toast. 'To the fine lady who thinks well of all, may she never come a cropper.' He gulped back the whisky and gave a mock bow. 'My stage awaits. Susie's promised me a couple of beers tonight if I entertain the tourists with a few folk stories. You coming?'

'Maybe later, I've a few things to sort out.'

CHAPTER 13

Freya had a change of heart and decided to go to the bar after all to watch Jack in the limelight as the spellbinding raconteur. A convivial hum drifted across the stable yard. Tonight promised to be lively. Inside, the flagon of locals mixed with jocular tourists – from where had they materialised? Perhaps they were intent on reconnecting with a rural idyll in some fest of nostalgic longing, yearning to hear tales spun into fantastical yarns of wild beasts and faeries, of sprites and phantoms haunting the moors in a demented quest for souls. Susie had bought in barrels of local real ales for the occasion and lined them up on precarious racks behind her, the brass beer pumps forgotten in favour of the simple tap and cork arrangements of yesteryear.

Freya pushed through the crowd towards the

motley crew of locals propping up the bar. She found Jack and Tom chatting, lifting their pints in unison, and taking hearty gulps.

'Toffee!' Tom sighed with pleasure.

'Nope, not getting that. Pecans perhaps, and a hint of Christmas pudding?' Jack held up his pint to catch the light. 'Look at that, clear as a whistle. Surely, ambrosia in a glass? A finer pint of Fitzwell's Folly have I ever tasted?' He took another swig and elaborately chewed it over. 'Shame they don't use the water from the well though, it'd be purer.'

'Yep, shame about that.'

'Fitzwell's well?' Freya interrupted.

'Ah great, you came!' Jack said. 'Yes to that or rather no. Poetic license on the brewery's part. It's Fitz's well, or to be more accurate, Fitzford's well. Now, there's a legend I could tell you about that.'

'Thought there might be,' Tom said. 'Here we go again.' He commandeered a chair, stood up on it and gave three sharp claps as if he were a ring master taming a ring of chattering chimps. 'Now then, m' lovers, let's have a bit of hush, shall we? For your delight and entertainment, and for one night only – except next Saturday. And possibly the following Thursday. Is that right Susie–?'

'Get on with it,' someone shouted.

'Alright, alright, keep your hair on. So, without further ado, give a big hand for our very own weaver of words, teller of tales and guarantee-er to make a short story long–'

'Oiy,' Jack piped up.

'Quite right, quite right,' Tom held up a hand of admission, 'Only kidding. I give you, the one and only, Jack of the Moors.' Expectant applause rippled through the crowd.

Jack perched himself on a bar stool by the fire, and with a lazy foot on the bottom rung and a pint in his hand, he began the timeless act of oral remembrance.

'*Long ago, when the moors stood remote and the valleys deep, when time was marked by dawn and dusk, seasons by first frosts and Christmas snow, lambs at Easter and summer with strawberries and cream, or Michaelmas and mulled cider in autumn. And when stone circles still held magic, and stars a web of wonder, when, in a certain light and with the wind blowing through the tors, pixies might still be seen carrying banners of mist and sacks of mayhem.*' Jack paused momentarily to let the scene soak in.

'*There was once a certain Moorlander, Fitzford by name, who along with a fine maiden – we'll call her Cecilia, for none was so blinded by love as this young beauty – set off on a glorious summer's day to watch the skylarks and take in the splendour of the wilderness. By and by, as the sun dipped from its zenith, and the* grasshoppers rasped in the afternoon heat, Fitzford looked for a place to rest a while with his beau, and foolhardily, for he should have known better, left the safety of the well-trodden track to pause at a stone circle. That the circle was remote and far from prying eyes, some might suggest passionate amour was in his mind.'

A wolf-whistle warbled from the back of the room. 'Quite!' Jack acknowledged, then, with a glint in his eyes, he leant forward and continued. 'Now…the mischievous pixies, or piskies as us Moorlanders call them, saw their chance to play havoc, so long had they waited for some frivolous fun. Summoning the mists around them, they caused the hapless pair to become disorientated and lost. But the piskies were not yet done with their mayhem. A curse fell upon the pair and they were condemned to walk around the moor, lost and alone for all eternity, searching for a way out of the wilderness and for the spell to be broken. That these Moorlanders should leave the safety of the well-trodden track without so much as a compass or map, alone out there on the moor with nobody knowing their whereabouts was inexcusable, any canny moor dweller knew this to be totally foolhardy.'

Tom shook his head in mock drama, 'Still is, still is. Be warned you city folk, moor's no place to go unprepared, 'specially when night's a-coming.' His bent finger panned the room, and the tourist received this wisdom with wonder in their eyes and reverence in their hearts.

'Absolutely, I drink to that,' Jack said, raising his glass. *Now, it was not the end of poor old Fitzford and his lady friend. Fitzford, familiar enough with the foibles of piskies, knew that drinking from a well would break the spell. Thus, they searched to that end, spending the whole night wandering and searching, searching and wandering, through bog and heather, over tor and brook, until eventually, falling upon a spring they fell to their knees, gave thanks and drank. All at once, the mists lifted, and the couple, recognising familiar ground found their way back to safety. However, little did they know that they could have saved their night's long travail if they had only but turned their coats inside out. The piskies' plan would then have been foiled and the spell broken. Fitzford, being so pleased as to his escape, returned soon after to stone-line the well for perpetuity and for the saving of other wanderers, erecting there a cross in thankfulness for their safe deliverance. So, to this day, the well, blessed and sanctified, continues to provide comfort and relief to all who lose their way out in the wilderness.* Jack winked and took a deep bow in recognition of the tumultuous applause.

Freya joined in enthusiastically. 'That was brilliant, Jack. Well done! Shame it isn't true though.'

'Says who?' Tom frowned. 'Don't you go trashing our folklore. Them's there for a reason.'

'He's right, you know,' Jack added. 'Just because something seems fanciful doesn't make it untrue. You'll see.'

Here was Jack again talking in riddles with his proverbial catch-all phrase, *you'll see*. Being with him felt like waiting for Christmas, as if time would magically endow wisdom upon the patient child. How much remained of her patience with Jack, was quite another matter.

The following morning the first frosts of autumn lay under a crisp sky. Freya turned up the thermostat in her room, pulled on a second pair of socks and slipped on Beckett's old gardening jumper. Soil and lanolin and the tang of the outdoors filled her senses. These past few days, living in Beckett's world here in Brohn-In-The-Moor, she came to a gradual realisation of a great living flow and interconnectedness of all things: seasons passing, habitats, geology, decay and rebirth. If she returned home – and now the word 'if' made that tentative – she would look beyond her immediate concerns and seek out the wondrous world of nature whenever she could. And thanks to Allegra and her openness in the chapel, perhaps she would go back to Mass, sit in a side aisle at the back, be no bother to anyone, just gaze and ask nothing from God but the quiet of being there.

Freya collected a pen and a large sheet of paper

and spread it out on the bed in front of her. She dithered for a moment, then wrote her and Beckett's names in two circles and linked them with a line. In a starburst she jotted down the facts so far: *Beckett arrived spring, worked for Jack, did Susie's gardening.* Then she followed with the questions: *stayed at inn? In this room?* – though this didn't make any difference except she liked the idea of him having been close. *Why the secrecy of Brohn folk? Did Merc know Beckett?* The task grew difficult after that. She wrote the words, *died on a hillside* – simple, hollow, monumental – and with thoughts from Good Friday, she whispered, '*Eloi, Eloi.*'

After this she scribbled: *Where? Margin Tor? How???* From here she worked away at all the possibilities, even considered the unlikely scenarios of conspiracy and murder. She refused to give in to the idea of his suicide. She evaluated the clues Beckett had left: the seed packet and map bringing her to Dartmoor, the cryptic note, *Jack and Gil went up the hill,* the message of encouragement written in flowers urging her to keep on searching. But why so little contact with him in the months before his death? And why so sporadic and sketchy? Other random ideas hung unconnected near the bottom of the page: *an affair? With Susie? Gambler!*

Freya stared at the page. The right side resembled a web of spiders, the left remained blank except for her name. She tapped her pen against her teeth, and in a painful moment of clarity, she realised the one factor she had not accounted for was her own role in Beckett's death. Her mind reeled, took regressive steps back to his last visit to her little terraced house, and her comments to him about settling down, making something of himself, and why he always seemed broke – a lifetime of little criticisms chipping away at his self-worth. Then she thought back further, to her implied martyrdom picking up of the pieces after their father died, then being left to cope alone with mother's terminal illness while he sought work as an itinerant gardener. And afterwards, the petty disagreements about what to do with their parents' house.

She thought of the very last time she saw him. He had stopped over to leave some of his belongings at her place. They had a terse dinner together before he took off to the pub. He came in late and the worse for wear, stumbled about in the dark, knocked over a chair, and was gone by morning. The previous visit by comparison had been slightly more successful. He stayed a week, spent his days cooking and gardening while she worked. When she got home, the daily newspapers were folded on the jobs section and circled hopefully with red pen. They went to Mass together on Sunday. He seemed lighter, happier. But then around 2am that night, she was awoken by shouts coming from Beckett's room. In the orange neon of streetlights glowing onto the landing, Freya crept to his door and listened. He appeared to be having a frantic one-way conversation with himself.

'Got to be deeper. Make it deeper,' Beckett was saying.

She turned the handle and peeped through the crack in the door. His dark figure was kneeling on the bed digging away at the covers as if he were a fox at a rabbit hole.

'Beck, what are you doing?' she asked quietly.

'Never going to be deep enough. Got to try harder. Got to bury it.'

Freya pushed open the door. A fan of light spread out on the bedroom carpet and her silhouette stretched into the room. His duvet lay in a heap around him, the sheet sprawled onto the floor. He breathed erratically and his skin burnished with sweat. She took a step towards him. His arm shot out to bar her. 'Keep back. It's bad,' he warned.

'What's bad? I'm here, you're safe.' Freya sat on the bed and pulled him down, so he rested back on his haunches. He stared into the pit of his bed, and like a mad man, took to the appalling gesture of wringing his hands.

'Stop it, Beck. You're scaring me.' She grabbed his

shoulders and shook him awake.

After that they sat in the kitchen with the fan heater blowing around the stale fetid air of dinner mixed with beer breath. Freya made sweet tea while Beckett crumbled a biscuit on the table until it was a heap which he could bulldoze around with his fingertip.

'What was that all about?' she asked.

He shrugged and packed the crumbs down into a reconstruction of its former self.

'Is this a reoccurring nightmare?'

'It's nothing.'

She grabbed her cup, crossed to the sink, and yanked the tap on full. A stream of errant water showered over her. 'Hell, hell, HELL! Look, if it's nothing why can't you tell me?' Then calmer she said, 'We all know dreams are stupid nonsense. Tell me and we'll have a laugh.' When he didn't answer she stepped forward and laid a hand gently on his shoulder. 'What was in the hole?'

Beckett sprang up, held a flat palm toward her. 'Stop!' he snarled. His chair scraped back, and he slammed the door on his way out. She was left alone in the kitchen to grapple with the resonance of his fury. So much for happy families.

Memories came easily in Brohn-In-The-Moor. Perhaps the desolate moors were a portal for the unresolved, or the George and Dragon emblem an amulet for the suppressed? Jack had told her about the symbolism behind St George and the Dragon; the eternal fight between good and evil with the dragon representing one's inner demons. With wry amusement, he said the pub sign hanging over the entrance was an ironic warning of the dangers of demon drink. She laughed too and they had another pint of Fitzwell's Folly in defiance.

Freya laid back on her bed and willed herself to remember all the times as the eldest child she dictated truth. She had always been a bossy child, willful, headstrong, defiant…infallible. In contrast, Beckett looked up to her, was compliant and seldom disagreed. He seemed to crave the security of certainty – the certainty that she was in control. Mother's perpetual illness heightened this. It had played out their entire lives, waning only recently as a healthy distance morphed into a gaping chasm.

On the day Debbie died, as Freya chased her across the daisy field, she had shouted back to Beckett, 'You stay here and don't move, or I'll give you another bloody nose to be getting on with.' And of course, she knew he would comply.

'Come back, please come back,' Beckett cried in his shrill, pathetic voice.

Freya took half an hour, maybe more, to return to him. Time seemed to have slowed down and she with it. Her legs struggled to complete the action of walking – lift, step through, land – as if the air had become a resistant sea with waves knocking her back before she could make headway. All her energy focused on keeping upright, moving forward, getting back to Beckett.

He was still where she had left him, sitting down alone next to the swings with his face bloody and dirty. As she got closer, he whimpered and whined complaining she'd left him too long. She was cross he hadn't the gumption to have simply gone home. For a few blissful seconds, the normality of feeling irritated with him restored her world to how it had always been. But the emotion was fleeting, slippery, cruel. Every single detail from the moment she entered the woods replayed through her mind, dim light, jingle-jangle rosary beads, the snap of twigs as she crept toward Old Tramp's Cabin, briars tugging at her legs, the caw-caw-caw laugh of crows in the treetops, her breath quick and light, the train rumbling over the tracks and the final hee-haw warning sound.

She struggled to grasp the fact that nothing could ever be the same again. Her mind searched for ways to escape, to turn back time. She would wake up in a moment surely. Someone would come along and say it was just a silly trick for a TV programme, *Candid Camera! Hahahaha!* Her ears filled with a peculiar whooshing sensation, a yellow blob of colour formed in her eyes and stayed there even when she squeezed them shut. Her stomach seemed to want to escape right up through her throat and out of her mouth. The sky, park, Beckett, swam around her. She collapsed onto the ground, passed out for a split second, and then vomited, as she had done all the way back through the woods and the field – a sour, hot, stinking mess. When the retching subsided and even the bile was spent, she sat next to him leaning her head on her knees. She shivered, couldn't speak, and when she tried to move, she retched again, until nothing else came from her except the salty taste of her own blood.

'You okay Frey, have you been running too hard? Has Debbie gone home?' he asked. His eyes swam searchingly across the park.

Freya jolted out of her trance. 'D…Deb…' She couldn't say her name. 'No Beck. She's gone.'

'Gone where? Where is Debbie? I want Debbie.'

He sounded silly, like he was five again and working up for a tantrum. Freya shook her head, but he'd guessed something was wrong. 'What's happened? I'm scared, Frey. There were sirens everywhere.' He sucked in his lips, afraid to say any more.

'Debbie's not coming back,' she whispered. 'She's in heaven now,'

'In heaven? I don't understand…sh-she was just here a minute ago. You mean she's…dead? Beckett struggled to take it in. 'Have you d-done s-s-something? Did you…?'

Freya turned her head away. A silent tear slid down her cheek. She had stolen his innocent spirit and crushed it into the dirt.

He curled up, cradled his knees to his chest, rocked and murmured as if he'd lost his senses. 'No, nope, nope, not real, not real, not *real*,' he said. 'Not happening. Just a bad dream, wake up silly Beckett, wake up, sleepy head. It's only a bad dream.' A load of jumbled up nursery rhymes tumbled from his mouth: 'Rock-a-by baby on a treetop, Humpty Dumpty had a great fall, Jack fell down and broke his crown, A-tishoo, A-tishoo we all fall down.'

Freya looked at him with detachment. She was aware of a numbness creeping through her, as if her heart had been ripped out and replaced with ice. She did not feel pity for him, only dread at what would happen next. She stayed, watching his madness unfold, unable to think of a single thing to do. As darkness fell, instinct took over, they should go home.

'Shush now, Beck,' she said at last. 'We need to go

back. We need to go home. You're so cold. Come on.' She laid a hand on his arm and he flinched away. 'Beck…Beck?' But he would not move. Freya watched the car headlights throw beams of light across the grass in the park. The colours of daylight faded to browns and greys and finally black. She clutched her school blazer around her and sang in a broken voice, '*Hush, little baby, don't say a word, Freya's going to buy you a mockingbird. If that mockingbird wont' sing, Freya's going to buy you a diamond ring…*'

She carried on through all the verses and began again. When the rhyme was sung out, she tilted her head to touch his. 'I know you're scared, but it's going to be alright. I promise I will always look after you, no matter what. You've got to trust me. Can you do that?' His head moved against hers in a nod. 'Well done. Now, because you are so good, I don't want you to think about this anymore. Don't say anything to anyone and everything will be alright. Do you see? You need to keep this a secret about Debbie, or I will get into big trouble. Then who would take care of you. Promise me? Okay?'

'Okay,' he said, his voice tiny in the darkness.

The events of that day were never mentioned again. Eight-year-old Beckett became withdrawn, clingy, easy to tears and listless. Nightmares dominated his sleep whilst conversely, Freya would have welcomed them, at least as a form of atonement. But they had not come. Instead, she experienced the dead sleep of coma, numb without dream or rest, and by waking, the flatline sameness of depression. Her days filled with the slow motion of one task following another, an automaton without feeling. As time passed, and the interest of the police and newspapers moved on to another tragic story, Freya learned to live with this burden she called guilt. In the years to come, maturity and insight added another term – *cowardice*, the lowest and most damning of all transgressions. She had tucked this self-knowledge into her rotten heart and there it lay, like a slumbering dragon.

Freya groaned with self-loathing, sat up on the bed and looked again at the spider map. Poor Beckett, carrying the burden of her secret all these years and never letting on, his constant running, running *away* from his pain. How could she ever have expected him to lead a normal life when she had done so much harm to him? She took the pen, wrote *Suicide* in bold capital letters, circled it, and drew a line directly to her own name. She listed all the reasons Beckett may have sought this as a permanent escape and all her own contributions to his death.

With her examination of conscience complete, she went to the wardrobe and pulled out his rucksack. She found his small photo album and flicked through the images until she got to one of them both together at the beach café, when the sun had shone yet her lips were blue with cold. She touched his smiling face. 'I'm so sorry, my little one. I should have realised what I'd put you through.' Whether she said it to the adult Beckett or to him as a child, it did not matter. She had robbed him of a happy life, burden with the secret of her guilt, and he had forever remained a vulnerable eight-year-old.

Freya glanced up. Beckett, or at least the manifestation of him from her imagination, was sitting on the chair by the window intently looking at some paper in front of him. He tapped his pen against his teeth, echoing her habit.

'Oh, Beck. I'm so–' He raised a stop hand as if she were breaking his concentration. 'What are you doing?' she asked.

'Just looking at stuff. Aren't you going to ask me?'

'Ask you what?'

'What you're too afraid to ask.'

She thought for a moment. The question remained as an ugly, amorphous stain on her soul, a stain that had nothing to do with forgiveness. 'No. I won't ask you that.'

'Then you'll never know, will you?' He turned back to his piece of paper and faded away.

Forgiveness by contrast would have been an easier thing to ask, but she could not do this either. It remained a luxury she did not deserve. A lifetime of penance, ten lifetimes of atonement could not begin to pay off her debt. Father Paul's words about the debt having already been paid floated past as inconsequential as dandelion seeds on a breeze. She fetched Beckett's wooden rosary, kissed the crucifix dangling on the end and even as she did so, whispered her apologies to Him for having nailed Him there in the first place.

She picked up the seaside photo of her and Beckett together. Something previously unnoticed caught her eye. There on the table amongst the plates of seafood and napkins, was Beckett's water flask, the one he took with him on hikes and bike rides and out into the fields when he was working, the flask she had seen a dozen times before, the one with the pattern of blue, red and black words repeating: *RIDE HIKE SURF*. The side which faced toward the camera had a small section of letters scratched out, not randomly as if by accident but purposefully. Instead of: *RIDE HIKE SURF*, it read: ■*I*■ ■ *H*■■■ *S*■■■. She gave an ironic smile, understanding the meaning straight away, IHS, the symbol for Jesus. As children, she and Beckett thought these letters were an acronym for Jesus having said, *I Have Suffered*. It was only later when they made their Confirmations that they found out the real meaning was as a Greek Christogram for the name Jesus.

If Beckett had taken their child-like interpretation at face value and scratched it out on the flask, could he then have been trying to say something but in a simple child-like way, that he was suffering and needed help? If this was the case, why, oh why, had he not just asked? It was of course possible that the message was not a plea for help at all, rather a simple statement of how he felt about his life. She stroked her finger over the image of him in the photo. *Dearest Beckett.*

On the other hand, could this be another of his cryptic clues? She needed to find the water flask to check. She was certain it was not at home with his other things. It had to be here at The Byre or in the main pub building. She started by searching her own room, under the bed, behind the furniture, on top of the wardrobe. Nothing. Perhaps he stayed in the room next door which Merc now occupied. But searching there would mean getting the master key from Susie and what excuse could she give. No, that was a nogoer, Susie was far too curious. But she could possibly wrangle an invitation from Merc. Easy enough with a sassy little suggestion of a nightcap, and then when he went to use the bathroom…What was she thinking!

No, she couldn't afford to be distracted by her silly infatuation with him and he was certain to expect more than chit-chat over a whisky. Besides, the flask might well be hidden in plain sight tucked inside a kitchen cupboard or amongst the lost property box behind the bar.

Freya set to work and checked the public areas of the bar then on to the communal areas of the Byre: the lounge, kitchen, hallway. It wasn't there either. As she sat contemplating her next move, she toyed with some pebbles displayed in a pottery dish on the table. The indigo glaze drew out the flint-grey of the stones evoking the natural landscape beyond, sky and scree, tor and granite. For amusement she tried to stack one on top of another to recreate a miniature Margin Tor. She managed four before the inevitable collapse. She turned the pebbles over in her hands and imagined Beckett doing the same, feeling for the perfect jigsaw fit to build his drystone walls. It occurred to her that if he had left something important for her to find, then surely it must be in the environment he loved. Which meant outside, either at Jack's farm or in the great wilderness beyond. But where to begin? The farm, all thirty acres of it, at least was a manageable entity. The yard, barn and house seemed a good place to start.

CHAPTER 14

An autumn sun rose over the crest of the moor as Freya walked along the track to Jack's Farm. Buzzards soared and rode high on the thermals, mewing out their eerie call to one another. When she reached the farm, Jack was in the yard leaning over the rusty heap of an old hopper with a wrench in his hand.

'How's your head after last night?' she asked.

'Pigging awful, thanks.' He straightened up and wiped his hands with a cloth. 'I'm getting far too old for that malarkey. Want a cuppa?'

'Mmm, please. I'm looking for something, Jack. When Beck was here working for you, did he leave a water flask lying around? It's about so big,' she sized it out with her hands, 'And has coloured lettering around it saying, ride, hike surf?'

'Can't recall seeing it. Have a look in the old barn while I put the kettle on. Suppose he could've left it up on the top field while he was repairing the stone wall. Might be in the animal shelter up there.'

Freya poked around in the barn and after moving about various discarded tools and lambing and feeding equipment, found a tool bag in the corner with BG written on the front in marker pen which bled into the canvas. Inside were Beckett's leather gloves with frayed fingertips – she tried one on and wriggled her finger about in the hole – a chisel, mallet, and trowel, but no flask. Perhaps it had been too much to expect. Doubts crept in.

'Here we go,' Jack called over from the farmhouse door and raised up a steaming tin mug. 'It'll keep it nice and hot. Thought we could take a stroll up to the top field and look around together. Why is it so important, anyway?'

She cradled the mug between her hands. 'I'm not sure yet. But it's the only lead I have.'

'You think he's trying to tell you something?'

'Possibly. Who knows? I might've got it all wrong anyway, but it's worth a try.'

They walked together up an incline towards a field gate. A piece of hardboard hung on it with an old wellington boot tied over the top to stop the wind from flapping it about. Someone had spray painted the words, *BEWARE, HORNY RAM*.

'Jack!' Freya giggled.

'Well, don't look at me. That'll be Tom's handiwork. Must have a word with him later.'

'No don't. I don't mind really. He's quite earthy, isn't he, not a prude like me?'

Jack opened the gate and stood aside. 'I think the term you're looking for is modest. There's a big difference.'

'Yes, I suppose. So long as I don't come across as po-faced.' She gave a weak smile. 'It's easy to be written off as a miserable old spinster who's embarrassed about the facts of life.'

'Or taken advantage of.'

Freya stopped and faced him. 'Here we go again, the Merc alert. Why is everyone trying to warn me off him.'

'Perhaps because we all know him too well. I just think you deserve to be happy.'

'With all due respect, what I deserve is not for you to judge.'

'That's not what I meant. Let's just forget it.' They carried on walking and after a few moments he said, 'I'm glad you decided to stay. I enjoyed being out on the lake with you yesterday. Seeing your face light up reminded me of when I first took Skye out. She must have been barely six?'

'Ah, your daughter. I thought so, from the photo back at your house. She looks like you, same pale eyes. Does she ever visit?'

'Not as much as I'd like. She moved to Northumberland last summer.'

'For work?'

'Yes, sort of. She's in a convent. So long as she's happy, can't ask anymore.' He smiled but the sadness in his eyes revealed his hidden sacrifice.

'It's funny,' Freya said. 'I thought about it too when I was a girl. Me and my friend Debbie used to put tea towels on our heads and pretend we were nuns.' She scraped back her hair in imitation of a wimple and Jack laughed. 'But then life got terribly complicated, and I sort of blew my chances. Well, it's all ancient history now.'

The bittersweet memory stabbed her heart. What might life have been like for Debbie, a kind-hearted girl, popular, friendly, gregarious? Not the convent with those beautiful brows. Probably marriage, children, maybe even grandchildren by now. As for herself, she had led an unassuming life spent marking time, the one good thing being her teaching, mostly accomplished with passion, lately with weariness. In truth, her temperament had ruled out any notion of a religious vocation even before the tragedy. It had just taken her a while for her to see that. Freya found it difficult to separate her pre-teen self with the person she might have become had Debbie not died. The disaster had crushed her vivacious spirit. Whereas before she had been fiery, tempestuous, adamant, and precocious but warm-hearted and kind; afterwards she was withdrawn and unable to raise the energy for ill-temper, any slip of an outbreak quickly quashed. She remained wary of passionate emotions for one simple reason, she feared herself and what she might do.

They reached the dry-stonewall at the furthermost side of the field. Jack patted the top-stones as if he were the proud owner of a fine filly. 'Amazing! Look at the workmanship. Every stone individually selected. Perfect fit.' He took a step back to take in the expanse of wall. 'Beckett was a fine craftsman. Good company too. Didn't say much but listened well, made you feel kind of important, as if you were the only person who mattered. Wasn't full of himself like most folk.'

'I miss him.' Freya stared sadly into the distant moors.

'I know.' Jack moved closer and wrapped his arms around her as a great bear might protect his young. 'I know you do.'

Freya rested her forehead against his chest, breathing in the faint smell of hay and engine oil. She felt protected, safe, and when Jack moved away, there was a fleeting sense of loss.

'I'll look from the right, you from the left,' he said, 'and we'll meet up in the middle. The wall's been so well built, we'll be hard pressed to find a gap big enough for a cigarette paper, let alone any water bottle.'

They checked both sides of the wall, but the search yielded nothing. After a while, Jack became distracted and took to hacking out thistles from the field with a fold-up multi-tool he kept in his back pocket. The plants, he explained, were a ruin for pasture. Was there anything he didn't know?

Freya realized the search was futile, not even a sparrow could nest between the stones let alone a flask the size of a milk bottle. She sat on the grass and watched Jack for a while, his back dipping and rising with every diligent blow of the tool. Her admiration for him swelled.

When he was out of earshot, she whispered to an invisible Beckett, 'You're going to have to help me. Where on earth did you leave it?' But he refused to appear, and helpful clues were not forthcoming. She gave up and wandered over to Jack. 'Thanks for taking the time to look with me. Guess I was wrong about the flask. I'll leave you to get on.' She turned away and was heading down the slope when Jack straightened up.

'Tell me again, what did the nursery rhyme note say, the one on the seed packet?'

'Jack and Gil went up the hill to fetch a pail of water. I don't think it means anything now. Most likely this whole thing is a wild goose chase anyway.'

'But you haven't checked the tor yet. That's a hill, isn't it? Come with me. I've a map back at the house.'

'No need, Jack. I know where the tor is. Thanks all the same.'

'Take it anyway, you may find it useful.'

He was trying to be kind. She may as well take it with grace than stand and argue. They returned to the farm and Jack retrieved it from the kitchen drawer. They did an exchange, her empty tin mug for the map. 'Will I see you in the pub later?' she asked.

'No, had a skinful last night. Maybe tomorrow. Good luck.'

Freya took the direct track leading up to the tor even though it was steeper. As she drew closer, the task ahead became apparent. The granite boulders had vast gaps between not just the stones, but the different formations themselves, making at least three distinct stacks to be searched, the highest perhaps thirty feet tall. She searched at ground level first, checking all the spaces that were large enough to insert her arm.

After an hour, she grew weary of the prevailing wind pestering her and rested behind some rocks. She opened out the ordnance survey map, more for interest than because she believed it would be helpful. Even then the wind worried and wuthered around the stones, snagging and tugging, lifting at the map's corners so it might take flight high over the landscape, free with its secrets. Unlike Beckett's map, Jack's didn't have any markings on it. Freya spent a while orientating herself before she found Margin Tor sitting out to the east of the map amid a spiral of orange contour lines. A few centimetres away, the italicised print indicated a stone circle with a cairn where the ancient Moorlanders buried their dead. It read *Bada's Circle*, an Anglo-Saxon name meaning battle. In contrast, to the right of this was Brohn-In-The-Moor, a name meaning brothers of the moor, with the jug icon representing the pub for those very much still in the land of the living. A blue blob, the symbol for water, small enough to miss, was dabbed at the foot of the tor. It read, *Pail Pool*. Freya looked about her but couldn't see it. She climbed up onto the lowest of the boulder stacks and took in the view: the barren wilderness of the moors and the craggy dark beauty of the rock formations, beyond that the lush green valleys and the distant grey sea. Below her feet, ground out from the granite by aeons of erosion, was a perfect eight feet wide circular pool filled with water and ribboned with ripples. Jack's insistence that she take the map made her wonder. She wouldn't have been aware of the pool or known its name without it. If this was indeed the hill Jack and Gil had climbed in Beckett's rhyme, why had they gone there for but to fetch a pail of water?

She crouched next to the pool and dangled her fingers into the water. They appeared as pale sea creatures swirling in the murk. She tossed in a few pebbles to gauge the depth. The first plopped the surface but did not sound the bottom, neither did the next, until she threw one in the size of her fist. A dull clang of stone hitting metal rang out. She knelt, pushed up her sleeve and plunged her arm into the cold water. The pool seemed bottomless. She took off her jacket, slipped an arm out of her jumper and laid down. This time she reached in until her arm could go no further, and her shoulder brushed the surface of the water. Her fingers probed, discarded the hard sharp rocks until they found the round even shape of something manmade. She struggled to get a grip on the slippery metal. She stretched in a little further, ignored the wetness soaking

201

into her clothes, managed to upend it, grab the ring, and bring it to the surface.

'Alleluia,' she offered up in thanks. A green slime covered the flask but without a doubt, it was Beckett's. The words *RIDE HIKE SURF* were still visible and wrapped on repeat around the outside until the break, ■*I*■■ *H*■■■ *S*■■■ – I have suffered – appeared. Freya weighed it in one hand. It was heavier than expected. Then she shook it, no water but too heavy for empty. The top would not budge. She wiped off the sludge and tried twisting again using her jumper for traction – still jammed tight. She rammed the lid into a space between the stones and twisted but this only succeeded in scraping more paint off the words. As a last resort, she found a long slim pebble which was small enough to insert into the finger ring of the lid and used this as leverage. After a lot of grunting and tugging, the seal gave way.

Inside she could see a rolled-up document, though this would not come out at first because the paper had sprung loose from its original tight roll making it too large to manoeuvre out through the narrowed top. With some fiddling and patience, she managed to wriggle it out. She scanned the document, turned to the second page, and a third, and to a separate letter.

'Oh, no, no, no, Beckett. What have you done?'

She moved into the shelter of the tor and re-read, hoping she'd gotten it wrong. A couple of yellowing pages had been hand-typed with an old-fashioned typewriter and the heading, *Title Deeds*, and underneath, *57 Fairbrook Road, Warrendean, Hampshire* – her childhood home, and since her parents' deaths, the property she and Beckett jointly owned but now rented out. The accompanying letter consisted of two bright white sheets churned out from a modern laser printer. A red and purple solicitors' header read, *Faddon, Faddon & Doble.*

> *Dear Mr Greene and Miss Greene*
>
> *I acknowledge receipt of your letter dated 20th July, requesting assignment of 57 Fairbrook Road, to a third party, gifted through deed transfer. In order to proceed with this application, I require you both to complete the enclosed pro-forma, signifying your formal intentions, and to sign and witness where indicated (leave date blank) and return to me at the above address.*
>
> *I enclose the standard contract for terms of engagement and my fee scale. Please also be aware that this transference may be subject to the usual taxes from Her Majesty's Revenue and Customs.*
>
> *Yours sincerely*
>
> *Hugh Faddon, Senior Partner*

Freya looked again at the pro-forma. There, next

to Beckett's loopy signature was her own – impossible since she had never seen the document before in her life – or as near a copy as could be forged. Her imagination galloped ahead searching for any rationale, however outlandish. No matter what scenarios she came up with, nothing could begin to explain what Beckett had done, or rather what he intended to do, as the document had not yet been formally witnessed and returned to the solicitor. This, at least, was a blessing. But why on earth would he have even thought about getting rid of their parents' house? And without telling her? For sure, managing the rental could be annoying at times, especially the gaps between tenancies when money flowed out instead of in. The tenants themselves could be demanding or destructive, sometimes both. Thus, the income seemed paltry in relation to the effort expended. But selling had not been an option either of them wanted. However, the letter implied not a sale but a transfer, and no mention of money. What right did he have? And who would Beckett want to *give* away the house to, anyway? She could not believe any individual or organisation would be worthy, let alone that the pair of them would agree on such? Beckett, so kind in many ways, gave no indication of any great altruism. Still, to be fair he was always the first to dip his hand in his pocket at a charity tin. Good intentions or no, he still should have talked to her first. Unless that is…because he had no choice.

She rubbed a hand over her throbbing forehead. The police investigations reported 'financial irregularities,' a generic term mopping up anything from dodgy tax returns to major fraud. As far as she knew, none of this applied. However, she had recently learnt of Beckett's gambling problem, and Jack seemed to think of his 'little problem' as anything but little. When Jack said he had handed Beckett leaflets for *Gamblers Anonymous* and urged him to seek professional help, she thought he was exaggerating. Might even Jack have underestimated the extent of Beckett's gambling and the trouble he was in? Using the house, their *parents'* house, to pay off his debts entered a different league altogether. How could he even run up such huge debts so rapidly? Susie kept a slot machine tucked under the stairs in the inn, but he would have needed to be playing round the clock and for much larger stakes than a pound-a-go for this to be the culprit.

Furthermore, Jack and Tom played cards for money. Jack had been adamant it was just for pennies – unless he had been lying. Could this be where Beckett lost so much money? And what about Merc, was he involved too? Susie had said on Freya's first day that Merc liked a 'flutter'. And where did all this take place? At the inn?

Freya pushed back a rising sense of unease. If any of this were true, they had all lied to her: Jack, Merc, Tom, Susie *and* Beckett.

Freya rolled up the documents and tucked them in the inside pocket of her windcheater. She screwed down the top on the water flask, lifted her arm and was about to throw it back into Pail Pool when she changed her mind. Her conclusions were wild speculation without a shred of proof, she must give them all the benefit of doubt, especially Beckett. Throwing away one of the few mementos of him would be churlish.

CHAPTER 15

Back at The Byre, Freya went straight to her room, stripped off her damp clothes and changed into some old jogging pants and a sweatshirt, intending to stay there for the rest of the evening to concentrate on being furious with Beckett. She tried summoning him into the chair by the window, just so she could see his gentle face and not believe her latest, hurtful, hateful imaginings about him. She focused on not being angry, allowing her subconscious to soothe away any anxiety so she could formulate the required hallucination of him. Nothing seemed to work. When hunger roused her from her mental gymnastics and she stood to rustle up some dinner, Beckett appeared crossed legged on the end of her bed.

'You're angry with me, I can tell,' he said.

'Tell me something I don't already know. What were you playing at? You had no right. And forging my signature too. That's unforgivable!'

'Unforgivable,' he echoed. 'Really? For something so small I'm to be damned?'

'Hell, Beck. You know what I mean.' She hurled a pillow at him. He dodged sideways and it crashed into the chest of drawers.

'Temper, temper! Best get that under control. It could lead to all sorts of trouble.'

'Well, thank you. Below the belt, even for you.' A hot mantle of shame wrapped around her. In frustration, she raked her fingers into her hair, gripped hard and tugged until the pain replaced the truth about herself.

'That's really going to help,' Beckett said.

'Shut up. Shut up. *Shut up!*' She flopped back on the pillow and focused on the hot-pins sensation prickling over her scalp and the distracting throb of illicit pain. When she sat up again, Beckett had gone. She went to the bathroom, splashed cold water on her face and brushed her hair, though it seemed to protest and wouldn't lie normally as if it were a free-spirited wig she had lost the right to call her own.

On the way to the kitchen, Freya passed by the door to the lounge. The table lamps and open fire gave a warm ambience to the room. It would be pleasant to eat there tonight to take away the cold worry of what might possibly be. Then Merc stepped into her line of vision. He was practising some imaginary golf swing.

She stopped. 'What are you doing?'

He completed the movement before answering. His arms swung, rose, and swooped down in one beautiful flowing swing. 'Practicing for the game next week. I want to impress.'

'Impress?'

'Yes. In my game, appearance is everything, lassie. When I make a good impression on the fairway, they trust my diligence and commitment, my attention to detail and that I know what I'm talking about.' He lined up the putter with the golf ball on the carpet and prepared himself for the shot.

'Oh, so that's how it works,' she said, his world of schmoozing and rapport so alien to her she thought nothing of teasing him for it. In teaching, qualifications and experience were the things that counted. 'Are you any good?'

'Aye, not bad.' He swelled with pride. 'Pretty good actually.'

Freya suppressed a laugh. Modesty came hard to men such as Merc, though to give him credit, he had the confidence to pull it off. She watched as he shuffled his feet into position, performed minute trial runs and hovered the putter a few inches from the ball, before tapping it lightly into the waiting receptacle – a paper cup – ten feet away.

'Can I have a go?' she asked.

He handed her the iron. She copied his stance, her shoulders with a slight stoop, her arms straight as the iron in her hands, and tapped at the ball. It curved to the right and stopped two feet short of the target.

Merc bent and placed a second ball on the carpet. 'Have another wee go.'
She hit it a little harder this time and it shot past the cup and rolled under the sofa.

'Unlucky. Here, let me show you.'

Merc moved behind her and as he wrapped his arms around her to help with her positioning, she became aware of his proximity, his scent, his muscles through his shirt, the buckle of his belt, the warmth of his skin on her hands. She straightened up.

'Maybe not.' She handed him back the putter.

'Ach, have another go. Do it like this.' He demonstrated in front of her, as if putting were the easiest thing in the world.

Freya concentrated and after a few more practice

shots and when she was sure she had perfected the knack, she putted for real. The ball found the target with such force the cup spun around. He suggested a competition, best out of ten which they took it in turns, beginning with Freya. The first four of her shots slotted into the cup with ease.

Merc matched putt for putt. 'Beginner's luck,' he said.

'I think you mean skill.'

He laughed and she was pleased she had managed to amuse him, after which her aim deteriorated, and she missed the next few goes. Apparently, Merc's game had worsened too.

'You're letting me win,' she said.

He raised his eyebrows. 'I've never thrown a game in my life. I've an intense dislike of losing. The trick is to think like a winner. Your turn.'

Whilst she didn't quite believe him, she did appreciate the sentiment and tried hard to justify his admiration. Think like a winner, she told herself, and on the final shot, when Merc was one hole behind, she repeated the mantra with an earnestness excessive to the circumstance. The ball saw home and she raised her arms in triumph. 'And that's how you do it,' she exclaimed, jiggling on the spot.

'Sure is.' Merc beamed, scooped her up, twirled her around and placed her back on her feet whilst keeping his arms clasped firmly at her waist.

An unknown and irresistible urge suddenly possessed her. Without logic or reason, she desired his touch, his kiss, for his body to be pressed against hers. Her head swam. She willed Merc's response, sent out desire from her eyes. As if she had spoken that yearning aloud, he moved in closer and kissed her, at first with small exploratory movements, then as she responded, with confident commanding lips. Self-consciousness fell away, she relaxed. For the very first time, she was willing to abandon herself to another. Everything she had heard about passion began to make sense – wondrous, ecstatic, sublime, satiating – and at the same time, its power frightened her. She was beguiled, intoxicated. Contentment spread through her like warming whisky on a cold day.

She would have been gratified to remain like that in his arms but after some minutes – she had no sense of time passing – his kiss became urgent, harder, and then a probing tongue. She hesitated, held back, grew alarmed. She was aware of his hand in the small of her back pulling her into him, the other lifting her jumper, and a sense that he was taking rather than she giving to him.

'That's more like it,' he whispered into her ear.

'Are you having fun, lassie?'

It might have been the word 'fun' itself, or the libertine, if not lecherous way he had said it, but her passion turned to disgust. She pulled back, turned her head away, resisted the urge to wipe his saliva from her lips. She wanted to spit out the stale-coffee taste of him. Had this noble gift of passion become little more than a leisure activity? Mightn't he just as well have asked her to join him on a rambunctious fairground ride all in the name of fun?

'So, what's wrong now?' he asked.

'Nothing…I just…can't.'

'Ach come on Freya, where's the harm? Let your bonnie hair down for a bit.'

She tried to wriggle from his arms. 'Sorry.' She thought she should say more, make it seem like it was all her fault, that it was her not him, but that wasn't true. He repulsed her with his excessive hunger and his casual expectation of the sacred.

He gave a long sigh and released her. 'Okay, if that's what you want. But I'm warning you, I'm not for the persuasion game. I've better things to be getting on with. Guess you're not as sophisticated as I thought.' He began to walk away then turned back. 'And Freya, you might want to think about the signals you're sending out. We used to have a word for lassies like you.' He said no more and left the room.

The idea horrified Freya, to be labelled a tease. How could she have been so naïve? Though no wonder, hadn't she been fawning over him like a besotted teenager since the moment she met him? She even encouraged him with her little Miss Confident act and her whisky-swigging drinking session, had even egged him on at the hotel, accepting his romantic rose-filled lunch with coquettish smiles. She should have known there was an expectation of pay-back, that this good-time-guy was not the sort of man looking for a serious relationship. Jack, Susie, Allegra, hadn't they all seen it coming and tried to warn her? And now she looked a fool. Why hadn't she listened? Freya groaned. Her inexperience and vulnerability were like a neon sign saying, *come take advantage!* On some deep level hadn't she known that about him anyway and didn't want to burst that thrilling bubble called infatuation.

Freya returned to her room drenched in his aftershave. She showered, brushed her teeth, changed clothes and still it permeated the very air she breathed. As she finished drying her hair Beckett appeared again on the end of the bed. She switched off the hairdryer.

'You're the last person I want to see right now,' she said.

'Oh, that's nice.'

'Out with it,' Freya sighed.

'Alright, I will. I told you so.'

'Beck, you're nothing if not predictable.'

'I never liked him.'

'So I gather.' She switched the hairdryer back on and shouted over the noise, 'You're not helping. Go away.' And the Beckett of her conscience faded.

She needed a distraction, a cup of coffee and one of Susie's homemade casseroles in the bar, perhaps a chat with Tom or one of the locals. But when she walked in Merc was sitting there perched up on a high stool with his back to the door. Susie was leant over the counter engrossed in a conversation which Freya couldn't hear but guessed was amusing because Susie suddenly threw back her head with mirth. Freya turned to leave.

'Ah, Freya love,' Susie said spotting her and suppressing a giggle. 'You look like you could do with a drink. What can I get you? Wonky Wassail, whisky?' She winked at Merc. He turned around still wearing that smirk which didn't fade even as she glared back. 'No, nothing. I was looking for Jack,' then remembered that Jack had already told her he wasn't coming to the inn that night.

'Yes, he's tucked over there by the fire.' Susie waved a vague hand in the direction of the inglenook where Jack sat staring into his pint and ruminating. His face was full of uncomfortable thoughts.

'Hey, you're miles away. Penny for them, nothing bad I hope,' Freya said. 'I thought you weren't coming tonight?'

He looked up, momentarily dazed by the interruption. 'Changed my mind. Wanted a word with Merc.' He cocked his head towards the bar. 'Looks like he's otherwise engaged.'

'It didn't take him long,' she said under her breath and slid along the bench next to him. Quick on the uptake, Jack swivelled to face her, his eyes pouring out sympathy. Freya held up a hand. 'Don't waste it on me. I've only myself to blame. Everyone warned me.'

'Right, I'm going to have it out with him.' He half-rose and Freya pulled him down.

'It's sweet of you Jack, but I can handle this.'

'If you say so. Best to find out now, eh? He didn't, did he—'

It was Freya's turn to frown. 'No and don't ask. Now, can we change the subject?' Jack grumbled out a host of obscenities, loosely aimed at some imaginary castration of the scoundrel. She told him about being up on the tor wasting time searching for the flask in the crags between the boulders when it had been hiding in Pail Pool all along. 'But then you knew that didn't you.' she said.

Jack ran a hand over his stubble. 'Oh,' he mouthed.

Freya shut her eyes; her worst fears realised. 'How?'

'Beckett asked me back along where a good place might be to hide something small. Didn't tell me what it was, and I didn't ask. It was only when you became so adamant about the darned flask that I put two and two together.'

'Weren't you even curious?'

'I figured he'd tell me if he wanted to. That's the thing about Brohn-In-The-Moor. Like I said before, people pass through here all the time. It's a staging post. The wilderness and big skies draw souls. It's a place to rest and clear the head, figure things out, make resolutions. Most move on. Some of us stay. Huh, guess that means I'm stuck.'

'Rigby?' she offered.

'Hmm, stupid I know.'

'Come on, Jack. You didn't mean to hurt him. That would be very different.' A stab of guilt flashed through her. 'What would it take for you to feel better about everything?'

'If I only knew that I'd grab it with both hands. You're right. Theoretically, I know I'm forgiven.' He pointed up to the deity of the ceiling. 'Rigby's wife wrote me a letter after the inquest saying what a great skipper I'd been. How Rigby looked up to me. Thanked me for making all the arrangements, the repatriation, memorial service, and stuff. It's funny, I could've coped with a rebuttal, but it was her kindness that got me in the end. I felt, still feel, like such a fraud.'

'Jack, when we were in the garden together, you talked about faith and wisdom, yet it doesn't seem to apply to you. There is no case to answer. Troubles come enough of their own accord. I would say choose your battles more wisely.'

'That I do, believe me, that I do.' He glared over at Merc.

'Forget about them. They're not important. Isn't this more a matter of perception?'

'You're now going to dazzle me with some psychobabble.' He paused in the action of lifting his pint to his lips. 'You want one?'

Freya waved away the distraction. 'Hear me out. You perceive yourself to be Jack the Elder, Jack of the Moors, wise skipper, always in control, responsible, knows the sea and all its moods. Your crew are your family, and you jolly well take care of them. Right?'

He set his pint down and stretched his legs out

under the table. For a few moments, he stared at some vague spot just short of the far wall. 'I suppose.'

'And then this tragedy happens, a combination of bad luck and time pressure mixed in with unpredictable weather and an absent-minded crew member – literally the perfect storm.' She shifted forward. 'What if the way you're feeling is less about guilt and more about your actions that day contradicting your long-held beliefs about yourself? It might not be about guilt at all.' She needed Jack to take this gift of mercy, even if she could not accept it for herself. 'You already know you're forgiven by God and Rigby's wife – not that there was anything to forgive in the first place. Perhaps on some level, you even forgive yourself for what happened. But you can't forgive yourself for not being the person you thought you were.'

He nodded slowly. 'Possibly…I might need some time to think about that.'

'It's just a matter of miss-matched self-perception.'

'How do you know all this stuff? Years of navel-gazing?'

'Huh, no.' She slumped back in her chair. 'I've known exactly what I am.'

'Lucky you.'

'No, not really.' She tried to keep her voice light,

as if it were some throw-away comment which didn't mean anything. 'You haven't asked me what was in the flask.'

'Okay. Tell me, what was in the flask?'

'Only the deeds to our parents' house, the one me and Beckett jointly owned. *And* a letter from a solicitor regarding a transfer of title deeds to a third party. To whom, I do not know, but I intend to find out.'

Jack whistled through his teeth. 'Why would he–?'

'Exactly. I've been thinking about that. It's got to be something to do with his gambling. It's the only explanation. Do you think it could have got this much out of hand? I know you don't like to tell tales, but I need to know. It involves me now, Jack, and right now you are the only person who knew about his problem.'

'Leave it with me, I'll do some digging.'

'Good. I'm going to check out the slot machine under the stairs, see what the stakes are.'

'I shouldn't bother, they're only for pounds. Would take a month of Sundays to run up that much debt.'

'I'm going to look anyhow.' Freya got up. 'Think of the drip-drip of attrition. It all mounts up.'

She went into the hall and found Tom feeding coins into it, absorbed by the flashing lights weaving their way up the console display, enticed by the tinny digital sounds bashing out from some hidden speaker and lured by the prospect of quick riches. Wheels whirled and clicked into position – cherry, cherry, melon, sack full of gold. A dull clunk-clunk dispensed two-pound coins of winnings. Tom took a quaff of beer and wiped his mouth with the back of his hand, then fed both coins back in quick succession. Freya watched fascinated, gained the measure of the machine, watched for predictable patterns, advised Tom on his next move, what to hold, what to free spin, until she was thoroughly bored and ready to report back to Jack with her findings gleaned from Tom. The machine spat out a '*not too shabby twenty smackers*' most nights and rarely, perhaps once in a quarter, a hundred-pound super jackpot. All well and good but surely Beckett wouldn't have wasted his effort on such paltry odds, and as Jack had said, it would take a month of Sundays to rack up debt amounting to the value of a house. Surely, he must have had another outlet.

As she walked along the corridor back to the bar, she heard an argument breaking out. She rushed to the doorway in time to witness Jack shove Merc's shoulder. Merc in turn grabbed Jack by the front of his sweater and pushed him up against the wall. A stool scraped, toppled over and the glass fell and smashed.

'You touch me again, pal–' Merc's voice was terse,

measured.

'Yeah? Yeah? And you'll do what? Silence me? Well, I've got news for you; I'm not playing your–'

'Careful. Wouldn't want certain *information* to get out now, would we?' Merc stood nose-to-nose with Jack.

Susie rushed forward. 'Stop it, both of you. We're all in this together.'

'No. No we're not,' Jack hissed. 'I'm not with this low life.'

'You bet you are,' Merc shoved his forearm hard up against Jack's throat and Jack gagged.

'What the heck's going on?' Freya stepped towards them, but Susie held out a warning arm, barring her path. 'Keep out of this.'

'Well then,' Merc said, pushing his arm harder into Jack's throat. 'Aren't you going to tell the lady?'

Freya looked from one to the other. 'Tell me what? Well…Jack?'

Jack glanced sideways to Freya, then back to Merc, and gave a curt shake of his head.

'Thought not,' Merc said and released his grip.

'It's nothing,' Jack said to Freya. He rolled back his shoulders and took a step towards her. Freya stepped back. 'Nothing to worry about' he repeated. 'Just a misunderstanding. Leave it be. Come on, I'll take you back to your room.' He took hold of her at the elbow and began to brisk-step her towards the corridor.

She wriggled free. 'No, Jack. Tell me now.' This was a new side to him which she struggled to reconcile to the 'good-old-Jack' persona she had created.

'Not here.' She followed him to the exit and made their way to The Byre.

'Well?' she asked again when out of earshot.

'It's nothing' he said with ridiculous emphasis. Just a few financial...*irregularities*. We made a deal back along and now it has come back to bite us. It'll blow over.'

Freya remembered the police using that exact phrase – *financial irregularities* on their report into Beckett's death. 'Oh, Jack. You're not involved in anything illegal, are you?' And though left unspoken, by implication, had Beckett been too?

He sighed. 'Not strictly speaking. Depend on who's doing the asking.'

'Can you sort it out...explain things?'

'It's not that simple. Wish it were.' When they reached her room, he said unnecessarily, 'We're here,' and took hold of her hand. 'I'm sorry you had to witness that. It's a messy business. Appears my integrity has slipped. Maybe I'll see you tomorrow, that is if you're still speaking to me?'

'Yes, of course. Night.' Freya let herself in and closed the door behind her with a gentle click. Just when she thought she was making headway with Jack, he had done something stupid and unnerved her, and moreover, she now wrestled with the possibility that Beckett too was involved in something illegal. Perhaps deviancy ran in the family.

CHAPTER 16

The next morning Freya decided on a cooked breakfast in the pub having only had beans on toast the night before because of all the commotion. She sat in the window seat sipping her tea.

Susie brought over a large plate of bacon and eggs and set it down on the table in front of her. 'Here you go, full English. Oh, and this came for you.' She produced an envelope from her apron pocket. 'I forgot to give it to you yesterday. Sorry if it's urgent.'

Freya hoped it was from Father Paul with news but was disappointed to see a red and purple patterned border on the front – not quite his style. Inside was its matching postcard. Elegant continental writing invited her to join Allegra in a tearoom in Stannaton for afternoon tea. She checked the date: Thursday at 3pm – today. She flipped the postcard over: *I'll pick you up at 2.30pm. Looking forward to seeing you, Allegra x.* Too late to decline and a presumptuous expectation of acceptance.

Just before 2.30pm, Freya stood waiting underneath the creaking sign of St George and the Dragon. It took a few minutes before realising the empty car parked awkwardly on the verge was Allegra's. Inside, the bar seemed to be deserted, unusual for this time of day considering Susie could usually be found somewhere clearing up or sitting at a table with her account books. Freya waited a moment then decided to take another look at the slot machine in the hall corridor. It sat idle with just an occasional flash of coloured lights and the odd blip of a sound to draw in any passing punters. She dug into her jeans pocket for a pound, then checked herself; what on earth was she doing?

A door opened in the stairwell above her, and feet started slowly descending the stairs. Freya caught the end of a conversation. Susie was saying, '…and if it gets out the brewery's gonna be the least of my worries.' And Merc said over her, 'Nothing's going to happen–.' Allegra then cut them both short, 'Just listen to the two of you. Do you not *care* about anyone?'

Freya took a step back under the staircase out of sight, as if she had just taken on the role of an undercover spy. In the process she managed to knock against the slot machine springing it back to life. A synthetic trilling sound erupted and lights zig-zagged up and down behind the console display. She winced. Cover blown.

From above her, Susie cleared her throat. 'And needless to say, all the proceeds from the Halloween party will be donated to a local charity. Should keep even you happy, Allegra.'

'We will see, talk is cheap,' Allegra replied.

Freya toyed with the idea of feigning a sudden and compelling interest in the blasted slot machine pretending that she hadn't heard any of it. The word 'coward' popped into her mind, then a phrase, 'confrontation adverse'. She should stand her ground, step forward – she hadn't intended to overhear after all. Whatever they were trying to cover up needed to be challenged, and why had she got the feeling this had something to do with Beckett? She thrust her hands in her jeans' pockets and went casually to the bottom of the stairs, pre-empting the encounter not with counter-questions but a simple, 'Hi, there…Ah, Allegra, I thought I heard you. You ready?' The word coward surfaced again. She was self-conscious; her arms felt all wrong, her elbows stuck out like wings as if she were about to take flight. She *looked* like she had been up to something. Merc led the way down the stairs and as he neared her, he puckered his lips in a mock kiss. Disgusted, she turned her head. What on earth had she seen in him?

Freya and Allegra drove out of the village towards the moors in polite and predictable conversation. When they rounded a bend and Margin Tor came into view, Allegra steered the car into a passing-place and switched off the engine. 'It is stunningly beautiful, is it not?' she said.

'It's taken a while, but yes. I think it's growing on me.'

'I know exactly what you mean. You will get there, I promise, I did. To think I used to be dismissive of anything that did not pamper or entertain me. I thought beauty was a diamond solitaire on a manicured finger, or a marbled dance floor in a grand palazzo. Lovely though they are, they are not the real deal. Someone very special helped me to see that. He took me up there,' she stretched her arm toward the tor, 'on a scorching summer's day. We watched the buzzards circle overhead, ate cheese sandwiches and drank lukewarm tea from a flask – tasted awful – you English and your tea – but I had the best of times, worth a thousand magnums of champagne.' A sadness passed over her. 'I knew I had got my priorities wrong. I felt a fraud next to him... then it was all over. Too late.'

Allegra fondled a silver ring on her left ring finger and Freya then knew. 'You're talking about Beckett, aren't you?'

'How–'

'I know my brother. The ring is a Celtic knot, what else would he have given you? He wasn't religious in the sense that he didn't go to Mass very often. Though he kept a rosary in his bag, whereas I never could.' She gave a wane smile to answer Allegra's unasked question. 'We have history, me and the beads. Long story, Catholic school and all that. But in a way Beckett was more in touch with God than I'll ever be. It was as if he could stand on the hills wondering at the greatness of creation and just know. My friend Father Paul wouldn't have me nag him about church, said to just leave him be.' Freya turned to face her. 'And why else would you bring *me* out here? Not to gloat about my foolishness, surely? No doubt Merc told you about my recent frigidness with him. So, unless you really are cruel, which I don't believe you are, it has to be about Beckett.'

'Yes, Merc did tell me, and I thought, good for you, about time he knew he cannot always get what he wants. Enough about him. With Beck, well, I had hoped we would…anyway.' Allegra sagged in her seat.

'I'm sorry. I did try to encourage him to settle

down, but increasingly he craved these big open spaces. He'd been distracted for months, searching for goodness knows what.' It was easier to tell half-truths; searching *for* seemed so much more dynamic than running *from* and all its repercussions. 'How could anyone compete with his love affair with the natural world?'

'Peace…he was searching for peace,' Allegra said and started up the engine and pulled away.

Freya had the shocking realisation that Allegra knew him all too well, that she was party to his innermost thoughts and feelings. For all of Freya's encouragement for him to settle down they had merely been lip-service on her part. The truth she had come recently to see was that she was afraid for him to settle down, afraid for the consequences, afraid for the inevitable secrets which would be shared, and Beckett knew it. He had made an escape bid and begun a private life which she had not been invited to share.

'Beckett once asked me if I trusted him,' Allegra said. 'When I said yes of course, his mood changed. He went quiet and said I really should not because he absolutely knew you could not trust anyone, that even the kindest people in the world were capable of the most terrible things. I laughed at the time; he was not capable of hurting anyone. It was only later I understood he had not been talking about himself, that something traumatic must have happened to him. Someone had let him down spectacularly. He did not say what or who. Poor Beckett.'

Freya's insides twisted. It was now she who wanted to run. In a panic, she considered her options: feign illness so Allegra would take her back to the inn, then emigrate, take on a new name, reinvent herself, do cleaning jobs to survive. However tempting it was pointless, she could never run from herself. Neither could she join Beckett in suicide – ten thousand times worse; not the slumber of oblivion but an eternity writhing in guilt.

'He didn't say anything to me,' Freya said. This in mitigation was the truth. 'I guess if you can't find peace here among these wild places, you never will.'

Freya was thankful Allegra didn't push the point. From then on, the conversation was light. She chatted about the hotel, her family back in Italy, some of the places she had visited: Australia, New Zealand, the Azores, the Caribbean. Freya listened, nodded in the right places, laughed when Allegra laughed and was relieved when they parked up in Stannaton and went into a little tearoom on the High Street. A bell tinkled on the back of the door as they entered. Light was scarce in the low beamed room though white walls and bright pastel furniture went some way to lighten it. They chose the table by the window,

Allegra sitting with her back to it, her hair a corona in the sun. They ordered tea and scones from a waitress with plaited hair.

'This isn't just about Beckett or a nice afternoon out, is it?' Freya asked. 'You could have told me about you both at The George.'

'The George has ears.'

'And secrets!'

'Yes, and secrets. I am doing someone a favour, Jack actually. He is a decent man.'

'Is this something to do with the ruckus he had with Merc last night?' Allegra's allegiances appeared to have shifted.

'Partly. There is no nice way of saying this, Beckett was in it up to his neck with the gambling ring.' She raised a horizontal hand to her neck in emphasis.

'A *gambling ring*?' Freya's eyes widened. 'Not Beck. He wouldn't.' Yet she knew her protests were futile. Hadn't Jack all but implied that? And Beckett had form, the betting slips from *Ladbrokes*.

'I wish I could say otherwise. He was in it far more than Jack or I could handle. We pulled out days before things got out of hand, though Merc stayed.'

'Jack involved too, why didn't he say?'

'Because he could not, which is why he asked me

to help.'

'But why couldn't he?' There could be no excuse. They had discussed gambling before, and Jack had played the innocent. There had been plenty of opportunities for him to own up.

'I really cannot tell you that. Please leave Jack out of it.' Allegra leant forward and squeezed Freya's hand, her knuckles yellowed like picked over bones. 'Jack is not the one you should be chasing. He is the good guy. You are a smart lady, do your digging elsewhere.'

Freya pulled her hand away. 'Okay. Let's start with you. What do you know?'

'I swear, that is all there is.'

'Not quite. The gambling ring involved you, Beckett, Jack, Merc. Who else?'

Allegra hesitated, shifted her eyes around the room and then satisfied said, 'Tom, but he only lasted the first session, a solicitor called Hugh, and an ex-convict Merc met in Marbella. I think he flew back when the police, how you say, got wind of him staying in England.'

'And that's all?'

Allegra nodded.

There were so many unanswered questions – where did it take place, which game, what stakes, was criminality involved? But Freya judged that Allegra had said all she was willing to give. After the sandwiches and scones, Freya asked to borrow her phone. She stood outside in the damp air watching the tourists flit between the gift shops and camping outlets, wondering why they chose to shop rather than experience the wilderness of the moors after travelling all this way. Most likely for the same reason as she – town as comfort zone, the rugged landscape a threatening reminder of this primeval thing called nature.

She tapped in Father Paul's number. His assistant answered. 'Hi there, Father Paul Atkinson's office. Roz speaking. How may I help you?' Her Canadian warmth poured down the line like thick maple syrup.

'Roz, it's Freya.'

'Great. How you doing?'

Roz was a theology intern Freya had met on her visit to Father Paul after Beckett's death. She had liked her from the outset, and they had developed an instant rapport. Freya told Roz about the quaint little inn she was staying at, the beauty of Dartmoor, the characters she had met: Jack the kindly uncle figure – ignoring the fact their age difference was less than ten years, Merc the flashy guy with the sports car, Susie the ultra-efficient landlady who didn't miss a thing, Tom, the salt of the earth. Freya had yet to summarise Allegra.

'You know, I should come visit,' Roz said. 'Get to see the real England.'

There was that word again, *real*, as if Roz and Father Paul lived in some theological bubble halfway up Jacob's ladder instead of a small village just outside Salisbury. However, Freya could say with honesty that Father Paul was more in touch with real life, with people and their problems, than anyone she had ever met. It was as if being slightly apart from the world made him more perceptive.

'When everything is sorted and it's all over,' Freya said, 'I promise I'll show you around.' What would constitute 'being sorted' and 'all over,' Freya didn't yet know. Neither had she thought about what life might look like after she had found out the truth about Beckett's death. Would she want to stay in Brohn-In-The-Moor, or would she go back to her old life and teach again? And if so, would a return visit here be sweet, bittersweet or just plain bitter?

'When it's all *over*? Freya, are you sure you're okay? You sound kinda ominous.'

'Really, I'm fine. Is his lordship in?'

'Okay, if you say so. I'll just get him.'

Roz's steps faded away and were soon replaced by the clip-clip of Father Paul's brogues over his parquet floor.

'Freya, how are you?' His voice radiated concern. 'I've been worried for you. I do wish you'd let me fetch you home, or at least come up and help. I've a few spare days, really it wouldn't be too much trouble I can assure you.'

'Paul, you are sweet, but no thanks. Have you any news for me?' There was a pause and an audible sigh.

'Not as much as I'd hoped.'

Freya slumped and leant back against the tearoom window. 'Oh well. You did your best. Thanks for trying.'

'I said, not as much as I'd hoped, but there is some news. Monkcombe isn't such a common name. I had a good poke on the internet and there are ten possibilities, five up north somewhere, three in the midlands and two along in the South West. My apologies, I should have asked you this before, do you know her first name?'

Freya straightened at the hope of seven leads and sagged again as she realised she didn't know the answer. 'I'm trying to remember. It was such a long time ago, and in those days, we just called everyone 'auntie' so and so or 'Mrs' whatever ... Just a sec.' She searched through a slide show of memories. 'Oh, I know. I think Debbie used to say that she could get away with opening her mum's letters when they were addressed as just D Monkcombe because it was the same initial as hers. She'd get a clip round the ear for it, mind. She found out a lot about her mum that way. Like the time she hadn't kept up with the repayments for Radio Rentals and they were going to cart the telly off any day.'

'Ha, Radio Rentals, there's a blast from the past. And did they?'

'I guess so. Debbie would come over to mine and watch Top of the Pops every week. That is…until she died.'

'Oh, Lord. I am sorry. What happened?'

An amorphous darkness pressed on her heart, and she was silent. Father Paul allowed a moment to pass before he said, 'Well, we'll have to take a leap of faith. Let's assume it's D for now. That narrows it down a bit.'

Father Paul's pen scratched over some paper as, she presumed, he crossed out names. 'There's a Deidre, miles away up in Bridlington. A Doris in Torquay and another Deidre in Paignton. Probably best to start with these two in the West Country. Now your move. What do you want to do next?'

She hesitated, swallowed back the tightening knot in her throat, tried to breathe. She knew what she ought to do. Temptation curled around her resolve and she searched for another way. 'I see,' she whispered after a few moments. 'Thank you, Paul.'

'My dear girl, I respect whatever decision you make without question. You seem to have some unfinished business. You do know I'll be there by your side, no matter what? Surely, this…thing, cannot be that bad? Can I just remind you that you thought it important enough to ask me for help in the first place?'

'I know that,' she answered, her voice frail and distant. Father Paul had an excellent reputation as a spiritual director and was in great demand. His probing and truth seeking exposed raw wounds, mitigated only by his utter kindness.

'So…it is serious. Take heart. In order for the light to shine, there must be darkness.'

Freya took a deep breath. 'When can you come?'

'Tomorrow.'

'Thank you, Paul. There is one more favour. Please could you ring Faddon, Faddon and Doble solicitors and make an appointment for us to see their senior partner, Hugh Faddon?'

'Of course. What shall I say it is in connection with?'

'Beckett Greene. On second thoughts, just say it is to do with title deeds. I'll explain it all to you on the way.'

'Intriguing. I love a good mystery. See you

tomorrow.'

The line went silent. Freya held the phone in front of her and stared at the screen for no other reason than she did not know what to do next. Then the phone suddenly trilled as a call came through. The screen flashed up the name Merc. Freya rushed back into the tearoom. 'Merc,' she mouthed as she handed it to Allegra.

Allegra took if from her, tapped the screen and terminated the call. 'Why spoil a nice afternoon?' she said, dropping it into her bag.

When they returned to The George and Dragon, Freya, exhausted and tired of company, went straight to her room. She changed into her pyjamas and sat on the bed to trying to figure things out. So, Beckett had been involved heavily in a gambling ring and neither Jack nor Merc had said a word, had in fact, all but denied even knowing him at first. It partly explained the secrecy, though that hurt most of all. Beckett was a kind soul who deserved to have some loyalty shown to him, rather than be cast aside like any old passing tourist who didn't add a jot to their community or environment. She had always thought there were givers and takers in this world, and Beckett was the former. He seldom asked for anything which he could not repay in kind, or failing that, in kindness.

There was a faint tap on her door. She dithered whether to answer it. Instead, she sat still and waited, hoping whoever it was would go away. Another slightly louder tap followed.

'Freya, are you in there?' Jack whispered loudly. 'Thought you might like to join me for supper. Are you there?' His voice climbed back to normal volume. 'If you're asleep, I won't disturb you.'

Freya tried not to smile, she wanted to stay angry with him. 'Yes, I'm asleep.'

'Okay, perhaps tomorrow.'

'Hang on, just a minute.' She dragged herself to the door. He stood in front of her with his head bowed like an errant child. 'What is it, Jack?' she asked.

'Can I buy you supper, or a drink or something,' he said to the floor. 'My way of apologising for the ruckus yesterday.'

'There's really no need.'

'I feel bad all the same, the scene with me and Merc. I suppose boys will be boys. I'm afraid we lack the diplomacy and finesse of your gender.'

'That's a lame excuse.'

'Yes. Sorry.' His chin sank lower onto his chest.

'Tell me another, such as why you lied to me about Beckett and the gambling ring.'

Jack's head shot up and darted from side to side. 'Shh. So Allegra's taken you for her little outing. Was it helpful?'

'Yes, you could say that.'

'And for the record, I didn't lie.'

'Sin of omission then?'

'Okay. Fair do's.'

'No doubt you have some explanation for that as well, but it'll have to wait. I'm too tired.' She closed the door.

'Tomorrow then?'

'No, I'll be busy. Good night Jack.'

CHAPTER 17

The autumn frost brought in a morning of long shadows and bright skies. The moor took on a luminescence which seemed to bring the tor within touching distance. While Freya waited outside the pub for Father Paul, the landscape presented an intensity and clarity she had not experienced before. The rhythm of sun climbing sky and wind chasing clouds, the sheer immutability of nature, filled her with a new-found hope. Though unconvinced of God's individual attention, she muttered a brief prayer of thanks for the beautiful day and that the day's unpleasant but necessary business be swift and, if not successful, at least illuminating. She had lain awake most of the night unable to find sleep for the relentless rehearsing of what she would say when the time came, her anxiety increasing with each spectre of worse-case scenarios come true.

Father Paul pulled up in front of her in his *Triumph Herald*, an ageing classic car which epitomised his character – solid, eccentric, and rather old fashioned. He wound down the window. 'Well, hello there! Glorious morning. Thought we might get a full English breakfast before we set off.' He sprang out of the car, pecked her on the cheek and ducked through the pub's entrance, his height incompatible with the shorter eighteenth-century folk it had been designed for. His immaculate clerical suit, with the flash of white at the throat, and the glinting gold pendant peeking through his shirt buttons were at odds with his grey tousled hair and gaunt face, though his warm smile contradicted any suggestion of suffering. At seventy, he displayed more energy than Freya thought she would ever have.

After captivating Susie with his effortless charm and having eaten an inordinate amount of breakfast which included two rounds of toast and two full pots of coffee, Father Paul declared himself ready to go. 'Just popping to the loo, won't be a mo.'

After five minutes had passed and he had not returned, Freya got up to investigate. She found him in the hallway looking alternately from the slott machine under the stairs to a group of photographs lining the wall opposite, as if he was a spectator at Wimbledon.

'Do you see this, Freya?' He pointed to a group photo of Susie, Jack and Merc standing smiling while Tom shook hands and congratulated another man which Freya didn't recognise. The half-face of a tanned guy just snuck into view, and a peeved looking Beckett shouldered up against a slot machine to the right of the picture. The underside of the staircase rose above them at an angle.

'Beck doesn't look too happy, does he?' She tapped the glass with her fingernail.

'And why would he. Take a look. That's a high stakes fixed-odds betting machine not your regular slot machine. We've seen no end of social problems caused by these vile things. How on earth they managed to install one here is anybody's guess. They are supposed to be strictly controlled by the government and are only licenced for betting shops.'

Freya pivoted around to look at the slot machine behind her. 'Well, it's not here now, thank God. Unfortunately, it makes absolute sense. Did you know Beckett was a gambler?'

'You know I can't answer that, old girl. I hate that label anyway, as if it defines the whole person.'

'I wish I'd seen this photo earlier. I would've known Beckett had been here all along instead of playing guessing games with these silly folk.' Their subtle betrayals had not been forgotten.

'A time for everything. Let's get going,' he said.

They took the faster, less scenic route out of Dartmoor, avoiding the hairpin bends and the narrow lanes without passing places. Even so, it still took half an hour before they rolled onto the smooth tarmac and double lanes of the A-roads where they headed southeast for the English Riviera. Traffic built up around the main coastal resorts and Freya worried they would miss their appointment with the solicitor.

'Relax,' Father Paul said in his chipper voice. 'Mr Faddon will make a point of keeping us waiting no matter what time we arrive. I see it all the time.' He took his eyes momentarily away from the road. 'He will imply he's very busy. Substitute that word for important.' The car swayed into the middle white lines of the road, and he corrected its course without fuss. 'And with it the suggestion he's doing us a big favour by interrupting far more vital work to squeeze us in at short notice. Pure psychology.' He chuckled. 'Ego's such a funny thing. Now, I think some explanations are due from you, don't you?'

Freya could hold off no longer. She relayed everything she had found out from the very beginning. She took her time, knowing Father Paul would digest every intriguing detail. His position as postulator for the beatification of saints involved a fair degree of detective work. It used to be nicknamed the Devil's Advocate. The role of sleuth suited his enquiring mind and his hunger for detail perfectly.

'You see, it's all muddled up somehow with the title deeds,' she said, summing up.

But Father Paul was ahead of her. 'So, Jack and Gil went up the hill.'

'Yes.'

'To fetch a pail of water.'

'Yes. What are you getting at?'

'Why else would Beckett have left behind the nursery rhyme note. I believe he foresaw trouble and took evasive action.'

'I was wondering about that. I thought maybe he hid the deeds out of shame because of what he'd done, losing everything in gambling then trying to clear his debts with my share of the house. I guessed he'd had a change of heart and wrote the rhyme down because, for whatever reason, he hadn't the time to go back and fetch them. I couldn't figure out why it had to be so cryptic though. Wait, are you suggesting…he hid the deeds to stop anyone getting hold of them?' Freya's voice was incredulous.

'Correct.'

'*A poisonous silence brings irritation and disdain*, that

was the flower message he left in the walled garden. I knew it! I knew he was trying to tell me something. He must have known someone was going to do the dirty on him. He was trying to guide me to the truth.'

'Perhaps, but there is the small matter of honouring a debt, gambling or no.' Father Paul pinched the top of his nose as if weary of Beckett's antics. 'Unless of course, ignoring the fact that the gambling ring was illegal, the debt was accrued under false pretences.'

'But who would...?' Freya struggled to believe that these, although imperfect people of Brohn-In-The-Moor could stoop that low. 'I can hardly think any of them would do such a thing. Perhaps Merc, at a push.' Her infatuation with him now a form of intense regret. 'Not Jack, surely?'

'Well, go with your gut instinct. There's probably a logical explanation.'

They were quiet for some minutes and Freya let her mind idle around the facts. She jolted forward. 'Oh, no. This could change everything. Might Beckett's death conclusively not be suicide after all? It might be...' she trailed off, unwilling to say the word.

Father Paul frowned, his face stern and punitive. 'Just hold on a second. Are you hinting at what I think you are? Let's be sure of the facts before we start brandishing unhelpful ideas like murder. Really, Freya. I expected better of you.'

Rebuked but undaunted, she tried again. 'Of course you'd say that. You always think the best of everyone.'

'And so should you. I like to think I know a lot about human nature, fallen as we are. Now understand this, the confessional dredges up all sorts of darkness, but it's a long journey from thought to intent, intent into action. Until we know more, we keep an open mind. Yes?'

They turned into the small car park of Faddon, Faddon and Doble and went inside. A young receptionist greeted them with a smile and the apologetic news that Mr Faddon was running late. Father Paul elbowed Freya. They were brought some tea and a plate of chocolate biscuits which Father Paul wolfed down while Freya flicked through a property magazine.

Fifteen minutes later, Mr Faddon came out of his office and greeted them. His slackened tie was nestled in an open collar too small to be done up. He was breathless, wheezy, whether through hard toil, or a reluctant five minutes on an exercise bike, Freya could only surmise. What was not in doubt was his identity. He was the same man in the photograph they saw earlier on the wall of The George and Dragon being congratulated for a win on the betting machine. Freya cast Father Paul a glance and he nodded.

Hugh Faddon led them through to his office, a characterless magnolia room with a faux leather chair and a desk devoid of any paperwork. They sat facing him in low chairs, giving the solicitor the advantage of height and superiority. Freya recalled her former employer inviting her to sit on a squat student chair whilst he himself sat atop the teacher's desk to dismiss her from her teaching post – he must have been beside himself with glee.

After the polite preliminaries, of which Father Paul performed with cheerful elegance, Freya waded straight in. 'Hypothetically speaking, how would I gift my property over to another person?'

'Ah, for that you'd need our conveyancing department,' Mr Faddon said. 'I'll arrange for you to see–'

Father Paul leaned forward. 'We're talking *gift*, not sale – no money will exchange hands. As senior partner you would of course know all the ins and outs.' He let the suggestion hang in the air.

'My mistake. As you see, I'm rushed off my feet.'

'Evidently.'

'The law has various avenues. I'll look into it. There'll be forms to sign, witnesses, guarantees of non-compulsion, especially among family members, possibly stamp duty, maybe inheritance tax. Depends who you're intending to transfer the deeds to Miss Greene.'

She had an uneasy feeling about him. His advice seemed intentionally vague. 'Well, certainly not to a family member. So, for arguments sake, let's assume it's me and I wanted to leave my house to a charity.'

'It'd be more usual to bequeath property via a will. But if you were adamant, I'd recommend you set up a trust so you can remain in the property until death. We can arrange that for you.'

'And what if I wanted Father Paul here to have my house straight away?'

Father Paul looked horrified. 'You know I couldn't accept it, hypothetically or otherwise. In theory, it would have to go to the diocese.'

'Oh, for goodness' sake, we're going around in circles.' Freya reached into her bag and pulled out the title deeds still rolled tight from having been inside Beckett's water flask. She held them up in the air as if they were a lamp which could shed light on the impasse.

'My deeds. I want to gift them to a third party who shall remain anonymous for now. Could you ask your staff to print me off the relevant forms to take away with me?'

Mr Faddon made a move toward the deeds and

Freya instinctively drew back. He studied her for a moment. Satisfied, he picked up the phone, spoke to a clerk and arranged for the paperwork to be run off immediately. He replaced the receiver, stood, and then offered out his hand by way of dismissal.

In the reception, Freya was advised by the young receptionist to collect the forms from an office on the first floor. She handed Father Paul the deeds but when she returned, he was not there. She waited a while then went outside to the car park, but his car was devoid of Father Paul. A few minutes later he arrived with the title deeds and the original transfer documents rolled up together like a baton in his hand. 'It's not often I come across a slippery character like dear Hugh Faddon, God love him. Clearly, he's lying. I thought about showing him these to gauge his reaction.' He slapped the roll on his palm. 'But in the end, and to his great disappointment, I didn't. Come on, let's get out of here.'

Once out on the road, Father Paul let out a laugh.

'What's so funny?' Freya asked.

'I've the mental image of Faddon as old Fagin in Oliver Twist, drooling over these blessed things. Couldn't wait to get his sticky fingers on them. I've a confession to make.' Freya arched a brow. 'I implied all the transfer details had already been filled in – names, witnesses, recipients, the whole caboodle – and he went for it.'

'Father!'

'I'll give myself three Hail Mary's and an Our Father as a penance.'

'So, who would be the lucky guy?' A question she had been wondering about since finding them.

'Merc, obviously. And bingo. Hugh had quoted something earlier about undue influence and coercion, so I happened to mention a certain photograph hanging on the wall in The George and Dragon. Then it was just a matter of reminding him that the said friendship might constitute a conflict of interest which the Law Society could find very interesting.'

'So, they were in it together, whatever 'it' might be. Could I be right about…you know what, after all?'

'He's slippery alright, but, no, I don't think so. They lack both the passion and the cold-heartedness for anything more than dodgy dealings. Though I'd be interested to dig a little deeper to see what else they've been getting up to.'

As they approached the coast, dark clouds tumbled in from the sea. Freya eyed them with unease. 'We could head back and miss the worst of it,' she said, her resolve to go through with the real task of why she had brought

Father Paul here in the first place, weakened. An array of legitimate excuses waited in a long line for an airing thus postponing the moment when she would come face to face with Debbie's mother and confront her own past.

'We're not sugar,' he answered. 'We won't melt. A little bit of rain didn't hurt anyone.'

'Paul, isn't it getting a bit late in the day to go visiting? Don't old people like an afternoon nap?'

'They can sleep afterwards.'

'But what about this business with Merc and Hugh? I could ask Jack what he knows? We need to get on with it before they all get talking.'

'He's unlikely to offer up anything useful. Besides, Hugh's most likely on the phone to Merc alre–'

'The phones in the village aren't working and there isn't a mobile signal,' she said, just as she remembered she had once seen Merc on his mobile in the pub.

Father Paul found a place to pull over and switched off the engine. 'Have I come all this way to help *you*, or to help Beckett, God rest his soul? Beckett, I can quite adequately pray for at home. You on the other hand, are the more pressing of the two.'

'On the other hand, I think you could be right,' he said. 'Perhaps some time to reflect…I intended to book into The George and Dragon tonight anyway. We'll resume in the morning.' He leant over to the glove compartment and took out a leather-bound breviary. 'Take it. Have a look at the page marked by the green ribbon. *Peace I leave you, my peace I give you. Do not let your hearts be troubled'*. Tomorrow we will drive out to Torquay and Paignton, and afterwards, I'd like the truth.'

'I'm scared,' she whispered.

'I know you are. Courage, old girl.' He reached up and traced a small cross on her forehead with his thumb in benediction for her weary soul.

CHAPTER 18

In the evening, Freya left Father Paul chatting to Susie in the bar of The George and Dragon and went to visit Jack. She expected to find him in the yard tinkering with some old machinery or in the stalls feeding the calves and settling them down for the night. Instead, the farm had an air of abandonment about it. The barn doors swung on their hinges, strands of hay blew like tumbleweed over the concrete yard, and tools sat discarded by the rusty hopper. She checked the calves and their water buckets and mangers – all full – at least they had been cared for. The farmhouse door had been left ajar letting in the chill of the oncoming dusk.

Freya called out for Jack, and getting no answer, went inside. A feeble and less than enthusiastic whistle came from the kettle on the stove. The lamp had not been lit, nor had the fire and it took a few moments for her eyes to adjust to the dimness. A grunt came from the direction of the sofa. She groped for the light switch and flicked it on. Jack was sprawled out with a tartan rug covering his legs and was clutching an empty whisky bottle to his chest. His chin sprouted grey stubble giving the impression of perpetual dishevelment. Startled by the light, Jack tried to sit up but flopped back, the effort being too much for his drunken body to accomplish.

'Honestly, Jack. What a state to get into.' She lifted the kettle and gave it a shake – enough for two cups of coffee – found the coffee jar, heaped two large spoonsful into Jack's one and placed it in his hand.

'No sugar,' he winced.

'He speaks. So, you're not about to die from alcohol poisoning?'

'Leave over. You sound like my life…wife. I mean wife.'

'It's freezing in here.' She knelt by the hearth to set a fire. The smell of wood smoke evoked cosy images of winter evenings snuggled up in front of it alone with Jack. Where had that thought suddenly come from? She would be leaving as soon as she had found out the truth about Beckett's death.

She built up a pyramid of paper, kindling and

small logs, the same way Beckett had shown her, then struck a match under it. The paper flared and curled as the flames took hold. The kindling didn't take long to catch and soon the fire glowed bright and emitted a golden ambience, enough for her to turn off the overhead light in favour of the softer lamplight from the side table.

'That's beller,' he said, grunting with all the temper of an angry bear. 'Thought you didn't want anything to do with the likes of me now you know I'm a lying thug.'

'I don't believe that for a second. Are you hungry?'

'Urgh, no. More whisky, over there, look.' He pointed to a painted cabinet with a trio of crystal decanters regimented in a line.

Freya poured one for herself but not for him and sat in the chair next to the fire. Even in Jack's current inebriated state, a sense of warmth towards him grew along with a willingness to forgive his subtle betrayals of silence and his boyish squabbles with Merc. There had to be a reason for his actions, and she wouldn't be fobbed off any longer. He had the information which could piece together the final days of Beckett's life. It was just a matter of waiting for him to sober up and start talking.

Jack was staring into the fire and taking tentative sips of hot coffee. At this rate, it would take all night.

Already she would have to cross the moor in the dark to get back to the inn, something she had promised Jack she would never do. She considered staying the night, helping him up to bed and sleeping herself on the sofa in front of the fire with the embers glowing in the grate. She was beginning to think of Jack's house as an icon of home, a technicolour contrast to her own sepia fortress of a terraced house waiting impassively for her return. But what would Father Paul think if she didn't get back tonight? A picture of him charming Susie and the rest of the locals came to mind. He wouldn't miss her. Most likely he had retired early to his room to recite the litany of the hours – compline if she remembered correctly. He would just think she had got back too late to say goodnight.

Freya made some sandwiches for them both despite Jack's protests – wholemeal bread filled with slabs of cheese and homemade chutney. She placed the plate next to him and though he shuddered, a few minutes later he was tucking into them with gusto.

'Is there anything you need me to do for the animals?' she asked, recalling an uncle once moaning about his chickens and Mr Fox.

'Don't think so. Oh blimey, the hens.'

'I can do it. What do I do?'

'Best I do it.' He stood, then steadied himself on

the back of the sofa. 'On second thoughts, would you mind? Torch is in the porch. Make sure they're not roosting on the calf shed roof. Shoo them down if they are.' He waved his arms as if herding an imaginary flock. 'Corn is in the barn if they give you any trouble. Shoot the bolt across when you're done.'

It was not the hens that worried her but the thought of being alone in the dark barn. Her recent escapades in the field shelter out on the moors mingled with the sinister events of Old Tramp's cabin haunted her. Dark spaces equated with trouble in her mind. She took a heroic breath. She had to do it for Jack's sake; feathers, gore and dead chickens strewn about the place in the morning would be even worse.

A moonless sky draped a dense black pall over the farm and when she stepped out from the porch, the floodlight tripped on briefly before cutting out again. She shone the torch beam over the roof and into the calf stalls looking for wayward hens. A row of blue-green cow eyes shone back at her. Some lowed their melancholy grumble, a sound deep and primordial, yet somehow familiar, as if an agrarian heritage had been written into her genes. She thought of her years teaching history: medieval man in tunics and hosiery of coarse wool, ploughs pulled by oxen, corn dolls, wassail and folk stories told by the fireside. She loved Jack for keeping alive this ancestry, that their wisdom be taught through the voices of the past.

She stopped. Loved? She *loved* Jack? She played with the possibility, dismissed it as ridiculous, then reconsidered. She'd felt comfortable with him from the beginning and able to be herself. He had been nothing but courteous, caring, concerned. Where Merc attracted with good looks and fine living, Jack presented himself with humility and patience. Merc took what he wanted, whereas Jack asked and offered. But what of the moot point, his secrecy, his lies, his sins of omission? How could she really trust him if he kept important information from her? Allegra's words came back – 'He's the good guy.' Again, there must be a good reason for his silence, and it seemed somewhat to do with compulsion and very much more to do with Merc.

The clouds parted and the moon cast a silver glow into the yard. Freya checked for hen silhouettes on the roofline and finding none, looked inside the barn. The torch swept from side to side, mopping up the darkness. She found over a dozen of them perched on the oak crossbeams and in amongst the straw bales. After deciding to leave them be, she turned to leave and for a moment thought she saw a dark shadow out of the corner of her eye. Freya hurried out of the barn, slammed the doors shut and wriggled the bolt into the stay. She didn't waste any time crossing the yard and hoped it had been nothing more than a trick of the light.

Jack had sobered a little and was clearing up the kitchen when she returned. 'Come and sit down for a minute,' he said, taking her by the hand and leading her to the sofa. She feigned protest. Though she had come to the farmhouse with the intention of getting answers, now her thoughts ambled on this new-found feeling of…whatever it was…love possibly?

'Please,' he pleaded. 'I want to say something.'

Bewildered, she sat with her hands folded in her lap.

'Freya, this thing with Beckett, I've been a hindrance, I apologise.' He rubbed the flat of his hand over his stubble and exhaled. 'What I did, I did for the best of intentions. Help comes in many guises.'

'Then tell me what I need to know.'

'I've given my word. I can't betray a *promise.*'

His stubborn pride reminded her of Beckett and all the silences he had kept. 'A promise! Jack, what the heck's been going on?'

'Steady.' He patted down the air with his palms.

'This has everything to do with Merc, hasn't it?'

Jack looked away and his mouth contorted as if he

had eaten something sour.

'Thought so. You already know Allegra told me about the gambling ring. Oh, and what else do I know? Hmm, let me see, a certain Hugh Faddon and the title deeds to mine and Beckett's parent's house.' Freya willed him to react, but he seemed not to have heard, his attention focused instead on the flames in the fireplace curling around the logs. She helped herself to another whisky and poured one out for him too. Perhaps a drunken Jack would be more willing to talk.

His gaze followed her as she crossed the room. He stood, took both the glasses and put them down on the coffee table. 'Truth will out. Trust me. Truth will out.' His concerned eyes carried the responsibility he bore for her and yet he was also smiling.

'Oh, Jack. You confuse me. I want to be angry with you, to hate you...but I don't. Tell me what to do.' She rushed at him, fists intent on pounding his chest into getting an answer but in those few steps her heart decided. She buried her face in his shirt and rested there. He remained there, tall, calm, strong, then in a gentle slow motion, he drew a hand through her hair, down to her cheek, and there let it rest. She lifted her hand to meet his, turned her head and placed a series of kisses into his palm.

He let out a low pleasurable moan. His fingers

brushed her cheek. Light and delicate strokes explored the contours of her face; eyebrows, nose, lips, his touch so gentle she could weep. A single tear slipped loose from her eye: a diamond hanging on the tip of her lashes. His thumb lingered there, soaked up the sorrow and placed it to his own lips. She trembled.

'You're cold,' he whispered.

'I'm–' she searched for the word to reflect these new feelings. 'I'm nervous.'

'I'll look after you.' He kissed her forehead, enfolded her in his arms.

She was motionless, her mind engaged in battle; her past or future, being true to her atonement or allowing herself the undeserved luxury of happiness? Her teeth chattered and Jack reached for the throw from the sofa and draped it around her.

'Thank you.' Her voice sounded far off. 'Jack, this can't be. There's something…I've done.' She could hardly bear to say it. 'I'm not who you think I am, not who you want me to be.'

'No…don't *We know what we are. But know not what we may be.*' He sat her down on the sofa and fussed with the throw around her.

'Quoting Shakespeare is only making this harder for me,' she sighed.

'Then I'll make it easy. I know you Freya Greene and you deserve to be happy. And thanks to you, I see that I do too. I've got to put Rigby behind me–'

'You don't know everything about me.'

'Here's the thing. I do.' His eyes seemed to penetrate her soul. 'You need to put Debbie behind you too. You can't go on wasting–'

'What?' Freya said. 'How do you…?' Her world collapsed around her. 'No one knows what really happened. Not even Beckett.'

'Believe me, he did. The poor guy got drunk one night drowning his sorrows after some heavy losses. Merc didn't help. Kept the whisky flowing. That's what he does, plies them with drink. Loosens their tongues to get the upper hand. Knowledge is power so they say.'

Confusion mixed up the words until they swirled into one another. He was talking about her, then Beckett, but all she was hearing was Merc. An invisible vice seemed intent on squeezing every ounce of breath from her. 'Slow down, Jack,' she panted.

Jack squeezed her hand and gave a consolatory smile. 'Beckett let it slip that you'd…that you killed your friend Debbie, when you were just a kid.'

Her eyelids clanked shut with the finality of a jail door. It had now been said and could not be unsaid, as if this alone had somehow chained it to fact – irretrievable, damning, real. Jack said something else. Why was he still talking? Why was the world still turning?

'You were just a *kid*, Freya, for God's sake. There must've been some sort of mix up. We all get confused when we're little. Beckett was beside himself next the morning when he realised what he'd gone and done, that he had broken your secret.'

Freya stood, stumbled toward the door, grabbed her coat, and ran.

CHAPTER 19

The clouds parted and a silver thread of a path wound its way through the dark moorland, over the sodden grass and the depleted heather, upwards towards the jutting granite of Margin Tor, and beyond into the black heart of the night. Like a somnambulist lost in a dream, Freya staggered forwards, her eyes fixed on the glistening track in front of her, caring only that she ran as far away as possible from the fantasy that Jack had created. The bright moon lay down a harsh frost underfoot. She shivered, her windcheater useless against the cold.

After some time wandering, she saw that the tor ahead was unfamiliar, not the thumping fist of Margin Tor, but a sharp stack of rugged boulders thrusting out of the earth in a well-defined defiant peak that she had not seen before. As she approached, the path skirted off to the right, down the hill and toward a large barn with a roof bright in the moonlight. It mattered little that this landscape was new terrain, for wasn't her life now a new terrain – unexplored and hostile?

The cold sank into her small body by degrees until she could bare it no longer. The instinct for survival refused to be silent no matter how much she wished she could join Beckett in the grave. Her broken spirit gave in to her weak flesh and the barn ahead became an irresistible temptation.

The huge heavy doors opened into a cathedral-like space with a wooden cruck vaulted ceiling befitting an ancient tithe barn. Dust swirled in the moonbeams spilling in from the ill-fitting roof tiles above. On each side of a central atrium haybales were stacked in tall columns soaring toward the beams. Freya stepped forward into the heart of the barn, her moonlit shadow elongated in front of her. The sounds of the moor faded away and an expectant silence descended. Suddenly the barn door slammed behind her. The comfort of her shadow disappeared. One step more and she was standing centre-stage in a shaft of moonbeams. The play began.

A dark figure scuttled in the wings to the right. Stage-left, a girl wearing a school blazer tip-toed past her oblivious to her older self, observing, judging, and stoic with resignation. Freya could no longer run from her past as she had from Jack, and from Duncan, and all the other graces that would have made her life complete. *Conscience betrays guilt.* Sin had consequences. And her guilt lay near to that old disused railway signal box.

Old Tramp's Cabin had always been a place of excited fear, a place where older kids drank contraband and told horror stories to the wide moon faces of the gullible younger ones, where they came of age on piles of dirty blankets and stacks of sticky magazines. To young Freya, it was a place of chicken and dare, where initiation rites required night-time excursions on Halloween. And finally, where tempers frayed and evil triumphed.

The young Freya tip-toed towards Debbie, her breath held, eyes narrowed, arms outstretched and ready to pounce, sneering at the sheer ease of it. Debbie suddenly lurched forward, not a sitting duck then but a renegade hunter dragging Freya down onto the filthy floor. 'You're such a bitch!' she hissed, slapping Freya hard in the face. 'That's a present from Beckett. And this is from me.' Her claws scraped down Freya's cheek.

She flinched, her eyes smarting from both the pain and the welled-up sense of inexcusable betrayal that Debbie could do such a thing – her best friend in all the world.

In the resulting brawl Freya held her own, was underneath, gained ground, then on top and astride her again, fighting off Debbie's flailing arms, all the while spewing out hatred and spittle. 'S'all your fault. You should've told me about the bishop. You watched me make a complete idiot of myself and you didn't even say nothing – on purpose! Now McGann's gonna be on my case all the time. Should've been you that got that detention. And Kev's Valentine card was meant for me not you. You knew I fancied him. You stole him from me. And you've taken Beck from me and goddamn nearly killed him!'

'Gerr'off me.' Debbie arched her back and heaved Freya off then clambered on top of her. 'You're just jealous coz nobody likes you. I only hung with you coz I felt sorry for you. The others are right, you're just a fleabag cow.'

Debbie shoved at Freya's forehead with the palm of her hand. There was a dull audible thud as Freya's head hit the floor. Then she grabbed a handful of hair and yanked. The unmistakable crackle of hair being wrenched from scalp mingled with Freya's scream. This seemed to satisfy Debbie, and with a triumphant smile she scrambled off, sent an unnecessary kick into Freya's side and fled.

Freya lay there dazed for a moment. A rising fury consumed her, as if a wild animal had taken over and destroyed all sense of what it meant to be herself. Now, ferocious, violent and with the energy of a beast, she sprang up and out of the cabin in pursuit of her prey.

In the barn the moonbeams which had so generously illustrated the memory show disappeared and left Freya in a world not of bleak darkness, but of helpful illumination. If she had the temptation to justify her actions – an eye for an eye, a tooth for a tooth – she did not. No excuses. The fact remained; she had succumbed to rage and Debbie ended up dead, no matter how much the preceding fight at Old Tramp's Cabin had been a fair one. Shaking, Freya reached for her pocket torch and switched it on. The barn, returned now to its normal state, appeared benign, neutral. Just as she was contemplating what she should do next, Beckett strode into the torch beam from the dark haystack columns to the right. His hands were thrust into his pockets and his windcheater was casually undone. He stopped and turned to face her. 'Who's scared now?' he said and with a slow shake of his head, faded away.

A screech owl cried out in the hollow frost of the night and Freya shuddered. Yes, she was scared for sure, but the question inferred someone else had also been scared – Beckett. It all made sense, the incident on the boat when he seemed terrified of her, his nightmares and his pitiful digging into the bedclothes trying to bury something – to bury her wicked secret. And all the while, since that day in the park, he had been afraid of her. The question she had refused to ask him back at The Byre had been this. He saw her as a murderer.

She stared into the empty space Beckett left behind. Everything was a sham. Her thinking all this time that they had an unshakeable bond fashioned not just from familial ties, but from unconditional and mutual trust and admiration, when in truth she had taken his love for granted and a wielded power over him which ultimately crushed him. What kind of sister would do such a thing? *Monster!*

His cryptic flower message had said, '*In death there is mourning, but a poisonous silence brings irritation and disdain. Justice comes from dying to oneself. I offer you encouragement, patience, and energy in adversity. I hope this brings you success. Farewell, my dearest sister.*'

Revelation came late. All this time she thought the message had been to encourage her on her quest to find out the truth about his death. She had not considered the other interpretation – his direct challenge for her to face her own past and the damage she had done. He had brought her here to sort it out once and for all. Did she have the courage to do just that? Undeniably, she had begun the process by asking Father Paul to find out a few things for her and yes, she had intended to see it through but the whole sorry business with the house deeds, the intrigue around Merc and that rogue solicitor Faddon had thrown her off task. And she willingly allowed herself to become distracted, knowing full well she had procrastinated for far too long. The slumbering dragon of self-knowledge now resurfaced to accuse her – *Coward!*

Freya's heart bled a little more and carrying on seemed all but impossible. Even so, the tiniest whisper of hope broke through and unbidden, grace entered. Empty and open-handed, Freya whispered a simple prayer, *I'm so sorry, Lord. Help me!*

CHAPTER 20

The road leading away from the moor sparkled with midnight frost. Freya had no idea whether she was heading in the direction of Brohn-In-The-Moor, Stannaton or Exeter, but so long as she kept going it didn't matter, any town would do and from there she could set about putting things right in her own life. Solving the mystery of Beckett's death could wait for now.

She walked with purpose, conviction, straight backed and arms swinging as a soldier marching to war. After half an hour a car rumbled some distance away and she paid little attention to it even as it got closer, slowed and illuminated the road ahead of her with its headlights. She held her steady march, neither curious nor afraid of who might be following. When the road widened, the car manoeuvred to her left and matched her pace. A few metres later the driver wound down the window, stuck an arm out and bid her stop.

Father Paul's face shone pale and worried in the moonlight. 'Will you please stop?' he called. When she continued walking, he stopped his little *Triumph Herald*, hopped out, lent back against it with folded arms, and waited.

She glanced over her shoulder and stopped. 'How did you know?' she sighed.

'I was worried when you didn't come back and phoned Jack.'

'But the phone lines are down.'

'Evidently not. Jack said there had been a misunderstanding and you had taken off over the moors. He would have followed you but the drink and driving, you know. He wanted to say sorry and asked to start again.'

'He had no right getting you involved.'

'My dear girl, it is past midnight, minus five out here, and what's more, you do know you're barely half a mile from where you started? You'd be going round in circles all night if I hadn't found you.'

Here on Dartmoor, it seemed to be a reoccurring theme; to be lost and in need of finding. She thought of Jack's folklore story told in the cosy atmosphere of the

George and Dragon to a grateful crowd lapping up his old wisdom. Foolish Fitzford destined to wander the moor for all eternity unless he finds the well to break the curse, or simply turns his coat inside out. Well, she was doing that all right.

'Paul, I've got this.'

'There's nothing wrong in asking for help.'

'I know, and I have.'

'How do you know I'm not the answer to your prayer.'

Freya gave an ironic smile despite herself. 'Too corny, even for you.'

'At least you smiled.'

'You can't imagine.'

Father Paul approached and gently took hold of her shoulders. 'Come on! Come with me. There's something I want you to see.'

Despite her objections she followed him back to the car where he threw a tartan rug over her and started up the engine. 'It's just up here.' A three-point turn later, they were heading back along the road from which they had just come. He pulled over onto a gravel ledge where the land fell away and the night sky, velvet dark and strewn with stars, swallowed the landscape.

'Freya, look. Heaven's so close you can almost

touch it,' he whispered, his ageing eyes taking on a fresh glow as if wonder be the fountain of youth. 'Now try telling me we are alone when each moment is radiant with beauty. Independence can be a good thing, mostly, until one becomes an island. Beware then of the freak tide that overwhelms the shore. I often wondered about the disciple in the garden who ran away naked as Jesus was arrested. Naked! Of all the details, why naked? Then it occurred to me. *We* are that disciple. When it comes to it, when we abandon Him, we are all downright naked and alone.'

Correction at any age hits hard and if it were not for his utter gentleness, Freya would have gotten straight back out of the car.

'You're preaching Father.'

Father Paul's brows knitted together. It had been a long time since she called him Father – a blow struck to their friendship. 'And for the record, it wasn't me who did the abandoning.'

'Are you sure about that?'

She flashed hot, flustered, uncomfortable. His words pierced and twisted, slicing through the armour she forged for herself so long ago. In truth, it was not God who had the monopoly on abandonment, she did. Poor Beckett. Poor Duncan. Poor, poor Debbie and now Jack.

After a while, Father Paul sighed into the stillness.

'I want to tell you something, something it took me a long time to admit. Years back when I was a young priest keen to make a name for myself, I got ahead of myself. I was so pompous and arrogant, cavalier even. I thought I had my life sorted. I was doing well, my peers sang my praises, my work was getting noticed. Then disaster! It didn't end well.'

'Paul, with respect, I hardly think a few spiritual struggles and an inflated ego are a matter of life and death.' Even as the first words escaped, she watched on horrified as the petulant child within took control of her mouth. How much more could she sabotage their friendship? The due apology locked in her throat.

He made a sudden sideways movement and she thought he was going to fling open the passenger door and demand she get out. Instead, he tipped forward into the footwell and drew out a thermos flask from the bashed-up leather bag he took everywhere with him. 'I forgot,' he said, holding up the trophy. He poured steaming tea into the little plastic cup and placed it in her shaking hands. 'Should thaw you out a bit,' he muttered.

The tea, sweetened with sugar but nevertheless welcome, revived and cajoled her back to her senses. 'Sorry,' she said.

'I am not immune to hurt, Freya. Now, shall I continue?' She nodded. 'It was back in the early eighties when stock market money set the tone. The whole continent seemed obsessed with the dream of success and power – cars, music, decadence. There was an air of unrestrained confidence in this idealised thing called lifestyle. The seminary had prepared me for pastoral life but not for my own ambition. I'd set my sights on Rome and all the cosmopolitan and artistic life it would bring, more precisely, on working for the Congregation for the Causes of Saints. I thought nothing of frequently hoping on a plane over to the Vatican or wherever, under the pretext of investigating various spiritual phenomena.'

On the one hand, Freya could imagine him fitting very nicely into the Rome-set with all his endearing affectations, but on the other, he was such a down-to-earth, compassionate person that he would see through superficiality in an instant. He cared about souls, not outside appearances. Maybe it was just that quality which suited his postulator role now. He could spot a fake a mile away. As for herself, she thought spiritual phenomena were the result of an overactive imagination. 'Even with faith I wouldn't believe those silly stories,' she told him.

'Oh, some were convincing alright, others were just plain wacky. 'Ha!' Father Paul chuckled. 'I've had my share of crying statues and toast with the face of Christ burnt onto it. I've had my pet projects too – an interesting case involving little miracles, accelerated sanctity, an amulet necklace, and a statue of Our Lady of Walsingham.'

'Sounds like you're leading up to another joke.'

'Unfortunately, not a joke this time,' he said with gravity. 'I came across the necklace, this one to be precise'. He delved under his collar and retrieved a gold locket which glinted in the moonlight. 'This was in an archive box in the Vatican library. The label simply said '*Sanctus Plasmator*' – Saint Maker. Curiosity got the better of me. The emblem was uncannily similar to the one I'd seen on a statue at the shrine in Walsingham. I thought perhaps I could re-unite it. Or maybe I had a mind to test its claims. Either way, I kept it.'

'Paul, you didn't?' Freya arched her brows.

'My dear, one can justify anything if one has a mind to. It hadn't even been catalogued and there were so many artifacts just sitting there gathering dust. About this time, I was seeing a young Italian woman to give her spiritual direction. It was soon apparent that it should have been her giving *me* spiritual direction, not the other way round. Ah, Maria, such a beautiful woman in all respects.'

'I'm not sure I want to hear anymore. Such a night of revelations!' Freya considered the consequences. Paul, a self-declared thief, albeit a Robin Hood returning the locket to its rightful place perhaps, or a fallen angel willing to have his head turned at the first beauty to come his way. She didn't want to think about it, she needed him to be who she thought he was.

'If you have quite finished putting me on a pedestal, I'll explain. She had a unique gift; to make one feel special, as if one were valuable, loved. And I loved her. I say 'loved' not because I was in love with her, at least I didn't think so, but because of the inadequacies of the English language. Knowing her felt like a religious experience. She epitomised beauty and love. I gave *her* the locket because she was worthy of it.'

Father Paul fell silent, and Freya felt again the strange tug of hallowedness on this ancient moor. Who was she to judge on love when for all accounts she had neither known nor given real love?

'What happened?' she asked tentatively.

'Perhaps the locket worked its magic. She grew in sanctity. But where there is light, darkness follows. It settled upon her poor unstable husband. He took to getting all sorts of crazy ideas, drove himself quite insane. And there was a child, a sweet boy of about six who became the focus of his father's madness. He was convinced the child would somehow, someday destroy him. Of course, we took the chap to all the right psychiatrists, had the psychology reports done and they

declared him mentally fine. He was extremely good at…'
Father Paul struggled for the word.

'Gaslighting?'

'Yes, that's it, gaslighting. Because of what was happening to Maria, and possibly because of the 'saint maker' locket, in time I *knew* it had to be demonic possession and an exorcism was needed. My mistake was in thinking I could do it on my own. I didn't seek the bishop's permission. Predictably, the chap ran rings around me… He ended up killing Maria and turning the gun on himself…So, you must let people in, old girl!

'And the boy?' Freya asked wide-eyed.

'Felix, he survived, grew to be a fine man. You'd like him.'

'Thank goodness. Did you find out if the locket had special powers?'

'Ah, now that's a story for another day.'

'It wasn't your fault, you know.' Freya leant over and kissed Father Paul on the cheek. There were echoes of her conversation with Jack and the plight of poor Rigby.

'No, indeed. I am not responsible for his actions, but I didn't help matters either. It is as it is, and events cannot be changed. What elevates us is our willingness to accept our failures, learn from them and grow, don't you agree?

CHAPTER 21

Dreams came in waves, bizarre and surreal, carrying Freya on eagle's wings high over the moors. Her soundless screams of protest were unheeded by the creature, its talons gripping ever tighter, crushing the breath from her. Then without warning she found herself falling, falling, arms flailing and body spiralling down, down toward an ancient tor. Then she was sitting on a boulder watching on passively as a frightened little boy clung to a young Father Paul, a mass of blood and gore at their feet, and men in dark uniforms ushering them away from the supine bodies. There among them she saw the lifeless eyes of Beckett staring up at her.

More than once she woke confused and sleep-paralysed, sweat beading her forehead and soaking through her hair. It took a few moments to come to, only for drowsiness to lure her back into her fretful dreams. Dawn came with relief and Freya threw herself into the shower to wash away the fogginess of the night.

She found Father Paul in the bar sitting by the fire with a pot of tea and a newspaper. He raised his eyes above his reading spectacles. 'My dear, you do look rough!'

'Just what a lady wants to hear.'

'Come, sit down, sit here. Have some tea.'

Susie brought over more tea and took their order for a full English breakfast – bacon, eggs, sausages, mushrooms, beans, with black pudding just for Father Paul. They discussed the day's itinerary. The plan was to head to Torquay first to a care home with the dubious name of *Heaven's Gate*, mainly because it was nearer and if they struck lucky, they would be back in time for lunch. The other was slightly further away in Paignton with the rather more sensible name of *The Elms*.

'How will I know for sure it's Debbie Monkcombe's mum?' Freya asked. 'It's been so long… seems like a lifetime ago.'

Father Paul considered for a moment. 'Well, if the years haven't been kind to her, and her memory is all muddled, we'll just have to pray for a sign. Do I detect a note of scorn coming from across the table?'

'Since when has God answered any of my prayers?'

'Let's just see.'

'Freya, love,' Susie interrupted as she set down the cutlery and condiments, 'I think he's telling you to have faith. Wouldn't do any harm now would it? Helped me with the flood and everything. I've still got my pub, haven't I?' She gave a self-satisfied smile and headed to the kitchen. In amongst the crashing of pans and the clinking of cutlery being loaded into the dishwasher, they caught snippets of her in a one-sided conversation presumably putting in the day's food order over the phone – *keep on ice, old trout,* and *picking up fresh samphire while you're about it.*

Father Paul ignored the white finger signpost pointing the way off the moor and to Stannaton, and instead took the opposite road toward Margin Tor. It took until the road rumbled into a track for Freya to notice what was happening, her thoughts being so pre-occupied with rehearsing the conversation she would have with Debbie's mother in a short while. 'You've gone the wrong way,' she said.

'Debatable, old girl,'

'No, I'm sure. This just leads up to the tor and Jack's– Oh!'

'He cares for you.'

'He cares for the drink.'

'Freya!'

'Sorry. That was uncalled for. Sorry Jack,' she murmured to the ether. 'I'm struggling with all this.'

'Will you ever let go?'

Their car pulled into the yard and as Jack rushed out to meet them the flutter of a little bird sang in her heart. He threw open the car door, pulled Freya into his arms and without resistance, she buried her face into his shirt and sighed with gratitude, a homecoming of sorts.

Jack insisted on making a pot of tea and when Father Paul excused himself for the loo, Jack reached across the table and took her hand.

'We're none of us perfect,' he began, 'I've messed up. You made me see there is no point in moping, it's time to move on. I know a good thing when it comes my way, and by God, you're a good thing. Just say yes.'

'Jack…I don't know…I want to but…' She searched their entwined hands for certainty.

'But I've been untruthful. I know that. It was for the best of reasons, but stupid. Come sailing with me tomorrow. Weather's going to be perfect. I'll bring a picnic, a bottle of wine.' Freya gave a playful frown. 'Point taken, elderflower cordial then, and I'll come clean. You'll get the whole story, start to finish, no-holds-barred.'

The journey's end seemed as tangible as a rainbow

and yet just as elusive. Would the truth about Beckett's death finally be revealed by Jack? A shiver of dread ran through her and she questioned whether she really wanted her almost perfect image of Beckett to be sullied by unpleasant facts. What if it were undoubtably suicide, could she come to terms with that and lose hope of him in heaven? Or what if he were part of Merc and Faddon's exploits? Or if Jack was, too? After awakening her heart, she didn't want the pain of loss twice.

Father Paul hovered at the kitchen doorway before he chose his moment. 'In a spirit of decisiveness Jack, she'll be at the quayside tomorrow at eleven. Now time to go, Freya.'

Freya eyed-up the building from the roadside and grimaced, her already knotted stomach griped in protest. *Heaven's Gate* was a purpose-built care home in a 1970s housing estate on the outskirts of Torquay, set apart from the touristy seafront some two miles away. The flat-roofed building with its pebbled-dashed walls and disproportionately wide windows gave off a despondent institutional feel to anyone unfortunate enough to find themselves on its threshold and in need of such care. Father Paul showed no such reluctance and bounded up the path with all the enthusiasm of a puppy expecting to be fussed over. And as soon as the door was answered by a young Filipino nurse, he was. On seeing his clerical collar, she ushered them inside with a joviality quite in contrast to the dull exterior. Freya and Father Paul sat in the waiting room on high-back vinyl chairs while the nurse fussed over finding them some tea and biscuits.

'It's like the dentist,' Freya said. The lavender scent of old ladies' linen cupboards mingled with an antiseptic undertone giving the perfect balance of pathos, all that was and all that is yet to be. She recalled a scripture passage that even as a child she thought too sad, *when you are old you will stretch out your hand and someone will lead you where you do not wish to go*. And Freya would rather be anywhere else than here.

After the manager had attended to some minor mishap in the dining room, he approached them with an outstretched hand and a broken cup and saucer in the other.

'Excuse the mess,' he said, glancing at the dark stain sinking down his trouser leg. 'Occupational hazard, I'm afraid. At least it's only tea.' He insisted on giving them the guided tour – *here's the dining room, the games room cum library – not used as much as hoped despite the large print books, the TV lounge – much more popular!* The residents' bedrooms along the top corridor were small single bedded affairs with hoist and commode paraphernalia and a regulation floral bedspread that matched the curtains. They were led to a room on the south side where a bird-like figure plucked pilling fabric from the arm of a well-loved chair.

'You've got some more visitors, Doris. Aren't you the popular one?' he said with an exaggerated volume. Her head snapped in his direction where upon, despite the Parkinson's disease that rendered all smooth movement impossible, she fixed a determined stare at him. 'It is *Mrs Monkcombe* to you, young man. Do call the manager for me, I have been waiting for the taxi for hours. My son is expecting me home soon, don't you know.'

'As you very well know, I *am* the manager.' Then aside to them, 'It's her little game she plays when she feels she isn't getting enough attention. And there isn't a taxi coming. Her family left her here six months ago and haven't visited since. Have they Doris?' he ended loudly.

Mrs Monkcombe seemed so small and fragile that Freya almost willed her to be Debbie's mum so she could visit again and take on the role of a dutiful loving replacement daughter. But Debbie's mum she was not. This Mrs Monkcombe bore not a hint of the vague recollections Freya had of a tall chic lady with a keen sense of style, a chignon bun, and the most elegant hands she had ever seen. Even as a child, she envied those beautiful nail-polished fingers, and despite her attempts to emulate them with cheap coloured varnish from the market, she never did manage to come even close. Debbie however, along with her perfect seagull-wing brows, carried the look effortlessly even with the most cheap and garish of colours.

Freya pulled on Father Paul's arm. 'She isn't Debbie's mum,' she whispered. 'Her fingers are all wrong.'

'Her poor hands are riddle with arthritis!'

'She's too small.'

'Everyone shrinks.'

'It's not her.'

'Alright, if you say so. Let's make our excuses and go.'

'Can't you do anything for her? Bless her or something.'

'My dear girl, as if I would leave without doing so.'

The manager had been distracted with the resetting of the reclining chair remote control Mrs Monkcombe had muddled by pressing all the buttons at the same time. 'She did this earlier,' he said, 'when the two solicitor chappies called in. It's like buses, no visitors for ages then two lots come along at once.'

Freya was about to ask but Father Paul beat her to

it. 'Solicitors you say. You don't happen to recall their names do you by any chance?'

'Gil and Gladden, Haddon, something like that.'

'Faddon?'

'Yes. Nice chaps.'

Freya and Father Paul locked eyes. Now there was no denying it, Faddon and Merc were working together. The scene in Faddon's office over the deeds had almost confirmed the link between the two of them and Beckett anyway. But what would that have to do with *her* past? It couldn't be a mere coincidence, could it? No prizes for guessing who alerted them to Mrs Monkcombe and her whereabouts – Susie!

'They bought some lovely flowers.' He nodded over to a red and orange arrangement shoved into a glass vase. Freya's conscience twinged, she should have thought to bring a gift and now it was doubtful they would have time to buy anything for the next Mrs Monkcombe.

The genteel atmosphere of *The Elms* could not have been more of a contrast. The row of Victorian villas along the seafront road on which it stood gave off an air of confidence which only those steadfast industrialists could impart, and which Freya always made sure she drew attention to in her history lessons. From the fancy gables to the ornate ironwork porch, the colourful encaustic tiles in the entrance hall, to the intricate cornicing on the ceiling, no detail had been spared.

'This is more like it,' Freya said as she stood in reception with a bunch of garage-bought flowers waiting for the receptionist to finish her phone call.

'Hmm…book and cover. Need I say more?

'I'm not a snob.'

'No,' Father Paul agreed flatly. 'There is nothing wrong with beauty, indeed it is to be sought. However, I spend an awful lot of time in these places, believe me, even the fanciest of them can be as grim as a workhouse. Thankfully, most aren't.'

'We ought to sign in,' Freya said spotting the visitor's book. She looked down the list for that day. 'Oh no. They've beaten us to it.'

Father Paul checked for good measure. 'Gil & Faddon, Family Solicitors. What's their game I wonder?'

Sunlight streamed through the French windows of Mrs Monkcombe's elegant ground floor room. A vase of pink lilies filled the room with rich scents of vanilla, jasmine and cloves which momentarily overwhelmed Freya and she needed to steady herself on the door frame. Unaffected, Father Paul strode towards the silhouetted figure sitting enjoying the views of the garden.

'My dear lady, how wonderful to meet you,' he said crouching to her level.

Awoken from her daydream, she turned and smiled. Freya gasped. This was definitely her, Mrs Monkcombe, the same long hair swept back into a chignon bun albeit now white with age, the same elegant facial features despite the ravages of time engraving a network of lines upon her face as beautiful as any etchings on a crystal glass, the same graceful hands painted with a hint of pink nail polish – without a doubt Debbie's mother. And now that she knew for sure, there was no more time for an imagined reunion with a perfect script of contrition and forgiveness. Gritty, shabby awkward reality awaited. With her Gethsemane moment upon her, Freya's resolve momentarily faltered. Wouldn't her revelation destroy any peace which Mrs Monkcombe had found over the years? She looked happy, peaceful. Why disturb her winter days on this earth with the tragedy of that other day such a long time ago? And mightn't the shock kill her, she was very old after all? There had been too much death, death was the robber of friends, family, hope, joy, present and future. Why risk another death?

Freya shook her thoughts away; *a poisonous silence brings irritation and disdain.* Mrs Monkcombe deserved the truth, and the truth would set her free, even if the implications of what she was about to say could have personal repercussions for herself beyond anything imaginable – police, trial, jail? But the deed had to be done; *justice comes from dying to oneself.* Without further hesitation, Freya approached Debbie's mother and knelt at her feet.

'You won't remember me Mrs Monkcombe, it was a long time ago.'

Her opaque eyes struggled to see, and she lifted Freya's chin and turned her face to the light of the window. Her jaw jabbered in silent practice while she worked up to speech. 'Ah yes Cynthia, I remember you. You are the pretty one.' She brushed a lock of hair from Freya's face with a quavering hand. 'So very pretty.'

A wave of affection came over Freya and she took Mrs Monkcombe's frail hand in her own. 'I always thought Debbie was the pretty one.'

'No, my dear, Debra was not blessed with looks and certainly was not one of my bridesmaids. I was quite definite I did not want *her.* And she was far too large for the dresses and besides, she was already married to Fred so would have to be the matron of honour and I had already asked Pam.'

'Mrs Monkcombe, I'm Freya, Debbie's friend.'

'Freya, you say? I don't remember the name. I know all of Debra's friends and she hates being called

Debbie, though I quite like it. We were all in the youth club together. Oh, the dances we went to. I was quite something you know, with the quick step and the waltzes, the Big Band Sound, and the Swing. We had so much fun, such good times. I can't think why we stopped going.'

Freya tried again. 'No, not Debra, Debbie your *daughter*. You remember?' In her mind she added – *you have to remember!* Mrs Monkcombe wore the far-off expression of one lost in the loops of dementia time. Father Paul laid a hand on Freya's shoulder and squeezed in commiseration.

'A daughter? Goodness me, not yet. Michael is still away at sea but when he gets back, God-willing children will come along.'

Freya offered up the limp garage-shop flowers they had rushed to buy. 'These are for you. Yes, it was a lovely wedding, Deidre. I was so pleased to be your bridesmaid. You were the most beautiful of all brides.'

Mrs Monkcombe grew in her chair as a radiant smile illuminated her face. 'Let me give you something.'

'No, there is really no need,' Freya protested.

'But I would like to. See that cupboard over there,' she pointed with a slender finger. 'There is a box on the top shelf. Could you get it down for me?' Freya retrieved the box and placed it in her lap. 'Ah, this is the one,' Mrs

Monkcombe said, retrieving a small rattling box from inside. 'There, you have it, dear. I cannot recall where I got it from.' She pressed it into Freya's hesitant hand.

Freya already knew what it was without looking. She opened her fingers to a plastic rosary tub with the gold indented image of Our Lady on the lid and the words *Our Lady of Perpetual Sorrows*. Freya's had been pink, this one was white, the sign of purity – Debbie's. She turned it over and found the scratched markings of Debbie's initials on the bottom etched out with a compass point in their maths lesson. She opened the lid. Small white beads coiled around a crucifix. They were cute, reassuring, innocent. 'Thank you. I shall treasure it always,' she said with sincerity.

There was a knock at the door and a care worker popped her head round, 'Here's the papers I guess you came for. I thought they said they were sending someone round to pick them up this afternoon. Bit early but never mind. Deidre said she's signed them. I've rung and left a message on the answer machine like they instructed.'

'Yes dear. I signed them just as they said to,' Mrs Monkcombe added. 'I liked the Scottish one, quite dishy. If I was not already married…' she gave a giggle and Freya joined in, only too aware of Merc's charms herself.

Father Paul took the papers and rifled through

them. 'We need to go, old girl. Time is of the essence.'

'But Paul, I haven't done what I've come to do.'

'That is as may be, but the task is futile. You will only confuse her more. It would be a mercy to spare her.' He turned to the elderly woman. 'Now, permit me to give a blessing for the blushing bride.' He raised his hand in benediction, '*May the Lord bless you and keep you, may His face shine upon you and be gracious to you, in the name of the Father, the Son and the Holy Spirit. Amen.* My dear lady unfortunately we must go now.'

In the corridor Freya quizzed him about the rush. 'If it wasn't for your charm, I'd say you were almost rude.'

'Rude but necessary. Here, read this.' He shoved the papers into her hand. The thick cartridge paper, no doubt chosen to give a sense of officiality and timeless trust, had the purple solicitor header of *Faddon, Faddon & Doble*, and underneath the subject title, *Intention to Pursue Legal Remedies*. She scanned down. Amongst the sentences she caught the gist of it *Civil Action, Plaintiff: Mrs Deidre Monkcombe, Respondent: Miss Freya Greene; Pursuit of damages relating to death of Debbie Monkcombe on 14th February 1977; Deprivation of family life and enjoyment; Sum of £400,000,* etcetera. The other paper expressed terms of engagement for pursuing the claim on her behalf and in the very small print at the bottom of the page their astronomical 50%

fees (with provision for them both to receive 25% each as separate companies) of all damages granted prior to legal costs. Freya's knees buckled and Father Paul needed to scoop her up under the arms and lead her to a chair before she collapsed.

'I half expected something like this,' he said, 'though they were quick off the mark by anyone's reckoning. I think this necessitates a thorough explanation, don't you?'

In all the help he had freely offered her over the last few months, Father Paul had not once asked nor expected to be given the details of what it was that bothered her conscience, and for this she was grateful.

'Give yourself a minute. I'll be waiting in the car.' He took out a purple stole from his bag and held it up. 'Under the circumstances, this may be helpful though it is for you to decide.'

'I don't need to decide. I've been waiting all my life for this invitation and yet dreading it.'

'The invitation has been there all along, you need only to have taken it.'

'I know, I know…I've always chickened out in the confessional. And now here it is, but do we have time? Merc and Faddon know we are on to them and will be plotting a countermove.'

'Freya, old girl, we are talking about the creator of time. All things will unfold as it should be.'

CHAPTER 22

After a few minutes of reflection, Freya returned to the car and found Father Paul absorbed in his breviary with the stole draped around his neck and a wooden crucifix propped up on the dashboard. She sat in the passenger seat, avoided his eyes, and instead concentrated on Debbie's rosary entangled between her fingers. She snatched a few reassuring breaths and with her trembling hands settled in prayer, she began. 'Bless me Father, for I have sinned. It's been–'

'It doesn't matter, you are here now. Try and relax. The Lord is present and already knows your heart.'

'Oh Paul, it is not so much Him I'm worried about.'

'Then it is me. I am an obstacle.'

'I don't want to lose you.'

'If I judge you harshly, it is my sin, not yours. I ask only that you pray for me.'

She was amazed at his humility and kindness. A life without his friendship would be a great loss indeed. Perhaps the task might be easier with a stranger but if she had really believed that she would already have confessed. She took a deep breath and continued. As she retold her story her mind cleared as if a path opened through the forest and led to a sun dappled glade where refreshment awaited. However hard the admission of her wrongdoings – the shameful picture of her worst self-laid bare in all its evil – through even this a sense of relief and peace beckoned. The words fell as autumn leaves rocking gently to the ground. Father Paul received those words with neutral acceptance. He nodded his encouragement. Then she faltered.

'Take courage, go on.'

'Debbie left the cabin and I followed. No, I *chased* her. I was sure she had ruined my life, stolen my brother and my stupid valentine. She'd punched, kicked and pummelled me, and at the time I wanted to kill her, really kill her. I hated her!' Even saying those words aroused those terrible feelings. 'I was enraged. It felt as if a beast had truly taken possession of me. But I will not credit the devil when the responsibility is mine alone.' She closed her eyes in disgust. The events played out in her mind. She was twelve again and reliving every rotten detail. '*I see Debbie ahead of me, her long fair hair flowing behind her while my own is dishevelled. Bloodied tuffs of it are lying back on the cabin floor where she wrenched them from my scalp. My side hurts from the kicking she gave me.*' Involuntarily Freya rubbed the ribs on her right side. '*I want to get hold of her, smash her face in, gouge out those mocking eyes, rip off those seagull brows, make it so no one will ever fancy her again. I want to tear the school down, have Mr McGann suffer something horrible like a heart attack or some terrible accident so he can never make anyone look stupid again. And I want to shove the bishop's ring into his fat ugly face.*

I run with unearthly speed, possessed with rage. Debbie is breathless, slows, bends over with a stitch and I cannot believe my luck. I have her. Startled, she glances round looking for an escape, but there is none. She is trapped. The only route is the railway crossing behind her which is out of bounds, everyone knew that, and she would never get through the rusty and broken gate. In desperation she runs to it anyway, struggles, cranks it open and squeezes through. I follow knowing full well I shouldn't. But I feel invincible. The danger makes me hyper-excited. 'Now what you gonna do?' I taunt her. She looks behind her to the rails, looks to me, looks back again, eyeing up her chances. The gate on the other side is wildly overgrown with brambles and would be impossible to get through. The old wooden safety boards over the crossing end at an arms' width apart so she cannot run up the tracks or she'll be electrocuted. She goes to head back towards me. I block her. We side-step in a hideous dance. And she steps back, trips, lands on her bum and I laugh and laugh. I win, I win, stupid cow! I'm going to beat her brains in.

The rails, quietly at first, begin their tee-dum, tee-dum, tee-dum up the track. As they become a thumping clack-clack-thud, clack-clack-thud I realise a train is nearer than I thought. 'DEBBIE, THE TRAIN!' I shout. She struggles to get up because her leg is twisted under her. 'I can't, my foot's stuck,' she shrieks. The hee-haw of the train horn blasts out invisibly from behind the bend in the tracks. A hammer thuds in my chest. I shake uncontrollably, I can't breathe, I dither, turn back to the gate, take a step, reconsider, turn back, run to help, pull at her hand. 'It's my shoelace,' she cries, 'it's stuck in the plank.' 'Take it off, quick!' We both grapple but the laces tighten, and we can't get her shoe off. I glance up. The yellow front of the train speeds towards us and is so close I can see the driver in the cab. The brakes squeal, the horn blasts. Air is propelled forward and knocks me over sideways. In slow motion I seem to roll away, over the sharp flints bedding in the rails and into the ditch full of brambles and muddy rain. I smell fox pee, engine grease, burning metal. My head turns, locks eyes with Debbie, my hand stretches futilely towards her. She is ashen, wide-eyed, her cavernous mouth screams into the sound of screeching brakes. I scrunch my eyes tight, tense my whole body ready for impact. A dull thud. Then silence...'

302

Freya broke off, the horror of blood and gore still vivid. Father Paul's hand was in hers and she noticed a small bead of blood where her nails had dug into his flesh. 'I kept staring at that arm and couldn't understand why Debbie wasn't attached to it. Her little fingers were still stained with ink from the fountain pen she refused to throw out because she got it free in the *Jackie* magazine. And I was puzzled as to how I could fix Debbie's arm back on. I kept thinking I could get my sewing kit out and everything could be put right again. Then the shouting started, and the sirens wailed. Police, ambulances, men in hard hats and suits came. I realised then that everything had actually happened, that it hadn't just been a nightmare. I kept myself hidden in the undergrowth for what seemed like hours until it was almost dark, and then I remembered Beckett waiting for me in the park.'

Father Paul remained silent.

'I'm so sorry Paul. No one should have to hear that.'

'My dearest child. You have carried this far too long.'

'I killed her.'

'You tried to *save* her.'

'I was a coward.'

'You were a scared child.'

'I wanted her dead.'

Father Paul snapped back. 'Yes, only for a moment. A child does not know the full weight of death. But you did not push her and even if you had, you did not foresee the train coming. And you *did* go back to help her.'

'I saved my own life at the expense of hers.'

'Not true. Nobody can stop the force of an oncoming train. What good would come of you both dying except to relieve your own guilt? Don't you think you owe it to Debbie to live your life to the full?'

'Perhaps.'

'Take a moment. Tell me where your real guilt lies.'

She struggled momentarily to understand and uttered a silent prayer – *let me see Lord*. Again, as if a path cleared through the forest, her thoughts swirled into a litany of wrongdoings but settled on two. 'The sin of anger and the sin of omission,' she said. 'Of succumbing to rage and of failing to do what I should have done, that is, to have owned up and told everyone what happened. Debbie's mum would have known the truth and had closure. I added to her suffering.'

'Correct. Why didn't you?'

'I wish with all my heart I had. I'm so very sorry. I was ashamed, and terrified no one would believe me, that they thought I had pushed her into the path of that oncoming train because I wanted her dead. And I thought I'd go to prison.' She gave an ironic smile. 'You see, I am a coward after all.'

'I see a scared child before me. There is one more sin, perhaps the greatest of all.'

Puzzled, Freya ran through a check list in her head. 'I'm sorry. I can't think.'

'Why have you hidden for so long?'

'I've said I was afraid of the police.'

'You know that's not what I mean. Think. Why have you not accepted forgiveness?'

A well of grief surged in her heart. She saw her soul as a fragile egg which had been cracked open that terrible day to release a tiny dragon. This creature, at first helpless, fed on the breast of her fear, then took to the sky and soared, growing in size and form until it blotted out the light of her soul. 'I looked into my heart and saw a monster. How could Christ forgive such evil?'

'Name the demon!'

'I cannot.'

'Very well. We will talk again. For your penance say five Hail Marys and two Our Fathers.'

'Was Debbie's life worth so little?'

'For my part I shall pray and fast.'

'You would do that?'

Father Paul let out what seemed a never-ending sigh. 'There you go again. Debbie's life was worth Our Lord dying for her, and for yours' too for that matter. Anything we do is a mere gesture given out of love. Whilst we may seek atonement, the debt is already paid.'

'I understand. I know I'm stubborn. My whole life I have been the bossy one, the one always in control, the one who knows best. I decided to dish out my own punishment, to speak for God, to know better than He. The demon's name is name is *pride*.'

'Alleluia. Now, will you make your act of contrition?'

She knew only one, the childhood version the nuns taught her in her First Holy Communion lessons, *O my God, because you are so good…* The words did not matter for she sighed with repentance. Father Paul raised his hand in absolution and from his blessed hand warmth flowed. 'Be at peace, my child.'

They drove at speed back towards Brohn-In-The-Moor. Father Paul was lost in his musings while Freya considered how their relationship might change now that he knew the truth. Confession had liberated her, and she viewed the situation not with angst but with a sense of gratitude for past friendship. Father Paul had been a good and precious friend which she had not always appreciated. Whilst she enjoyed her relationship with him, some things were bigger than friendship, bigger than the comforting feeling of someone having your back, of being liked. Truth and goodness superseded all earthly things, and they were beautiful. Nothing compared to the peace she now felt in her soul.

'Got it!' Father Paul said suddenly.

'Got what?'

'I'm pretty sure I know what they're up to.'

Relieved that Father Paul had not been dwelling on the confession, she replied with a simple 'And?'

'Let's just see if I'm right. Do you have a mobile with you? We need to ring Merc.'

'No and no. No to the mobile, and no to Merc. He's the last person I want to speak to. Besides, I don't have his number.'

'Mine's in the glove compartment. Ring the George and Dragon and speak to Susie. Now, what shall we say?' They discussed a couple of options, settling on a white lie for delay tactics to keep Merc at the inn, asking Susie to say an offer of business had come his way which he couldn't possibly refuse. Father Paul had a friend with a classic MGB GT sports car, racing green, complete with chrome bumpers in mint condition which he wanted to sell. He was confident he knew the car well enough to pull it off.

The call was partially successful. They got through to the inn, spoke to Susie but Merc was not there. She said she would ring him straight away, though she questioned the urgency. Freya fobbed her off saying Father Paul had to get back to pack for his trip to Rome.

'Whilst we're on the subject,' Father Paul said to Freya after the call ended, 'the invite is still there for Rome. You'd enjoy it. Come.'

'Yes, why not,' she said smiling and meant it.

Freya sensed something was wrong the minute they pulled up outside the George and Dragon. It took a moment to put her finger on it: there were no cars. Merc usually kept his own and at least one other of his for-sale cars in the car park, and Susie's little work van always sat in the stable yard tucked in on the far left. The inn was empty inside except for Tom minding the bar and chatting to a solitary regular.

'Alright, m' lovers. What can I get ya?' he said, rising to his new role.

'We've no time for that that, Tom. Where's Su–' Freya said.

'I'd kill for a coffee,' Father Paul interrupted,

giving Tom his most charming smile.

'If you're sure we've time, though I think I need something stronger after the morning I've had.'

'Now, it's a funny thing,' Tom said as he set about getting the drinks. 'You know how protective Susie gets about her precious bar, well, couldn't get enough of me earlier, practically begged me to mind it for her. Slipped me a tenner and said help yourself,' he winked, 'would be rude not to. Gone to see Allegra, I think, at that stuck up hotel of hers.'

'Was Merc with her?' Freya asked.

'Woof-woo,' he whistled. 'Ark at the little green monster. Jealous, are we?'

'Not now, Tom.'

'I's just having a bit of fun with ya. No, not seen Merc all morning, won't neither, taken off he has, like a rat leaving a sinking ship.'

She and Father Paul exchanged glances, the same thought occurring.

'Thanks Tom. You've been really helpful,' Freya said.

'They don't call me a ratcatcher for nothing,' he called after them as they rushed to the B&B rooms in The Byre. Merc's bedroom door was propped open with a mop bucket, and the cleaner was still hard at work. Despite the smell of bleach and bathroom cleaner, the stench of his aftershave lingered like last night's fish supper. His wardrobe was empty, so too the drawers. The bathroom showed no sign of the usual paraphernalia and even his golf bag had gone.

'We're too late,' Freya said, collapsing onto the bed. 'I can't believe he'd just take off like that without an explanation. I'm still struggling to believe what I saw on those Faddon papers. I thought he liked me. Surely, he would leave a note or something?'

When they went to her room an A4 envelope had been shoved underneath the door. She ripped it open and found the same documents as those Mrs Monkcombe had signed earlier, only this time they were photocopied on cheap copy paper. Merc had scrawled over the front of it – *You should have said yes, lassie. I could have made this all go away! No hard feelings, Merc x*

'Bloody cheek of it,' Father Paul said. 'And a kiss too.'

'Good riddance. I don't need him.'

'We should call the police.'

'No, not yet. We need to go to Allegra's and see what the pair of them have to say.'

'The police would understand about what happened with Debbie.'

'It's not that. I'm not scared anymore. I'll take what's coming. If we get the police involved at this stage, they'll clamp up and I'll never know the truth about what happened to Beckett. These two might be my last chance.'

'You've Jack.' Father Paul said.

'Hmm… true. He did say he'd come clean tomorrow but no doubt the truth will be wrapped up in some ridiculous riddle or folklore story that I'll have to work out for myself. Best keep him out of it for now.'

The approach to Allegra's hotel was every bit as grand as she remembered though the trees had taken on the rusty shades of autumn. Slippery decaying leaves littered the gravel driveway and flowerpots flopped with gone-over flowers. 'Beckett would never have let the place go to pot like this. I wonder if he ever came here.' As if reading Father Paul's mind, she added, 'They were an item, he and Allegra. She thought it quite serious, said they'd practically got engaged.'

'You have your doubts?'

'You haven't met her. I didn't think she was his type. She's nice, friendly, of course, but exuberant and how shall I say…she's incredibly attractive and likes her little luxuries. I rather thought Beck would fall for the nature-loving outdoorsy type.'

'Opposites attract.'

'Maybe. Let's hope her loyalty to him is still intact.'

They were greeted with warm smiles in reception by the same concierge who had had the altercation with Merc on her last visit. He remembered her and her generous gift and came out from behind the desk extending his hand in welcome and putting himself at their disposal. Allegra, he explained, was in a meeting and left strict instructions not to be disturbed. However, if they were to inadvertently wander into the spa area, they would find her there. He would ring ahead to arrange for robes and towels to be made available. He then slipped them the access code for the door.

No matter how much the staff had endeavoured to create the atmosphere of an exotic oriental spa complete with tinkling water fountain, natural slate tiles and lemon and verbena scented candles, the unmistakeable and eye-watering tang of swimming pool chlorine ruined the illusion. When Father Paul emerged from the changing room semi bare-chested and with stork legs sticking out from beneath a white robe, Freya stifled a giggle. 'That's it,' he said. 'I'm changing back into my clericals. You can do it on your own.'

'Don't be such a baby. I bared my soul to you

earlier and now you're worried about a little bit of flesh. Come on, they must be in the steam room. It's over there.'

Freya opened the door to a wall of intense heat and poked her head into the steam. She could just make out parallel marble benches and two pairs of opalescent legs. She pulled Father Paul inside and they sat opposite them. As their eyes began to adjust, the ceiling vents let out a fresh gush of opaque steam rendering vision all but impossible.

'As if the heat isn't enough,' he muttered.

'Stop complaining. Try and relax.'

'Freya, is that you?' Allegra leaned towards her through the steam. 'What on earth are you doing here?'

'I expect that'll be something to do with me,' Susie said, materialising from the vapour. 'I'll kill that Tom when I get hold of him. Blabber mouth.'

'Never mind that. What's going on?' Allegra said rising to her feet.

'I think we would all like to know that.' Father Paul opened the steam room door. 'Shall we?'

Allegra donned a robe and led them to a bistro table by the poolside. An ice bucket held an opened bottle of champagne. She called over the pool attendant and asked for more glasses in rapid Italian. 'Why not,' she shrugged, 'I find it loosens the tongue.'

'I think Merc would be the first to agree with you there,' Freya said, looking her straight in the eye. 'However, there's been enough careless talk, hasn't there?'

'What do you mean?'

'She knows,' Susie said, toying with her glass. 'But how much I wonder. I'm guessing you're here for answers, right?'

'Surely the truth would be more appropriate.' Father Paul said.

Just then a hotel guest appeared from the changing rooms dressed in a floral bathing costume and swimming goggles. When all four heads snapped towards her and scowled. She retreated back to the changing rooms muttering something about a forgotten towel. Freya took advantage of the distraction, 'Susie, it was you who told Merc we were going to visit Mrs Monkcombe today, didn't you?'

'Who the heck is Mrs Monkcombe?' Allegra said, her eyes darting from Freya to Susie.

'The dead girl's mother,' Susie answered coldly.

Freya tensed and was about to respond with an ill-timed retort when Father Paul placed a hand on her arm – *noted and understood*. 'You also knew about his and Faddon's little attempt at fraud,' she continued. 'Well, Mrs Monkcombe signed the papers. I have them in the car if you still have the stomach for it, though I think you'd have a hard time in court persuading a judge of her sanity. Unless, that is, Faddon has an ally there too.'

'Whoa,' Allegra said. 'What's all this about papers and judges? I knew about the…' she clamped her mouth shut.

'Blackmail? Say it for what it is,' Father Paul said. 'Blackmail. Such an ugly betrayal, the worst in fact.'

A long pause ensued interrupted only by the pool attended bringing two fresh champagne flutes to the table. Freya could think of nothing more ironic at that moment. In a quiet voice she addressed Allegra, 'I thought you were my friend.'

'I was, I am. I swear I knew nothing of this latest scam. I already wanted to get out. I got to know Beckett and to fall in love with him, but I was in too deep and couldn't see a way out. I intended to tell him, but I did not get the chance…poor Beck. I am so sorry.'

'Why did you get involved in the first place?'

'I was not as heartless and calculated as you think.'

'Why care about what I think?'

'Because Freya, I believe we became friends. And you are the last link with the man I loved. At first it seemed so simple. Merc had come up with a ruse to let Beck dig his own grave, so to speak.'

315

'An unfortunate analogy,' Father Paul said.

'Merc was good at the cards, far too good. Hungry for more winnings, hungry for more of everything.'

Freya understood. She used the exact term herself. Merc lived in excess; luxury cars, expensive cologne, useful friends who had 'made it', and for all she knew, women as well. Endowed with charisma and good looks, he could have anything he wanted. Except, she noted with a sense of satisfaction, herself.

'All we had to do was play along, is that not so, Susie? Keep playing the cards, keep quiet, not be an obstacle. Before long, Beck's losses were significant. Horribly so. That is when I got nervous. I wanted to be out.'

'Hmph,' Susie snorted. 'You didn't try very hard. You were milking it as much as the rest of us.'

'No, that is not fair. I owed Merc money, more than I had thought. He sent some affluent customers my way and in return I was supposed to send him clients for his luxury car business. Only they did not materialise on my part. Faddon had drawn up a little business agreement with penalties thrown in. Then, after our romantic liaison he turned up with a little red sports car for me. I was only too ready to sign what I thought were the transfer documents. They turned out to be a loan agreement. I could kick myself for being so naïve. I thought it a lover's gift.'

'Naivety is not a sin,' Freya said. 'It seems Merc charmed us both. And you Susie, did he charm you too?' She suspected the answer but out of charity gave her the benefit of the doubt.

'I wouldn't be so foolish. Obviously, it was the inn. He'd bought the mortgage from the bank. But the repayments were a struggle, even at his discounted rates so I encouraged the gambling ring and the fixed odds terminal to boost my takings. And it worked…for a while. For the record, me and Merc have been an item for over a decade now. I allow him his little dalliances in return for the preferential payments.'

Allegra gasped and Father Paul cringed, but Freya was the one to speak. 'To reduce something so beautiful to a mercantile trade off!'

'Hey, it works for us.'

'Ladies, do keep to the point.'

'I have this, Paul,' Freya said composing herself. 'When did Merc tell you about my past?'

Susie stood, poured another glass of champagne, and plonked the bottle back into the ice bucket. She sauntered to the glass wall of windows which overlooked the garden. The flowers were bowing from the overnight rain and the leaves were yellowing in the autumn sun. 'He came to see me one night very chuffed with himself, said things had taken an unexpected turn to his advantage. Beckett had got drunk, spilled the beans about you and your little friend's death and bingo, more leverage. The idiot's only bargaining chip to stop Merc blabbing about you was your parents' house.'

So, Beckett had been trying to protect her all along and had fallen foul of Merc's blackmail. It was all *her* fault. If only she had faced the truth, gone to the police and explained to Beckett from the beginning what had happened to Debbie, he wouldn't have been so traumatised and vulnerable. There would have been no need for secrets, no need for fear.

'You saw nothing wrong in blackmail?' Father Paul said addressing Susie and Allegra.

Allegra spoke first. 'For Beckett's sake I did not want to do it, but Merc is a powerful man. He could ruin me. I thought if I could warn Beck, reason with him, he might be able to see sense and do something about it, pay off the debt with a bank loan. I thought I was getting through to him and that he would speak to you. Freya, I always believed there must have been another explanation for what happened to your childhood friend. It had to have been an accident and I told Beck so.'

'You're too generous, love. Susie said. 'Our Freya here deserves everything she gets.'

Despite her earlier sense of peace, Susie's words tore through her like a scab ripped from a wound. The old insecurities flooded back. She was a thing to be despised, rejected, unloved.

'What is this, a self-appointed judge and jury?' Father Paul interrupted. 'Only God alone can read our hearts. Who are you to cast the first stone?' He nodded over to Freya and she took strength form his reassurance. She knew she was still a work in progress. Accepting forgiveness needed not only grace but a willingness to change and let old habits die. She turned her attention back to the unresolved question of Beckett's death. 'If you knew about Merc and Faddon's shady business, you must also know what happened to Beck. I just can't believe it was suicide.'

Susie shook her head vehemently. 'No. I don't know, and that's the truth. Merc was adamant nothing amiss happened and that I should trust him. Sure, he's a crook but he's not a murderer if that's what you're thinking.'

Allegra became animated, 'Freya, please do not believe what the police say. I too cannot believe it was suicide. I have been over it a thousand times in my head. I saw Beck the day he died. We had had a lovely picnic at our favourite place out on the moor by Margin Tor. He seemed in good spirits, and happy. He said he had a plan. He would write to you offering to sell his share of the house to you at a reduced price and would pay off his debts, and mine too and we would both be done with Merc forever.'

'How convenient for you,' Susie said.

'For your information, I insisted it was not necessary and refused his offer to pay off my debts. Then Beck said he would help me run the hotel. We had so many plans for it: themed weekends, nature breaks, walking, birdwatching. I knew he was planning to see Merc that evening at the George and Dragon. He was convinced everything would be okay though I had a strange feeling about it and warned him to be careful. I should have known Merc would not be satisfied with a simple repayment.'

'We haven't all had your privileges in life,' Susie snapped. 'Merc grew up in a tenement in the Gorbals in Glasgow surrounded by filth and vermin. Do you blame him for wanting a better life?'

'For that, no,' Father Paul said. 'But at the expense of others, that I cannot agree with.'

Allegra continued, 'I thought Jack would look

after Beck. But Jack refuses to say a word about what happened on the tor. I guess out of some misplaced sense of family loyalty.'

'Oh, come off it. You kept your mouth shut about the gambling ring,' Susie said.

Freya reached over the table and squeezed Allegra's hand. 'I'm glad you had happy times with Beck, really, I am. It also confirms what I knew all along. There was no way he was suicidal. Something else must have happened. Susie, can you enlighten us?'

'Look, I've said I don't know. Why don't you ask Jack?'

'I intend to. Tell me one thing, were Merc and Beck at the inn the night he died?'

Susie turned back to the window and drained her champagne flute. 'Beckett came to the bar early and seemed in good spirits.

'You're drenched,' I said, and he just smiled and shrugged. 'Expecting your lady friend tonight?'

'She has a name, Susie, as you well know. Anyhow, she's now officially my fiancée.'

'Drat,' I said, 'I've missed my chance. Congrats. Champagne?'

'Maybe later. Wonky Wassail and top it up with the Fitzwell's folly.'

'A Snake Bite?'

'Let's hope not.' He glanced over his shoulder for Merc I supposed. 'Want to join me?'

'Well, I'm no drinker, seen too many landlords on the slippery slope, so I poured myself a lime and tonic instead. We chatted for a while, mostly about the veg growing in the kitchen garden and I joked about the formal garden he'd planted saying it was a bit posh. He smiled and said it was for someone special, Allegra I supposed. He ordered another drink then Merc turned up, all preened and cocksure of himself. He was splashing the cash alright, bought drinks all round. Tom thought all his Christmases had come at once. Bless him,' she chuckled.

'We've business,' Merc said to Beckett, and he nodded over to the corner. Wasn't long before things got a bit heated.

'You've got your due,' Beckett shouted standing up and knocking over the dregs of his drink in the process. 'Happy now?'

'Believe me, I've only just got started.' Merc rose and eyeballed him. 'There's the wee matter of interest. Why don't you be a good lad and save me the bother of fetching it down from Margin Tor?'

'You wouldn't dare!'

'Wouldn't I?' Merc wore that supercilious smirk of

his, then Beckett made a fist.

'You son of a–'

'Out, the pair of you,' I ordered. 'That's the last I saw of him. Tom got all agitated and excited, said he'd fetch Jack who should've been there half an hour ago anyway as he was supposed to be storytelling to the punters that night. By the time he arrived Merc and Beckett were long gone.'

Freya dipped her head while she tried to digest the events. A long silence followed only broken by Father Paul saying in little more than a whisper 'You told the police this?' Susie shook her head. 'Why on earth not?' he asked.

'Because Merc would be implicated, questions would be asked, I'd be dragged into it, the police would find out about the gambling ring. I couldn't risk that. And I trusted Merc.'

'Trusted?' Freya repeated. 'Past tense!'

'Ah, you're sharp.'

'Where's Merc now?' Father Paul asked. 'I suppose the MG wasn't to his taste. Pity, my friend really did want to sell it,'

'I wish I knew. I passed on the message from the nurse in the care home saying she had given *you* the signed papers from Mrs Monkcombe. Unbeknown to me, he bailed. Didn't even have the guts to tell me to my face.

After all these years covering for him, I get a lousy note saying he'd call when they were settled – *they* obviously meaning him and that creep Faddon – and a bloody *adios amigo* as a farewell. My guess is they're heading for the Costa del Crime. Good luck to them.'

'We've still time. They've only just left,' Father Paul said.

'Don't bother yourself, my love. They're long gone. Probably called in a favour from one of his yachting friends. He'll cover his tracks alright. Besides, I get the impression it wouldn't do Freya much good getting the police involved, now would it?'

Freya lifted her chin in defiance. 'I'm beyond caring what happens to me. Call the police if you dare. I only want what's right for Beck. He deserves the truth and as for me, I'll take whatever is coming.' She turned to Father Paul. 'Looks like everything rests on Jack tomorrow.

.

CHAPTER 23

'You came!' Jack straightened up from the bags of sails lying on the jetty. He took a step towards her with his great bear arms spread wide for a hug. Freya recoiled with a barely perceptible backwards tilt of the head. 'So, it's like that, is it?' Jack said. 'You sure you want to come?'

'She does,' said Father Paul. 'I'll leave you two to it.' He squinted up to the sun. 'Nice day. I'll wait for you, old girl, no hurry. I've some reading to do. Enjoy, enjoy.'

They watched Father Paul trot over to an oak tree, settle himself under it and take out his book. Freya turned back to Jack and kissed his cheek. 'Sorry, old habits die hard. Do you need a hand?'

He tasked her with loading the picnic hamper and buoyancy aids while he unravelled the sails and threaded the mainsail onto the boom. When they were ready, he pushed away from the jetty. Freya stood tall at the bow, shielding her eyes from the morning sun resplendent in a cerulean sky. Whether from the sudden thud of water bouncing hard against the hull or the crack of the mainsheet tightening on the pullies, the rooks took flight, cackling witch-like into the crisp air. If thoughts occurred of Dartmoor yielding yet more folklore omens upon such a beautiful day, Freya pushed them away. She was content to enjoy the moment before hard questions would be asked. First, they would have a perfect picnic of wholesome food from Jack's country pantry and enjoy the unchanging beauty of this landscape. Then, hopefully, a peace would wash over them connecting them to the timeless stream of abundance given, when full of happiness she'd recline in his arms and trust all things worked for the good.

Sailing was light, easy. A steady wind billowed the sails and propelled them zigzagging across the lake until tingling with sensations, they dropped anchor to drift on the chain while they picnicked. Jack opened the wicker hamper and handed her a doorstop sandwich wrapped in baking paper and a hardboiled egg. He took a bite of his own and still with a mouthful spoke, as if the food would somehow make the content of his words more palatable. 'Where to begin...? The night I found you, I already knew who you were. You see, I had been expecting you. And Beckett knew you would come too.'

'You did? And *he* did? That's impossible. Beck was dead by then, so how –'

'Did he know? Call it a premonition. Guess it was all the pixies and faerie stories I'd been telling him.'

The playful glint in his eyes escaped her, and she received the news with gravity. 'Jack, no more allegories and folklore. Be straight with me or not at all. I'm done with faerie stories, magic stone circles, dragons as amulets and these eerie moors as conduits for memories. As you are well aware, I've been seeing visions of Beckett since I got here.'

'And how is he?'

'It's not funny, it's total madness. That evening in your kitchen you said the mist delivers all manner of people, some running away, some running toward and that we all pass through here. What exactly did you mean?'

'How can I speak without allegories?' He ran a hand through his hair. 'Sometimes things happen, a conversation, a circumstance… or a death, which leaves us all at sea, our certainties disappear, we are no longer sure who we are. We need stories to tame the raw thoughts into a form we can process.'

Freya frowned, 'I guess that's why parables work

so well? They cut to the heart.'

'As I said, we all figuratively pass through here at some stage. It just so happens that Brohn-In-The-Moor gets more than its fair share of literal pilgrims. If I were to ignore the mischievous pixies or the delights of a pint of Fitzwell's Folly, I'd say it was the moor's rugged remoteness which draws them. It's a primeval landscape our souls recognise; a place of innocence and timelessness.'

'For once you make perfect sense. But Beck's premonition?'

'No great mystery there. He knew he was up to his neck in it. He might even have thought he was in danger. We talked a lot. He tried to provide just enough clues for you to follow him here to Brohn should things come to a head and the worst happened, but not so blatant as to alarm you if things were to settle down and go away. You would merely think he'd either been out in the sun too long or was having a bit of fun with you in riddles and rhymes. Only now we know there wasn't to be an afterwards.' Jack gazed over to the distant shore through moist eyes. 'I miss him. He was like a son to me.'

'Like a son to you! So how come you denied even knowing him?' Her voice rose an octave. 'And no nonsense about sleeping dogs and keeping schtum.' As Jack extracted a bottle from the basket, she caught his arm and pleaded, 'Give me a reason to believe in you.'

He uncorked the sparkling elderflower in silence, poured some into a tin mug and handed it to her. 'I will, you'll see. Back in the spring I placed an ad in *Farmer's Weekly* for a labourer – had to be good with animals, fencing, drystone walling and all that gubbins. I had a few replies, but Beck's was with a postcard from St Ives saying he could start immediately, was on his way and would be with me by the weekend. I liked that, the presumption and confidence. And the photo of the sailing boat on the front helped a bit too. But by Sunday night there was still no sign of him. I could've just dismissed it as him having second thoughts, but a real peasouper crept over the moors that night and a freezing one at that. I began to feel uneasy. Despite all my fanciful tales, the moor's no place to be lost in the fog. I checked the west road and the track by Margin Tor. Nothing. Then under a hunch, I went up past the stone circle and the standing stone, the one with the Celtic cross, and I just knew where he'd be.'

'I know that place. The moors delivered me there too. If the mist clears a little, you can see the field barn lights twinkle in the distance. You found Beck there,' she stated with certainty. She had felt his presence as almost a hallowedness before she fell asleep.

'I did, thank God. It was such a bitter night. A hot

meal and a nightcap later, he'd revived. I offered him the job there and then. He wasn't a great talker at first, and would let me ramble on, laugh at my jokes, listen to endless stories. Slowly over time we both came to understand each other. Boy, could he work. Good at it too. It was as if nature responded to his will, gentle and nurturing he was, like a stealth deer in the woods.'

'Yes, that was Beck. It's only here that I've truly come to know that side of him. I wish things could have been different…'

'Love is born from understanding.' They pondered the words letting them soothe and comfort, like the rocking of their boat upon the water. 'Despite that, I could sense something bothering him, some deep sadness. I would sometimes catch him gazing across at the moors, sighing along with the wind, and I wondered. You see Freya, those moments spoke. I recognised myself in him, and knew I had to help him any way I could, one lost soul to another. His stupid gambling was just a symptom. For me it might have been the drink.'

'Might have?'

'Fair point. Still a work in progress I'm afraid. I did all things humanly possible to stop Beck gambling, short of locking him up in one of my barns every Wednesday night, though I considered that too. So, I joined in too to keep an eye on things. In my naivety, I didn't even know The George and Dragon had a gambling ring until he mentioned it.'

'Why didn't you call the police?'

'You need to ask? Loyalty. Us Moorlanders stick together…Well, things started to heat up and I took a long hard look at the punters. I wasn't worried about Tom. He'd set a limit of two hundred quid. Sometimes he won, most often he lost, but he liked the banter and the camaraderie, so it didn't matter to him.' Jack refilled Freya's glass. 'Want another sandwich?'

Feya took one and chewed over the offerings. 'There's so much I didn't know about Beck. I'm struggling to take it all in.'

'At first Allegra had been besotted with Merc then it turned a bit sour. It was obvious he had some sort of hold on her, you could see it in her eyes. Frightened, I think. She'd get all emotional whenever she lost. And then she took up with Beck and was all for wanting out. As for Susie, well, she's a hard cookie, she and Merc both, peas in a pod. Come hell or high water she wasn't going to lose the inn and saw the gambling ring as a way to entice some hard spending. I supposed she had a cut of the winnings. Faddon and Merc, we both know they were working together. I think one-upmanship had as much to do with it as the money.'

'That tallies with what the girls said yesterday. Tell me about the blackmail.'

Jack swallowed hard. 'Blasted blackmail. If only Beckett hadn't blabbed…until then it was just a matter of minimising his losses. Pretty steep as they were. I offered him a loan. Ten-grand would have done it, no probs and it wouldn't have mattered to me if he never repaid it.'

'Ten-grand. That's a lot but not nearly as much as the value of our parent's house which must be worth about four hundred thousand pounds now, exactly the amount Merc is trying to sue me for via poor Mrs Monkcombe.'

'He's trying to do *what*? Sorry, I had no idea. What are you going to do?'

'Nothing for the minute. I heard him and Faddon are hiding in Marbella or somewhere.'

'Hell, what a mess. I should have told the police.' He shoved the remnants of a pork pie in his mouth.

'You didn't though, did you? I can hardly bear the thought of you betraying Beck. I'm still waiting for that reason to stay.'

'It wasn't for love or loyalty to Merc, that's for sure. Nor to the ladies, or for my own reputation. It was for *yours*.'

'I beg your pardon! You didn't even know me then.'

'I did. No, don't shake your head. At least it seemed like I knew you. Beck was a good judge of character, could suss someone out in a few seconds, though he was gentle in his judgements.'

'Tell me, was he afraid of me?'

'He adored you, and that was good enough for me. He'd get so animated telling me all sorts of funny stories about you and him, the way you played schools in your nursery and put on long rambling plays for your friends, and the wizen old nuns yielding sticks. You were his everything.'

Not everything she thought sadly remembering all his recent secrets.

'Then when he fell for Allegra, his heart expanded all the more. I felt glad for him.'

'I wished I'd known. I wish things could have been different between Beck and me. I would have loved having Allegra as a sister-in-law.'

'Love them or hate them, families are so necessary. I'm a silly sentimental old fool and since my wife died and Skye flew the nest, I was lonely. I wanted to make my own family again. I wanted Beckett as my family and that included you. You see…I loved you before I even met you.'

Freya's heart sang with hope.

'I didn't say anything because I swore I would protect you – at any cost. I had to spare you the anguish of public humiliation – all the tabloid lies making you out to be some kind of monster when you're not. I know you wouldn't have deliberately killed Debbie, not out of malice. There had to have been some unfortunate mishap or error of judgement. You were just a child, no doubt with a rush of overwhelming emotions and a hot temper to boot. But for the grace of God, we've all been there…And perhaps selfishly I did it in atonement for Rigby's death.

She received this news in astonishment. Jack had inadvertently made things worse by his silence but for the best of intentions. Here he offered the gift of love and acceptance, of understanding and revelation, something to be embraced and cherished. It may have taken her a while – too long in fact – to come to an honesty about herself, but at least Jack had given her time while Beckett challenged her to make peace with her past. *In death there is mourning, but a poisonous silence brings irritation and disdain. Justice comes from dying to oneself. I offer you encouragement, patience, and energy in adversity. I hope this brings you success. Farewell, my dearest sister.'*

She leant over and kissed Jack. 'Thank you,' she

whispered. 'So, what really happened the night Beckett died?'

'I beg you, Freya, don't believe what the police told you. His death wasn't suicide, though metaphorically he'd done that the moment he let slip the secret to Merc.'

'I never believed it was suicide. I don't know how to ask this it seems so surreal. Was he murdered?'

'Heck no. I gathered from Susie that he and Merc were having a hell of an argument about the deeds to the house. Somehow Merc knew they were hidden up the tor.'

'How so?'

'Anyone's guess. Nothing gets past the inn, eyes and ears everywhere. That evening he marched Beck up to the tor to get them. I'd been on my way to The George and Dragon for a storytelling stint when Tom came running up all het up and excited saying there's going to be a fight. I sprinted ahead and as I got close to the tor I could make out two silhouettes against the skyline so I made a beeline to it. Beck was on the highest boulder and Merc lower stooping into some crag or crevice like he was looking for something.

'I'm the king of the castle, you're the dirty rascal,' Beck taunted with his hands on hips.

'You got a death wish, pal?' Merc yelled as he started climbing up the rocks towards him.

As I got nearer, I bellowed, 'God damn it, Merc. Leave him be. It's dark and blooming raining. You're gonna get you both killed. He'll come down eventually.'

'Keep out of it, Jack. It's not your business.'

'It is now.' I knew I had to get between them. I know Margin Tor like the back of my hand. On the north side, the rocks form a natural staircase. I bolted up them like I was twenty again and had nearly reached Merc when stupidly I lost my footing. Merc, in some uncharacteristic act of charity, or just instinct, reached out and grabbed my hand. But by then the momentum just carried us both down.'

'*Jack fell down and broke his crown, and Gil came tumbling after,*' Freya whispered. 'How could Beck have known?' Her thoughts hovered over mythical lands and magical conduits, then to seeing the events through the eyes of faith – prophecy, truth, grace.

'Beats me. We cannot explain away mystery. Some things simply are. Merc was okay but I must have knocked my head and passed out briefly, then came to with Beck shouting, 'Jack, you alright? I'm coming down.'

'I'll be okay. Nothing's broken. Stay where you are, the rocks are too slippery. I'll run back and get a torch.'

'I'm coming down.'

He disappeared behind a boulder, then me and Merc heard a yelp and a thump-thump and thud. We locked eyes and knew it was serious. Merc let out some profanity. We found him curled up at the bottom of the tor, for all the world as if he were asleep.

Merc took out his satellite phone. 'Ambulance, Margin Tor. Hurry.' After the call he turned to me, 'Is he conscious?'

'I don't think so.'

'Just let me think a wee moment.'

'What's there to think about, bloody help him.'

But there was nothing much we could do. I held Beck's hand and put my jacket over him. He wouldn't have known anything about it and didn't suffer. I'm so sorry Freya. When the emergency services arrived, Merc slipped back into type. Acting all cagey, recounting some half-truths, making up the rest. Typically, he said nothing about the argument. Made out that Beckett was drunk and suicidal, threatening to throw himself off the tor and that we'd followed him but got there too late. Merc threw me that indolent challenging look of his. I knew the implications: blab and I tell. Secrets, secrets, curse those bloody secrets.'

Freya rose and the dinghy swayed. Her thoughts swirled like eddies in the lake. 'I need to go home now.

I've got to process all this.' She struggled to pull up the anchor rope which had snagged on some boulder or debris on the lake bottom. An awareness surfaced of some bridge having been crossed. Jack's account gave her the answers she was looking for confirming what she had known all along; Beckett would never have taken his own life. Perhaps it was the manner of his death, or the anguish and worry he suffered all his life for his mistakes – no, *her* mistakes, or maybe the awareness of a certain finality which unsettled her. With the busyness and practicalities of his death over, all that remained was for Freya to grieve in peace. If she could get back to her little terraced house, to her kitchen with the cheerful bunting, she could begin again. Perhaps in time Jack would visit. Maybe they would see each other, get married, possibly she would teach again – a thousand maybes. And she longed to return to her faith, to believe again, if for nothing else than to sit in peace and just be.

She tugged harder on the anchor rope and just as Jack rose to help, Freya heaved with every ounce of strength. The anchor suddenly gave way from its tether, the boat lurched, the sail caught the wind and the boom swung forty-five degrees. Jack took a blow to the side of his head and tumbled into the water. 'Jack!' she cried, as she strained her arm to reach him. His unconscious body bobbed, flipped over face down and his legs rose out behind him. The useless buoyancy aid floated away, its loose straps trailing like tentacles. 'Jack, hold on, I'm coming round.'

In a freak gust the sails bulged again and propelled the boat forward. She fought back panic and tried to think clearly and remember all that Jack had taught her on their last trip. *Grab the rope, pull in the sheet, leave the jib flapping, control the tiller, hurry.* A moment later the dinghy was back under control. She turned about, took a wide circle to manoeuvre back to Jack, but where was he? Her cheeks drained. Frantic, she scanned the lake aware that every second counted. *Jack, I can't lose you too, not here, not now. I love you. How much more does Brohn want from me?*

The wind drove waves across the water which swelled into a choppy sea. She saw a dark object in the water some fifty metres away and adjusted the tiller towards it. As she got closer, she saw with horror it was just a log and precious seconds had been lost. She scanned again. Jack was over to the right of her, face-up and floating on his back – *thank God!* She adjusted the tiller and pointed the bow in his direction. Her speed picked up but there was no way she would be able to pull up beside him. She let the sheet out, pushed the tiller hard away but turned the boat too quickly. She felt a great heave as the mast creaked, groaned, and toppled. The hull tipped sideways, she lost her grip, plunged into the cold water and gasped.

Freya held onto the mast to keep herself afloat, her buoyancy aid barely helping, and assessed the distance – *I can make it. I've got to make it.* She launched herself towards him in a frenzy of splaying arms and legs and excessive splashing. As she tired, she began doubting – *Lord, help me save Jack, I beg you!* For a moment she trod water, caught her breath, then switched into a calmer breaststroke which helped her glide gently up beside him. He was breathing, his colour good. If she could get him back to *The Dragon,* he would have a chance.

She made good headway at first by swimming on her back and cupping his chin, so his head rested on her shoulder. Kicking furiously, she gained a metre, lost a half when her legs got too tired and could no longer paddle fast enough to keep them both afloat. By chance, a wind-driven swell thrust them forward toward the boat and she managed to heave Jack over the mast with his head and shoulders supported by the sail. But then a return swell tore her backwards far away from the boat, too far for her to swim back, and far from any hope that her life could begin over and that she could at last be happy. A fear as dark as obsidian trembled through her exhausted, fragile body. *So far away, how am I ever…? I can do this, I know I can…just keep going, close my eyes, calm down, breathe, keep swimming.*

Her head dipped below the surface; her nostrils flooded with water. She bobbed up, coughed, spluttered, sank, rose, and sank again, her lungs filling with the wretched lake. Then a serenity never experienced before gathered her in, enfolding her as a beloved child cosseted in her mother's arms. She became aware of a great peace, a rightness that all things were ordered just as they should be, that all was well. Beckett swam towards her with the most radiant of smiles. He held out his hand and seemed to say *'welcome dearest sister'* though his lips never moved. She took his hand and from it flowed a stream of love so extraordinary that it appeared to possess all the colours of light along with all the angelic sounds of heaven and earth. Then, like a mermaid from the deep, Debbie appeared darting and looping around her, laughing in the shimmering water. She slipped a hand into hers and Freya too laughed with a happiness as complete and vast as the oceans. They swam upwards and upwards, through the weeds of crimson, silver, purple, blue and green, and the sparkling fish, iridescent and luminous, towards a great light glistening on the surface.

Still coughing up half the lake and unsteady on his feet, Jack staggered onto the shore with Freya carried in his arms. Father Paul ran to meet him and together they laid her gently down on the beach. Father Paul bent his ear low and listened for breath. 'Nothing,' he whispered.

'It's not over. I won't let it be.' Jack knelt before her, pinched her nose and placed his lips full over her mouth delivering two sharp breaths, then pounded rhythmically on her chest. 'Come on Freya, come on! We've come this far, don't give up.'

Father Paul took out the sacred oils from his beaten-up leather bag, unscrewed the cap with profound attention, placed the top of his thumb onto the opening and tilted the silver vessel sideways. A dribble of green oil cried to the ground. He traced a small cross on her forehead, then onto the palms of her cold lifeless hands. *Through this holy anointing, may the Lord in his love and mercy help you with the grace of the Holy Spirit…'* An internal battle ensued between his faith in 'Thy will be done' and his love for her. If Freya had simply slipped through the veil separating this world from the next, who was he to wish her back? Yet he wanted her to stay here on this earth, to be alive to the promise of happiness with Jack. *The foolishness of God is wiser than the wisdom of man. I do not understand your ways, O Lord.* He laid a hand on Jack's shoulder. 'Best we stop now,' he at last said.

Jack rested back on his heels panting with exertion and disbelief.

Father Paul removed the locket of Our Lady of Walsingham he wore around his neck, placed it on Freya's heart and bowed his head in silent supplication. A warm wind whistled and moaned, stirring up the autumn leaves to dance around her delicate body. Through their mourning Jack was the first to see the locket on her breast rise gently and fall and rise once more. 'Paul, am I imagining?'

Father Paul smiled, nodded, and gave thanks.

The End

ABOUT THE AUTHOR

Cymmone Imms grew up on a large housing estate near the sea with the joyful freedom to play outside until bedtime, and where the local Catholic church was an extension of home. Whilst raising a family, and a career in the police and community sectors, she watched and took note, pondering the stories she would one day write. She has an MA in Creative Writing from Bath Spa University, and currently lives in Somerset with her husband and an unruly kitchen garden. Her writing explores themes of memory, redemption, and transcendence.

Printed in Great Britain
by Amazon